PORTAL

Printed in Australia

Published by Toshiro Books

Cover by Kristine Slater

Internal design by A to B Editing – atobediting.com.au

Second edition: June 2025

Paperback ISBN 978-1-7641340-0-2

eBook ISBN 978-1-7641340-1-9

The author acknowledges the traditional owners of the land and pays respects to Elders, past, present and future.

A catalogue record for this work is available from the National Library of Australia

KATRINA McKEE

BOOK ONE

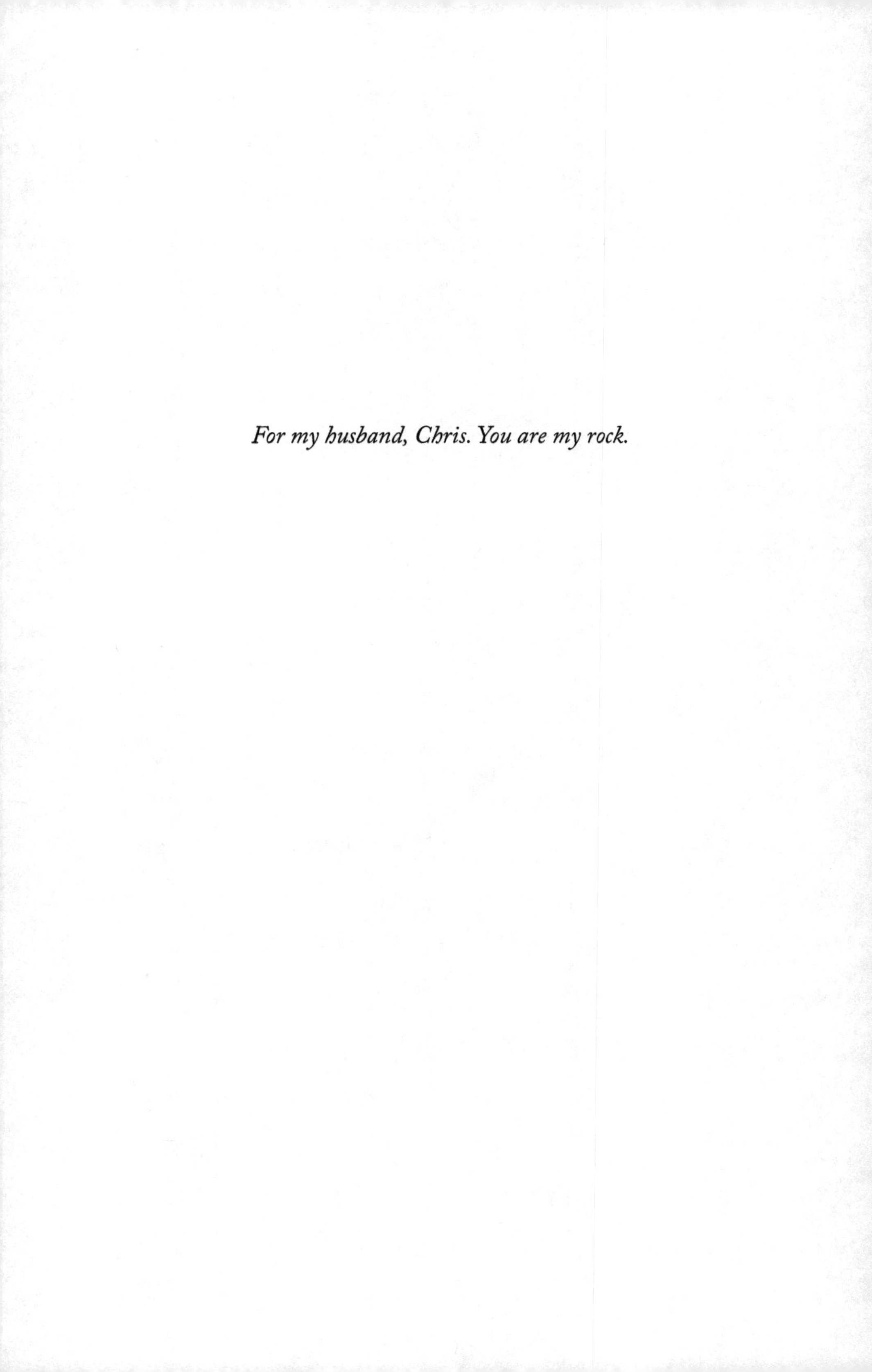

For my husband, Chris. You are my rock.

PROLOGUE

'Have you decided on how you're going to do it?'

Redmond huffed, not liking the interruption. He lay down his quill and turned to find George standing at the door to his office.

'Yes, as a matter of fact, I have.'

George smiled in greeting and stepped into the room. He still wore his coat, so Redmond knew he had just arrived, his hat tucked under one arm. 'So, how do you intend to do it?'

'I intend on writing journals,' Redmond explained, making a sweeping motion towards his desk. 'I will document the locations on the pages.'

'Is that wise? Anyone could find and read them.'

'Ah, see now,' – Redmond felt a sense of smugness – 'I will hide the location. You will need a code to understand.'

'That is clever,' George said. 'A code that only you will know, I assume.'

'And whoever I shall choose to be my heir,' Redmond said. 'The Keeper will always have access to the code.'

'And I will protect all,' George said. He looked at the desk. 'Is that the first one?'

'Indeed,' Redmond said, turning back to the book in front of him. 'I had them specially commissioned. They are made of the finest leather and paper. They shall stand the test of time.'

'And you will store them here.'

'I am having a cabinet commissioned. It will protect them until they are needed.'

George shuffled his hat, a faraway look on his face. 'It is sad that it has come to this.'

'We must do what is required of us,' Redmond said. 'We were entrusted with hiding the keys. We were chosen for a reason.'

'Because of our connections and wisdom,' George agreed. 'And your intelligence, good sir.'

'Don't be so hard on yourself, good fellow,' Redmond said. 'You have achieved much in the time we have been here. And you are to assist me in placing the keys in their hiding locations.'

'It will be quite the endeavour,' George said. 'I am rather looking forward to it. Have you chosen any locations yet? I have compiled a list myself.'

'Indeed, I have,' Redmond said. 'This is going to take us quite some time.'

'Time we have,' George said. He retrieved a pocket watch from his coat, looking down at it. 'Although not now. I'm afraid I have a meeting to attend.'

'Then off you go. I shall continue writing in my journal. That way, the locations shall never be lost.'

'Farewell, Redmond.'

'Enjoy your meeting.'

1

Sydney Madinah knew that Adelaide, being a city during peak hours, would be busy and congested. Compared to New York, it just didn't feel that way. She welcomed the clearer air and the lack of constant horns and spent a good deal of time taking in the local sights and getting to know what the city offered. Her experience as a hotel worker had taught her that guests always wanted to know what to try to what to visit and that speaking from experience rather than rattling off a tourist brochure seemed to go over better.

Her apartment was within easy walking distance from the Medina Grand Hotel, meaning she didn't have to buy herself a car. She hadn't had one in New York, and it was one less expense for the time being. The hardest thing had been getting used to the change in time zones. Her body clock had been fine-tuned to that of America's East Coast, and it had taken the better part of a week for her to stop feeling sluggish in the days and wide awake at night. It was good to be back in Australia.

It was still a week until her official start date when she set foot inside the hotel for the first time. She'd admired it from outside many times, taking in the heritage and charm of the old building. Her research had told her it was once the city's treasury building, built between 1839 and 1907. It had served not only as the treasury for the state, but had also been used by the government over the years as offices and cabinet rooms. They had redeveloped it into a hotel after the government had moved into modern premises.

Sydney couldn't help but wonder what quirks the old building had. Even as she stepped inside the modern glass doors, she could feel the history. The building had stories to tell, that was sure, and she made a mental note to learn more about the building so that she could answer questions from tourists and sightseers. She knew there were tours of the building from time to time, including in the building's 'tunnels' situated beneath.

She felt that the elderly man behind the desk talking to the receptionist likely knew every nook and cranny, and as she approached she caught sight of his 'Manager' name tag. This was undoubtedly the man she would replace, and he was probably moving on into retirement. He had a kind, weathered face, but eyes that told her he'd seen some things over the years. Her time spent working in hotels had given her a glimpse at quite a few crazy things and she doubted those would be the last.

He looked up at her, and she caught a look of recognition in his eyes. He'd seen her profile then.

'Miss Madinah,' he said, straightening. 'We weren't expecting you until next week.'

'I just wanted to touch base and get the lay of the land,' she replied, tucking her blonde hair back behind her ear. 'Ease into it slowly rather than jump off the deep end.'

He smiled and nodded in understanding, looking down at the receptionist. 'Better call up.'

'Yes, sir,' the receptionist said. Sydney saw her call an in-house number and announced her arrival to whoever had answered.

The man came around the side of the table, extending a hand towards her. 'Nicholas Keaton.'

'Sydney Madinah.' She took his hand in a firm shake. 'Have you been a manager here long?'

'Since it opened,' he replied. 'I understand this is your first management position.'

'It is, yes,' she said.

'It's an excellent hotel,' he said. 'I'll give you the tour once Miss Taylor gives the go-ahead.'

Sydney recognised the name of the woman who had conducted her job interview, and hearing footsteps, she looked up to see the red-headed woman from the online video conference coming down the stairs. She was as well dressed and clean-cut as she had appeared over the internet, and the way she walked and held herself told Sydney that this woman was confident and not one to take anyone's BS. The woman, Miss Taylor, extended a hand automatically towards her.

'Rita Taylor,' the woman said with a tight smile. 'I've been expecting you.'

Sydney accepted her handshake.

'Sydney Madinah. I'm not due for another week.'

'I appreciate the dedication,' Rita said. 'I've already got the paperwork ready for you, and your security and network profiles are already set up. Nick will give you the tour of the hotel and answer any questions you have regarding clientele. You can find me here if you need me.' Rita handed her a card with a floor and room number.

With that, she turned and started back up the stairs. Sydney had to admire her directness. She found it lacking in the industry, and having a no-nonsense PR rep was a breath of fresh air.

'I hope you don't find Miss Taylor too off-putting,' Nicholas said, tilting back slightly on his heels in slight apology. 'She's a lovely lady; she's just very…'

'Busy,' Sydney finished.

'She is that,' Nicholas said. 'Shall we begin the tour?'

Sydney nodded her consent. 'Yes, please.'

* * * * *

Despite its heritage exterior, the Medina Grand had all the amenities Sydney associated with a modern hotel. Whoever had been in charge of renovating the hotel had done so with care, maintaining the history while incorporating the new. There was an indoor heated pool with a sauna, several function rooms, a courtyard, and a well-equipped gym. Every room had a kitchen, some their own laundry, and guests had access to complimentary Wi-Fi.

It was clear to Sydney that they aimed the hotel more towards long-stay guests, particularly those of the business variety. However, Nicholas also explained the hotel's popularity for weddings and receptions. Sydney imagined the courtyard would be a popular location for wedding photos.

After going over the various guest rooms and the facilities, Nicholas moved them into the hotel staff areas. He introduced Sydney to different members of staff who were more than happy to talk her through their tasks and answer questions she had. Sydney quickly realised that Nicholas would leave her with a well-oiled machine. Everyone knew their role, and everyone seemed open and welcoming.

As they walked back towards reception, Nicholas cleared his throat. 'Just so you are aware, a few places in the hotel are off-limits, even to the manager. We have three permanent residents in the hotel, and we are not to enter their rooms unless we're invited or it is necessary for us to do so. The first is Mr and Mrs Hall. Mr Xavier Hall is a prominent businessman here in Adelaide, and Mrs Katherine Hall is a senior law firm partner. They live out of the hotel during the week and return to their property in the Adelaide Hills on the weekends.

'Our other permanent resident is Mr Kingston. He is a silent partner of the hotel and handles the business side of things. Miss Taylor works directly for him, and their office is within his room. They are very busy people, so we try to stay out of their way as much as possible. Mr Kingston is also the owner of the storage room I pointed out earlier.' Sydney remembered the doorway in the tunnels below with the 'Do Not Enter' sign. 'Access to that room is strictly forbidden.'

Sydney could understand the need for privacy, especially for the permanent residents. The hotel was their home; while some people enjoyed the room service and having a maid to tidy their room, others did not. 'They're aware I will take over as manager next week?'

'They are. I can tell you now that Mr and Mrs Hall are hard people to catch given their hours, but are a rather pleasant couple. Mr Kingston…' Nicholas frowned. 'I've always gotten along well with him, but he can be a bit… reserved when meeting new people. He is a hard man to win the trust of. Please don't be offended if he seems distant initially, but he'll warm once you get to know him.'

Nicholas led the way through a side door into the courtyard, Sydney taking in the tables and chairs. A middle-aged Aboriginal man stood near two older ladies talking, and Sydney could tell from how he was dressed that he worked there. Nicholas moved towards him. 'Simon, I'd like you to meet the new hotel manager.'

'So Rita was right,' the man extended his hand towards her. 'Simon Pierce. I'm the manager of the cafe and restaurant here at the Medina.'

'Sydney Madinah,' she replied.

One of the old ladies clicked her tongue. 'With a name like that, you were destined to work here.'

'Oh, hogwash,' her companion said. 'It's just a coincidence. That's what that is.'

'There's no such thing,' the first lady countered. 'Everything happens for a–'

'It does not!' the second lady interrupted.

'Careful ladies, or you'll scare the poor girl off.' A man from the following table cut in.

Simon sighed, smiling. 'I'm afraid this is something you'll get quite used to. Dot and Lizzie are always in philosophical disagreement, with Kian playing the peacemaker.'

'We're not in disagreement,' one lady said. 'Dorothy and I simply approach things from different angles.'

'Pretty sure that's a disagreement, Elizabeth,' Dorothy countered. She looked up at Sydney. 'Lizzie's a bit tizzy.'

'And Dotty is a bit spotty,' Elizabeth shot back.

'And I'm never going to have a coffee in peace,' Kian said. Sydney couldn't help but notice a faint accent, but couldn't quite place it. The man was in a suit minus a tie, his hair cropped close and his goatee well-trimmed. She picked him for a business man.

Dorothy and Elizabeth, on the other hand, were more casually dressed. Their clothing could only be described as neat casual. Both women had grey hair; Dorothy had a tight perm, while Elizabeth's hair was cut to shoulder length. From their empty bags, they intended to go shopping.

'Oh, hush you,' Elizabeth said to Kian. 'You enjoy it. Otherwise you wouldn't sit so close.'

'This is the best seat in the courtyard,' Kian said, raising his cup to his lips. 'I will not part with it because of you two.'

'So you're all regulars,' Sydney said.

'Tuesday through Friday,' Dorothy confirmed. 'A drop of tea before we go to the market, and another before we go home.'

'The Adelaide Central Market,' Nicholas said before Sydney could ask. 'It's not far from here. It's also open Saturdays, but the ladies here don't seem to do weekends.'

'I fail to see why you need to go every day,' Kian said. 'It rarely changes.'

'We have our reasons,' Elizabeth said. 'Better than being cooped up at home.'

'We've been going to the market for years,' Dorothy said. 'We get to know people and get some exercise while we're at it.'

'We'll probably outlive the market,' Elizabeth said with a laugh, Dorothy joining her.

'I live and work not far away,' Kian said, answering Sydney's comment. 'I find it a nice place to sit, have a coffee and catch up on some work. For the most part, it's rather peaceful.'

'Dot, I think we've just been insulted,' Elizabeth said with mock horror.

'I don't think there's any thinking necessary, Lizzie,' Dorothy said with equal false shock, a smile tugging at her lips. 'Mr MacDowell finds us to be loud.'

'Not loud,' Kian said calmly. 'More a… consistent buzz.'

'Well, I never,' Elizabeth said, one hand on her chest in feigned outrage but unable to keep the grin from her face.

'Never, ever,' Dorothy added.

'Careful, Kian, you'll have them rioting,' Simon laughed.

'That would make for something interesting for once,' Kian replied.

The two ladies gasped in mock exasperation, throwing their napkins over at him. A tiny smile twitched at the corner of his otherwise impassive face, although his eyes were sparkling with amusement.

'We better leave before the pitchforks come out,' Nicholas said with a smile, leading Sydney back inside.

'I take it that's a regular thing,' Sydney said, gesturing back to the courtyard.

'Kian is usually a lot quieter,' Nicholas admitted. 'He's more a… people watcher. Dot and Lizzie are the types that want to get into the thick of it.'

'And gossipers, I'm guessing,' Sydney said.

Nicholas nodded. 'They could also tell you about every conspiracy theory known to man. If you spend enough time with them, they'll have you questioning your existence and believing in aliens.'

'The universe is pretty big,' Sydney said thoughtfully.

'You'll fit right in,' Nicholas laughed, stopping at the front desk. 'And that concludes our tour. I hope you didn't find it too overwhelming.'

'The Medina is much smaller than the hotels I've previously worked at,' Sydney said. 'Not as much to take in.'

'Oh, you'll find she has her quirks,' Nicholas said. 'Most old buildings do. I sometimes wish the walls could talk.'

Sydney smiled. She had always found that, in some ways, walls did talk. The cleanliness of the hotel told her it was well cared for, but the floors, stairs and railings were well worn. Some areas were more worn than others telling her which areas saw more traffic. Some walls had slightly different textures, showing they were more recent changes to the original interior, most likely from when the building was converted to a hotel. The building spoke of classical elegance and the state's wealth when they built it.

Sydney was sure that the more time she spent there, the more the building would speak to her, and she looked forward to uncovering all the little secrets that the Treasury Building and hotel offered.

* * * * *

Before heading home, Sydney did a lap of the hotel's exterior, getting to know the location of all the outside exits. She took in everything, from where the windows looked (and therefore the view from the interior rooms) to the placement of the skip bins. Her former mentor had told her early on that it was as essential to know the outside of the hotel as it was to know the inside, as the hotel existed within a larger city and where and how it was placed within that city meant everything.

As she neared the end of Pilgrim Lane, the sound of hushed voices caught her attention. She knew it was rude to listen in on someone else's conversation, but something about how they talked hooked her in. She slowed, stepping further into the shadows, and strained to hear what was being said.

'–don't even know that I'm right about this,' the first man said.

'It's a lead and the best we've got,' the second man replied, his voice deeper and with the barest of an accent she couldn't quite place. 'I have faith in you–'

'I don't,' the first man cut in.

'You should,' the second said. 'It's certainly worth a look.'

'Have you thought about what happens if we get caught?'

'First, we won't, and second, when do you care about getting caught?'

'Since it's right next door, and we have to show our faces around here,' the first man said. 'I don't see why we can't do it in the daytime.'

'Because it's easier at night when nobody's around, and they'd never let us back in the day.' There was a pause. 'We're doing this. If you want to sit out–'

'No, you're not going without me,' the first man cut him off. 'If I'm wrong, I want to be the one to wear it when it goes balls up.'

'It won't.' The pause was longer this time. Sydney felt the hair on the back of her neck prickle.

'What is it?' The first man asked.

'I think somebody's listening,' the second man said.

Sydney took that as her cue to leave, stepping quickly out of the lane and onto Flinders Street and the foot traffic. Her heart felt like it was racing a mile a minute as she tried to piece together what she had overheard. It had sounded like the plans for a break-in, as if they were going to steal something. Given their proximity to the Town Hall, she could only assume it was there. Could she have overheard government employees planning a Watergate-esque plot?

Sydney didn't stop until she got to her apartment and locked the door behind her. She wondered if she should call the police, but she knew that simply saying what she had overheard wasn't enough. It didn't help that she hadn't seen who was talking. All that she knew was there were two men, and one of them had a faint accent. For the time being, there was nothing she could do about it, but she was confident that she would be awake all night trying to work out just what she had heard.

2

Two days after the incident in the laneway, Sydney returned to the hotel with a small bag over her shoulder containing all the signed paperwork. Over the past day, she had been emailing back and forth with Rita, who had sent her all the paperwork for her to bring in when she was ready. Even though it was still a few days out from her starting date, Sydney knew how much easier it would be to take the paperwork in early, so she'd read through it and completed everything as soon as she could.

The conversation she'd overheard in the laneway still bothered her. She'd monitored local news reports about any break-ins to the government offices, but nothing had crossed her news feed. The only robberies she'd seen were the legal kind that occurred daily in politics. However, she wondered if a break-in to a government building would go unreported on purpose to avoid copycats.

The same reception lady she'd seen on her first visit was behind the desk and smiled when she saw her. 'Mr Keaton is in the courtyard,' she said.

'Thank you,' Sydney replied, giving an answering smile before turning in the courtyard's direction. She'd learned on her initial visit that while the cafe/restaurant served breakfast for paying guests, it did not open to the public until midmorning for a light brunch before it closed to prepare for the lunchtime crowds and afternoon functions. There were a modest number of customers for being midweek, but enough to keep Simon busy. He gave her a nod as he prepared an order at the coffee station, a nod she returned.

She found Nicholas seated with the same two ladies from her last visit at the same table. Close to them, at his same table, she saw Kian typing on a small notebook computer, his coffee, and an empty plate within easy reach. To the casual observer, he seemed engrossed in his work, but Sydney could tell he was listening closely to the conversation at the nearby table. It was a serious topic given the looks on everyone's faces, and Sydney wondered for a moment if it would be better to come back later, but Nicholas spotted her before she could leave and waved her over.

'We didn't scare you away then,' Dorothy said with a smile.

'Not yet,' Sydney answered smiling and tucking her hair back behind her ear.

'That almost sounds like a challenge,' Elizabeth said with a short laugh, some of the tension lifting from the table as they invited her to join them.

'Miss Taylor said to expect you,' Nicholas said. 'That you were planning on finalising the paperwork.'

'She was right,' Sydney said, patting her bag. 'I like to keep on top of things.'

'There certainly is a lot to keep on top of, especially with the business with the church,' Dorothy said.

'Oh, Dotty!' Elizabeth huffed. 'You don't need to bother her with that!'

'Well, the hotel could be next!' Dorothy countered.

'You don't know that!'

'And you certainly don't know that it won't!'

'I don't think it's anything to worry about,' Nicholas said in an assuring voice. 'Nothing was taken, and no actual damage was done.' He must have seen the confusion on Sydney's face, because he turned to her. 'There was a break-in at the Pilgrim Church last night. Someone disabled the security systems and picked the lock. Police suspect it was probably some kids wanting to get pictures for online or something.'

Sydney immediately had flashbacks to the overheard conversation, the puzzle pieces falling into place. Something must have shown on her face because Dorothy gripped her arm, leaning in.

'You know something!'

'I just overheard some people talking the other day, that's all,' she admitted. 'A couple of men—'

'Hope I'm not interrupting,' a voice said behind her.

'Just the usual conspiracies and gossip,' Kian called across.

'Oh, hush you,' Dorothy shot back.

Sydney turned to find a young man standing nearby. He was dressed in semiformal attire: dark suit pants and a business shirt, but no tie. He wore his blond hair short with a slight spike, and he was of athletic build. A hotel nametag caught the morning light, and the wire hooked into one ear gave him away as hotel security. He had the natural tan of someone who got a lot of sun, even though he most likely spent a lot of time indoors for work, which told her he spent most of his off-time outdoors.

'Jake,' Nicholas said with a smile towards the newcomer, 'this is Sydney Madinah. Sydney, I'd like you to meet our head of security – Jake Peterson.'

Sydney tried to hide her surprise as she stood and took his offered hand in a firm shake. 'Pleased to meet you.'

'Yes, I know. I'm young,' Jake said, blue eyes twinkling with amusement. 'I get it a lot. I assure you I got the job by merit, not from being pretty.'

'You broke the security system,' Kian accused.

'No, I improved the security system,' Jake countered, fixing him with a levelled look. 'You're just bitter that I nailed shut that back door you've been trying to hack into all morning.'

Kian glared at him. 'You've made the system volatile—'

'The system is fine, thanks, and I think you'll find that the contract states that we can change the program out of our discretion—'

'Within reason!'

'All I did was streamline your spaghetti code—'

Kian slammed his hands down on the sides of the table. 'It wasn't spaghetti code before you got to it!'

'Gentleman, gentleman!' Nicholas said, raising his hands. 'Another time.'

'Yes,' Jake said, giving Kian one last glare. 'I came here for a reason.' He pulled a card on a lanyard from his pocket and offered it to Sydney. 'One security pass. We can set up a passcode and your system profile if you swing by the office later. We utilise both an internal and external system, so you'll be able to check your messages and bookings from home should you need to and make changes.'

'Saves you from having to come in should something arise with the system,' Nicholas said. 'Aside from all the paperwork and setting up the system, you should be ready to start.' He paused. 'There is, of course, the case of your office. I can take you through everything I have in there that you might need. We also still have paper copies of records that we keep downstairs. You'd be surprised how often people want them over the much easier digitised copies.'

'There was a frequent guest at the hotel in New York who refused everything but paper copies,' Sydney said. 'He used to pay in cash because he didn't trust the banks, and we had to keep one room without a keycard just for him.'

'Was he a doomsday prepper?' Jake asked. 'They believe someone will Dark Angel the world with an EMP bomb. Fry every computer, wipe out the digital currency, kill the power grid and all that.'

'You know what? I think he was,' Sydney said. 'He was always going on about the cold war never-ending, and that satellite dishes and mobile phones were mind controlling us.'

'I bet he had a bunker.'

'Oh, he did. He would show us pictures of it. Polaroid pictures.'

'There are some crazy people in the world,' Jake said.

'And they all stay at hotels at some point,' Nicholas agreed. He looked at Jake and raised a brow. 'Remember the X-Files convention?'

'That was a blast,' Jake laughed. 'I still have the tin foil hat one guy made me.'

Nicholas smiled at Sydney. 'This wasn't a tv show convention, but one where people believed the X-Files were real. I heard more stories about alien abduction in one weekend than I had my entire career.'

'You don't believe in aliens, do you, Nicholas?' Sydney glanced back to see two men approaching through the doors to the courtyard. They were both tall and lean, and both wore suit pants with button-up dress shirts that Sydney expected from business people, although neither of them wore a tie, and both had the top button undone. The one who had spoken was the taller of the two, and Sydney guessed him to be in his mid-thirties. His dark hair had only the faintest hint of silver at his temples, and he wore it at a length that brushed his shoulders. A soft curl fell almost into his eyes. He was a classically handsome man with green eyes that held a look she usually saw in men much older than himself.

The second man was younger and lankier in his build but equally fit. Fashionable glasses sat over his blue eyes, his brown hair cut short and neat, countering the day-old stubble on his jaw. He was almost boyish, but he held himself with confidence and grace. His head tilted slightly with curiosity as he looked at her, and she could see he was reading her the same way she was reading him.

Nicholas and Jake straightened at the sight of them, their eyes on the older of the two men, which told Sydney that this was someone important.

'Mr Kingston,' Nicholas said, smiling. 'We don't usually see you down at this hour.'

'I heard our new manager was here,' Kingston said. 'I thought I'd introduce myself.' He turned to her and extended a hand. 'You must be Sydney Madinah. My name is Kingston.'

Sydney took his hand, his ring warm against her skin. She saw something flicker in his eyes for a moment, but it was gone so quickly that she couldn't be sure if she'd seen anything. 'Pleased to meet you, Mr Kingston.'

'Just Kingston. No need for the "Mr".' He glanced up. 'As I've told Nicholas many times, but he insists.'

'Old habit,' Nicholas said with a shrug.

The second man extended his hand towards her. 'Raymond Barry. I'm a friend of Kingston's.'

'Who should be at work,' Jake said softly.

'I got curious,' Raymond said as he shook Sydney's hand. 'They won't miss me for ten minutes.'

'But it's never ten minutes with you.'

'It's close to his break,' Kingston said. 'I believe he said it was a slow day.'

'It's always slow,' Raymond said, pulling a face.

'Still, Jake is right; you are needing to get back to work,' Kingston reminded him. 'And so should I.'

'Does Rita even know you're down here?' Jake asked.

'She does.' Kingston turned to Sydney. 'Rita has time to finish the paperwork and sign off on the last details. She has a meeting in forty-five minutes, though, so you better not dawdle. You better get back to work yourself, Jake.' Turning towards the door, he pressed a hand into the small of Raymond's back and gave him a light shove. 'We'll leave you to it. Be seeing you at the going away party, Nicholas.'

After the three men had left, Sydney heard one of the older ladies making a soft sound of admiration. 'Handsome men, aren't they?' Elizabeth said.

'They look better going than they do coming,' Dorothy agreed.

'Oh hush,' Elizabeth laughed.

Sydney caught Kian's eye roll and couldn't help but smile.

* * * * *

One thing Sydney had quickly come to admire about Rita was her efficiency. The other woman knew how to manage time and organised her paperwork. She also knew what they needed and how to do it and understood all the relevant topics. It took them less than thirty minutes to complete the paperwork and get things in order, with Rita sending Sydney back to Nicholas to go through the documentation in his (soon hers) office. By the end, Sydney was confident to start working the following week.

She next stopped in the security office, where she found Jake and another worker watching the various monitors while sorting out an issue with a security key. It didn't take long to get set up on the system, with Jake loaning her a spare laptop to sit in the foyer and familiarise herself with the system. Thankfully, she found it to be like systems she'd used before, and the system's navigation was simple but effective. She made a note to bring her own laptop to work the next day so she could have the system software installed.

'Sir, you can't go back there.'

Sydney looked up at the sound of the warning from the receptionist and spotted a man leaning over the desk and reaching for something. She frowned as he seemed to find what he was after and grab it.

'Sir, you need to stop!'

Sydney put the laptop down and stood at the second warning, but the man was already on the move. From the word 'sir' Sydney could tell this man was not a guest, and he'd just stolen something from behind the receptionist's desk. Glancing at his hand, she spotted the flash of a keycard. Alarms rang in Sydney's head. Back in New York, on more than one occasion, she'd had to deal with cases of people trying to gain access to the hotel rooms of others for nefarious reasons.

'Sir!'

Sydney saw the receptionist reaching for the button under the desk that would sound the alert in the security office. The man hurried away, and Sydney knew he would be gone with his prize by the time security arrived. She decided without a second thought to follow him. It surprised her when he didn't head toward the main staircase but to the stairs that lead down to the former vaults below the hotel.

As she rushed after him, Sydney remembered the bar and the

various storage spaces that took up residence in the catacombs below the treasury building. This man was clearly not after a guest, but something in one of those two areas. He passed the bar area without slowing down, making a beeline straight towards the storage rooms.

'Hey!'

Sydney called out, trying to get him to slow, but he was a man on a mission. He didn't stop until he was directly in front of a door, swiping the keycard over the lock. Kingston's storage, she realised. The same room she'd been told was off-limits to everyone but Kingston himself. Whatever this man was after must be in there.

The man threw open the door and disappeared inside. Sydney hesitated for a moment and wondered if she should wait for security. There was probably a reason Kingston didn't want anyone in there and she doubted there was another way out. Curiosity got the better, and she stepped in the door.

She found herself in a small room with two other doors on opposite walls to each other. The thief had opened the door to the right and was staring at whatever was inside with a look of confusion. Whatever he was after was not behind door number one. He stepped back, slamming the door and rushing to the door on the left wall and throwing it open. He paused for a second, and Sydney ran towards him and grabbed his shirt.

'You've got to stop,' she said.

The man glanced at her quickly, and then stepped through the door. Sydney's fingertips just brushed the fabric as he stepped out of reach. She hurried after him, reaching for him again. This time her fingers found material and she yanked back, only for the shirt to fall as the man seemed to vanish. She blinked, barely noticing the rush of warm air as she followed him through the doorway, staring at the empty shirt in her fingers.

A fine layer of dust poured from the shirt onto the floor, where the man's pants and shoes lay in an unceremonious pile. He'd disintegrated. The keycard that had been in his hand hit the wooden floor with a slap of plastic and skidded a good foot away. Shock washed over her as her mind raced to process what had just happened.

'Not again.'

The voice came from her right and glancing up, Sydney spotted two people sitting and staring at her from what looked like a dining table. Sydney instantly recognised one of them as Raymond Barry. The other, an older woman, sighed and looked at Raymond.

'We need to change that lock.'

3

SYDNEY LET THE shirt slip from her fingers onto the floor, panic rushing over her. Behind her, she heard running feet, and glancing back, she saw Jake burst through the door and slide to a stop. He glanced at her before looking down at the pile of clothing on the floor.

'Shit,' he muttered.

'What happened to the additional security measures you promised us?' the woman said from the table. 'You said this wouldn't happen again.'

'I know, I know, I'm working on it,' Jake said, eyes not leaving what had once been a man. 'I got distracted.'

'With the new manager?' Raymond said, eyes falling on Sydney.

'Yeah. Also, a software update and a million other things.'

Sydney heard more footsteps behind Jake and saw Rita and Kingston step into the small room. Rita looked exasperated, while it surprised Sydney to see a look of almost amusement on Kingston's face.

'Well, this is awkward,' Kingston said, his eyes meeting Sydney's. 'Miss Madinah.'

'Mr Kingston,' she replied, trying to keep herself from hyperventilating.

She felt someone take her arm and lead her to the dining room table and sit her down. Rita knelt before her, gripping Sydney's arms. 'I need you to slowly breathe in through your nose and out through your mouth. Focus on your breathing.'

Relaxation techniques, Sydney realised. But how she could relax after she'd just seen a man—

'Sydney, I need you to focus,' Rita said again. 'I need you to breathe in, hold it for five seconds, then breath out through your mouth while counting to ten.'

'The keycard wouldn't have been under the reception desk, would it?' Raymond asked, looking pointedly at Jake.

Jake winced. 'Maybe.'

'Jake!' the older woman exclaimed.

'I'm sorry, Lucille, but where do you want me to put it?'

'How about in your office?!'

'Enough!' Kingston said, raising his hands. 'Enough. What happened, happened. It's unfortunate, but it happened.'

'Again,' Lucille said.

'Again.' Kingston conceded.

'What… did just happen?' Sydney asked, finally finding her voice. 'That man just…'

'Atomised?' Jake offered. 'Disintegrated? Dustified?'

'Not helping,' Rita said.

'Indeed.' Kingston sighed, brushing a hand through his hair as he seemed to think for a moment. 'Well, Miss Madinah. You've certainly stumbled your way in.'

Sydney felt her stomach drop as she remembered that this area was supposed to have no access. She swallowed hard. 'I'm sorry—'

'Don't apologise. You were trying to stop a thief. You're just lucky that…' he sighed. 'You're part of this now, so we might as well show you.'

'Upstairs?' Raymond asked.

'Upstairs,' Kingston confirmed.

'Oh, sure, leave me with the cleanup,' Lucille said.

'Technically, this is also cleaning up,' Raymond said, moving over to Sydney and offering her a hand. 'Let's go get some fresh air.'

Sydney took the offered hand, allowing him to pull her to her feet. She was a bit surprised when he led her away from the doorway she had entered and instead down a hallway. It was only then that Sydney noticed her surroundings more, realising that she seemed to be in some kind of apartment. They had been in a dining room with an adjoining kitchen, and as they walked down the corridor, she spotted doorways leading off into what seemed to be an office, at least one bedroom, a bathroom, and an archway that led into a living area. At the end of the corridor was a staircase leading upstairs, Raymond leading the way up.

Once they reached the top, they approached a doorway, Raymond opening it and leading the way out. It was then that Sydney realised Kingston had followed them. Raymond led the way through another corridor and up another staircase, bringing them to a doorway. He paused, looking back at Sydney with a mischievous twinkle in his eye.

'You ready?'

Sydney frowned. 'For what?'

He smirked and opened the door, leading the way outside.

It took a moment for her eyes to adjust to the light, Sydney taking in the sound of traffic, pedestrians and… trams? Sure enough, a tram was gliding its way down the street to her right. Sydney took in the unfamiliar surroundings and tried to place where she was. She knew she should have been outside the Treasury Building in Adelaide, but this looked like a different city altogether. Raymond led her around the front of the building they had just exited and over onto a grassy area. Sydney looked back at the building and frowned as she read the word 'Victoria'.

'Welcome to Melbourne,' Raymond said. 'The State Library, to be exact. That's Swanston Street in front of you.'

'Wait… Melbourne?!' Sydney felt her legs turn to jelly for the second time in an hour. 'How can… we were just in Adelaide!'

'The door you came through, the one that caused the man to disintegrate, was a portal,' Kingston said, pressing a reassuring hand into the middle of her back. 'One leads between the Treasury

Building in Adelaide and the State Library of Victoria here in Melbourne. Only people with certain DNA can safely use it. You have that DNA. The man that crossed before you did not.'

'So you're saying that if I didn't have the right DNA, I would have…'

'Unfortunately, yes,' Kingston said. 'Over the last month, at least three people have tried to access the portal. You're the only one who's crossed successfully.'

Sydney let herself sink onto the grass, thankful that it was soft and that it wasn't wet. There were people sitting all over the grass, seeming to be working with text books and papers. Nausea rolled over her, and she stared back at the bricks of the state library with its columns standing proud and tall. She felt like she was going to be sick. She began practising the breathing technique Rita had just taught her.

This was a lot to get her head around. That a portal like that could exist was something straight out of science fiction. It was the sort of thing you'd expect to be public knowledge, which made her wonder how many people knew about its existence.

'The only people who know about the portal were in that room,' Kingston said as if reading her mind, sitting down beside her. 'And it needs to stay that way, so it's safe to say that you cannot tell anyone about what you've seen today.'

'So nobody else knows?' Sydney asked.

'There's a couple of other people,' Raymond admitted, sitting on her other side. 'But they're sworn to secrecy. There are many reasons, but you've seen firsthand the main one.'

'So there's a portal,' Sydney said, trying to wrap her mind around what they were telling her. 'A portal between Melbourne and Adelaide, and only certain people can use it. And if you're the wrong person, you die?'

'Pretty much,' Raymond said.

Sydney studied the two men, looking from one to the other and trying to read their faces. She frowned. 'No, there's more to it than that. You're leaving something out.'

Raymond raised his eyebrows and looked up at Kingston. 'She's good.'

Kingston nodded his agreement. 'Rita can pick them.' He met her eye. 'The second door in Adelaide, across from the one that leads to Melbourne, is also a portal. But that door is different. It requires keys to activate it, and each key opens a portal to a different location across Australia and some parts of the world.'

She remembered watching the thief open that door, but he hadn't gone through it. 'But he didn't use that door.'

'He didn't have a key for it,' Raymond said. 'Without a key, it's just a door to a storage room. A dead end.'

'So, what was that back there?' Sydney said, gesturing back towards the library. 'It looked like an apartment of some sort.'

'That would be mine,' Raymond said. 'Mine and my mother's, anyway. That was the lady you saw, my mother, Lucille Barry.'

'You live under the library?' Sydney asked. 'Why?'

'I think that's enough for now,' Kingston said, standing. He offered a hand to Sydney to pull her up and then assisted Raymond the same way. 'You've already got a lot to wrap your head around. We'll tell you more in due time, but I believe you have some thinking to do for now.'

'What do you mean?' She asked.

'For a start, do you still want the hotel job after everything you've just seen?'

Sydney frowned. 'Of course. My knowing won't affect anything, will it?'

'Probably make things easier,' Raymond admitted.

'Second,' Kingston continued. 'Is a question of how deep down this rabbit hole you want to go? Is just knowing about the portal enough, or do you want to know everything? Be aware that knowing everything has its risks and dangers. It will put you in the sights of some very dangerous people. It's not a decision to be taken lightly, so I suggest you sleep on it.'

Sydney nodded, feeling there was a lot more to it that they hadn't told her. Like where the keys were, why Raymond lived under the library, and just why the portal existed in the first place and who had created it. All those questions would keep her up at night. But for now, she let them go. Her mind was buzzing as it was.

★ ★ ★ ★ ★

As predicted, Sydney found it nearly impossible to sleep. At first, she thought it might have all been some kind of dream, a nightmare, as the sight of the man disintegrating played itself over in her mind repeatedly. That whole thing made her feel sick. She entertained the thought of calling into the hotel and saying she'd changed her mind and catching the first flight back to New York and begging for her old job back, but she knew if she did, she'd never be able to get the answers that she so desperately wanted.

Instead, Sydney finished the last of her preparations for starting her managerial role, installing the software Jake had given her on a USB onto her laptop and using her new sign-in to sync everything up. She'd kept in contact with Nicholas, a man she was sure didn't know about the portal, and she caught up on everything she would need to know to start her new job officially.

When the starting day finally rolled around, Sydney dressed herself in dress pants, a blouse and flat shoes and headed into the hotel. The staff warmly greeted her. Nicholas stayed on for the first day to help oversee a smooth transition. Sydney easily fell into the manager's role, finding the hotel much easier to run than the New York one. Jake and Rita had both stopped by to check on her, neither mentioning what had transpired just days beforehand and keeping things strictly to business.

The first day quickly became the first week, remaining uneventful and so typical that Sydney questioned that what had happened with the portal had ever happened at all. That somehow, she had just dreamed up the entire thing while stressing about her new responsibilities and role. That was until Friday evening.

Sydney stuck her head into the security room, smiling as she spotted Jake playing a game on his laptop. The blue lights of the multitude of CCTV screens flickered over his face as he concentrated hard on what he was doing.

'Bye, Jake,' she said as she pulled her scarf out of her large bag hanging on her arm.

'See ya, Syd,' Jake responded, glancing at her quickly before turning back to the laptop again. 'Have a nice dinner,' he said to her retreating back.

She chuckled at the politeness of Jake. As she stepped around the counter, Simon entered out of the cafe to her right.

'Night, Simon,' she said.

Still smiling after one of the most effortless shifts she had ever worked, she felt a hand snake around her arm. The smile fell off her face as she looked up into the green eyes of Kingston, who had a firm grip on her arm and was walking with her towards to front door. Sydney glanced to find Raymond on her other side. He wasn't touching her, but he was close enough that she felt his body heat through her black wool coat.

'Miss Madinah deserves a delightful meal to welcome her to Adelaide, don't you think, Simon?' Kingston said over his shoulder as he continued to walk her out of the door.

It appeared to be a rhetorical question, as he had not awaited Simon's answer. Sydney was still shocked at the fait accompli that the two men seemed to perpetuate. As she blinked and some of her wits returned, she secretly tried to work her free arm into her handbag.

The brisk Adelaide night revealed a waiting taxi right at the front door of the hotel. Raymond stepped forward and opened the rear car door. He turned back to her and Kingston, and Sydney found herself sans her handbag.

'I'll take this for you,' Raymond said as he rounded the rear of the taxi to walk to the other side.

Sydney shivered; the mace her father had taught her to use during a crisis was now in the hands of a man she wasn't sure had her best interests at heart.

'Dinner, Miss Madinah?' Kingston asked her as he gestured to the waiting taxi.

Sydney weighed the public nature of their exit from the hotel and took the plunge to step into the taxi, where Raymond was already waiting with her handbag.

She had to hurry over into the middle seat as Kingston followed her into the back seat.

'The Italian Club,' Kingston told the taxi driver as she tried to curl in on herself and not touch either man filling up the spaces. The back seat of the taxi was not spacious, and she could feel both of them pressing in on her. She was trapped.

4

S YDNEY WAS SURE the Italian Club was a pleasant restaurant, but she found it rather hard to focus with the two men who had escorted her there sitting across from her. It had felt almost like an abduction, and she couldn't help the flashbacks to the incident with the 'portal' just a few days beforehand. She had been almost ready to brush it all off as a bad dream, but the reality of it had come crashing back.

It seemed like a casual affair with the way Kingston and Raymond were partaking in idle conversation about work, and they had ordered without having to look at the menu, which told Sydney they had been to this restaurant several times beforehand. She had followed suit and ordered as well, even though she knew it would be hard to eat until she knew exactly what was happening.

After they had eaten half of their meal, Kingston finally turned to her. 'I'm sure you're wondering why we invited you out tonight.'

She wasn't sure if she'd call it an 'invite', but she played along. 'I am, actually.'

'We thought we'd better finish filling you in on the situation, but first, we had to be sure you would not run,' Kingston said. 'You seem to have fitted nicely into your role as manager.'

'I wasn't about to let a… disintegrating man ruin my career,' she said, trying to lighten the mood with a smile. She was relieved when they smiled back, ever so slightly.

'Considering what you saw, you've handled it well,' Raymond said, pushing his glasses back up his nose. 'We half expected you to quit.'

'I'm not that easy to get rid of.'

'Apparently not.'

'So, Miss Madinah,' Kingston said. 'You've got questions; let's see if we can answer them.'

The questions came fast into her head, Sydney sorting them into importance. 'Where did the portals come from?'

'They built them when the treasury building and state library were constructed,' Kingston answered. 'They've been off-limits to the public since their construction. A man known as the Overseer oversaw their construction. He disappeared soon after they were completed, and no one has seen or heard from him since. At least not that we're aware of, given his name was classified and the people who knew it died over a century ago.'

'Who knew it?'

'That would be the people behind the two buildings, our relatives' Raymond answered. 'Kingston here is a descendant of George Strickland Kingston, who designed the original building that stood on the site of the Adelaide Treasury Building. My ancestor is Redmond Barry, who was behind the construction of the State Library of Victoria. They were the original Protector and Keeper of the portals.'

Sydney frowned. 'Protector and Keeper?'

'Keeper of the Keys,' Raymond continued. 'For the second portal to work, you need to have a key, with each one unlocking a different destination portal. They look like an ordinary brass keys to the naked eye, but there's more to them than that. We don't know how many keys there are – there could be hundreds. We know that Redmond Barry hid the keys all over Adelaide and Melbourne and recorded their locations in code in his journals.'

'The role of the Protector is much simpler,' Kingston said. 'The role is to protect the portals from those who want to misuse them and keep people from accidentally stumbling upon them and… well, you saw.'

The image of the man turning to dust played in her mind's eye, causing Sydney to shudder. 'You said only certain people can use the portals?'

'Yes,' Kingston said. He raised his hand, Sydney seeing his gold ring catch in the light. 'This ring reacts to anyone with the right DNA. No doubt you noticed it when I shook your hand.'

Sydney remembered how warm his ring had felt when they first met. 'I remember. But how does someone get the right DNA? Is it a genetic thing?'

'It appears so,' Kingston said. 'Some people have stronger lineages than others.'

'But where did the original linage come from?' Sydney asked. 'And the portals? Where did they come from? How do they work?'

'That information is lost to time,' Kingston said.

Convenient, Sydney thought, but it raised more questions than answers. 'So the Keeper knows where all the keys are?'

'Not quite,' Raymond answered. 'As I said, Redmond wrote their locations in code in his journal. The encryption key for the code died with him, so for the last few generations, the Keepers have been trying to break the code.'

'And did they?'

'Raymond's great-grandfather did,' Kingston said. 'But they killed him for that knowledge.'

'Wait… *killed*?!' Sydney felt her stomach flip at those words. 'People out there would kill to get the keys?'

'Of course,' Kingston said. 'In the wrong hands, the portals could be used for untold destruction politically and financially. Who knows which buildings around the world the portals could lead into, thus granting the user unlimited access to many things. That's why the Keeper and Protector are necessary.'

'So wouldn't it be better not to break the code?'

'Exactly what Rita said,' Raymond mumbled.

'Yes and no,' Kingston admitted. 'The problem is the keys are hidden in historic buildings, and buildings have a habit of being renovated and knocked down. Keys are lost or uncovered in the process, so it's important to find them and… relocate them to a more secure location.'

'But you don't know the code.' She saw something flicker across their faces. 'You do. You broke the code.'

'Recently,' Raymond admitted. 'At least I think I have.'

'The key was where you said it would be,' Kingston said.

Sydney remembered the two voices she had heard in the laneway behind the hotel, and it took little for her to put two and two together. 'You were the ones who broke into the church next to the hotel.'

Guilt flashed over their faces, along with Kingston's faint, accusing look. 'I assume you were the one who was listening in on our conversation.'

Sydney nodded. 'When two people are whispering like that, it's hard not to.'

'We need to watch ourselves,' Raymond said to Kingston. 'If Sydney could listen in, anyone could.'

'Indeed,' Kingston agreed. 'From now on, we should limit our conversations to my room.'

'But aren't we talking about it here?' Sydney said.

Kingston and Raymond both straightened slightly, glancing around them. Sydney couldn't help but do the same, but nobody around them seemed to be paying any attention to them. Everyone was engrossed in their meals and their conversations.

'So, who else knows?' Sydney asked. 'About the… you know what?'

'Jake and Rita,' Kingston said. 'Jake is our security, although he needs to improve given recent events. Rita keeps things organised and is also a registered nurse, should we ever need one.'

'Also, my mother,' Raymond said. 'Lucille. You saw her the other day. My grandparents on my mother's side also know, as my grandfather was the Keeper before me. Also my father, but he…'

Raymond paused, seeming to search for a word. '… travels. For work, I mean. He's in Europe at the moment. Has been for some time.'

Sydney caught the subtext to his comments: a broken home, but not a divorce. An absentee father, nonetheless. 'Do others know? I mean, that guy who…'

'A strong argument to say that, yes, others know,' Kingston frowned. 'From what we've seen so far, none of those who have attempted to access the por–' he caught himself. 'Storage room, have known exactly what they were looking for and haven't been able to use the doorway themselves, which leads us to believe that someone else is instructing them.'

'Someone who wants access?'

Kingston nodded. 'It wouldn't be the first time. As I said, someone who wanted to gain access killed Raymond's great-grandfather, and we don't know exactly how many people out there are aware of what's hidden down there. It could be a handful of people, or it could be hundreds. I'm more inclined to think the former.'

'Yes,' Raymond agreed. 'If it were the latter, Jake would have his hands full.'

'But what was that room in Melbourne?' Sydney asked. 'It looked like an apartment of some sort.'

'It was,' Raymond said. 'That was my home. The Keeper has always lived under the State Library. It's where Redmond's journals are stored, which gives me time to go through them when I'm not at work.'

'And you're a librarian?'

'And Archivist,' Raymond confirmed. 'I work primarily with the historical collection of the library. Mostly digitising books these days.'

Sydney turned to Kingston. 'And you?'

'Co-own the hotel. You could say I'm your boss,' Kingston said with a half-smile.

There was a minor threat in his words. It was unsaid and barely there, but Sydney picked up on it. She knew she had overstepped her boundaries already by going into the restricted area, and she knew she could well have paid for her mistake with her life. She swallowed, feeling a fresh wave of unease at the thought. 'So… now that I know about… you know. Where does that leave me?'

Raymond frowned. 'We will not make you disappear, if that is what you are wondering.'

'I think it is beneficial to us for you to be aware of the … doors.' Kingston half shrugged. 'It will make you more aware of people trying to enter the area, especially if word gets out that Raymond has figured out the code.'

'Do you think word will get out?' Sydney asked.

'It seems like it already has,' Raymond said softly.

'How? A mole?'

'It goes without question that we're being watched at the hotel,' Kingston said. 'Once they see that we're going to specific locations, they will realise what is happening, so incursions will become more frequent.'

'Then maybe it's not a good idea to keep the keycard under the front desk,' Sydney suggested helpfully. 'Wouldn't it be better to be in the security office?'

'Hotel policy kept it under the desk,' Kingston said.

'Then maybe replace it with a fake card. Keep the real one in your room.'

'That could work,' Raymond said, looking at Kingston.

'I'll talk it over with Jake,' Kingston said. He checked his watch. 'Getting late.'

'Best we finish eating,' Raymond agreed.

Sydney looked at her watch and was surprised by how quickly the time had gone. She took the hint that the discussion was over and instead focused her attention back on her meal. She still had a lot of questions, but she doubted she'd get any answers right now. Instead, she vowed to pry them out of them and the others over the coming weeks.

5

After the meeting at the restaurant, Sydney became hyperaware of the region around the restricted area. She couldn't help but suspect anyone who went down that way, including the janitor. Not only that, but she felt her ears prick up at any mention of Kingston even though she knew that there was bound to be discussion about him as a permanent resident of the hotel.

Life at the hotel seemed rather mundane after the first week's excitement. The highlight of Sydney's day quickly became her lunch break when she could go out to the courtyard and have a coffee with Elizabeth and Dorothy, and when he was in a chatty mood, even Kian. She learned that the two ladies were widowers and were born and raised in Adelaide. Neither of them had travelled, and the idea wasn't appealing, although Dorothy had confessed to wishing to visit Paris in her youth.

On the rare occasion, Jake would come out to join them, although his break was a lot shorter than hers. On one afternoon, even Rita had made an appearance. Sydney got the impression that the two of them were observing her, most likely still judging her. Sydney knew it was only a matter of time before they learned she was trustworthy. After all, you didn't become a hotel manager without keeping more than a few secrets.

As the Friday of the second week found her, Sydney was happy that the most significant thing to happen all week was a drunk guest leaving a tap on and flooding the bathroom, something a maid doing a linen change had caught before too much damage was done. The guest had initially claimed that the tap had turned itself on, but after Sydney had stood firm, they had admitted to their error and paid for the damage.

She was clocking out when she felt eyes on her and turned; she spotted Jake striding over to her. 'We've got a meeting,' he said.

'Where?'

'Kingston's place. Ten minutes.'

Thanking him, Sydney went about finishing her hand-off to the night manager, and then headed upstairs to Kingston's quarters.

Rita opened the door not long after Sydney had knocked, Sydney stepping into the room she'd only been in twice beforehand. The main living area of Kingston's rooms had been turned into an office. Rita's desk was at the front of the room near the kitchenette, whereas Kingston's desk sat at the far end of the room. The rest of the room contained an oversized couch and tv, with a window overlooking the street.

'Welcome to conspiracy central,' Jake joked from the couch.

'Be serious,' Rita said from her seat.

'Relax,' Kingston said as he rounded his desk to sit on the edge. 'Miss Madinah.'

'Mr Kingston,' Sydney said, wondering where she should sit. She decided on the space next to Jake, who happily moved up the couch to give her room.

Hearing the door open, Sydney looked up to see Raymond enter.

'Last one, as usual,' Rita chided.

'Yet still on time,' he countered.

'Since we are all here, we will start,' Kingston said, not waiting for Raymond to find somewhere to sit. 'Raymond found another key.'

'I think I have,' Raymond said, perching himself on the edge of Rita's desk. 'Until we look, we don't know for sure.'

'Where?' Jake asked. 'Close by?'

'Melbourne,' Raymond answered. 'St Paul's Cathedral.'

'Another church,' Jake said.

Raymond nodded.

'Wonder if this key will work,' Rita said.

'We won't know until we acquire it,' Kingston said. 'As Raymond is a Melbourne native and Jake is familiar with the city, I thought the two of you could go look.'

'Nice,' Jake said with a grin. 'Got a time?'

'There's a service tomorrow morning,' Raymond said. 'Although I feel it won't be hard to find.'

'What makes you say that?'

'The notes suggest it is around the entranceway,' Raymond answered.

'Try not to look too much like tourists,' Rita said. 'You might want to stay for some of the Mass.'

'Better than breaking in,' Raymond agreed.

'So, what time do we have to be there?' Jake asked.

'Not sure,' Raymond said. 'Early.'

Sydney frowned, pulling her phone out of her pocket and looking up St Paul's Cathedral. It didn't take her long to find the times for Mass. 'Eight am,' she said. 'The Mass starts at eight am.'

'As I said, early,' Raymond said.

'I was planning on surfing, but I guess I'm off to church,' Jake said.

'Better avoid confession, or you'll never get out of there,' Rita teased.

Jake frowned. 'I don't do anything–'

'I meant Raymond,' Rita said. 'He plays sweet, but I have a feeling his sin list would make anyone blush.'

Raymond gave her an innocent 'who, me?' look, but Sydney could see a smirk tugging at the corner of his mouth. Rita was right about him playing sweet. All Sydney could see was an innocent librarian, but there was something about how his eyes sparkled at Rita's comment that had Sydney wondering.

'Might be an idea for you to spend the night at the Barry's,' Kingston said.

'Won't be the first time I've crashed at their place,' Jake said. 'If you don't mind,' he looked over at Raymond.

'Mother won't care,' Raymond said. 'Especially given it's key related.'

'It's a plan then,' Kingston said. 'Let us know how it goes. And be careful.'

* * * * *

If there was one thing Sydney didn't like about living on her own, it was the grocery shopping. It was a necessary evil, as far as she was concerned. She made it a habit of going out on a Friday night after work to do her shopping. She absently wondered if maybe she should try to get it done earlier and try the market but knew that it would probably be impossible given her hours.

As she made her way through the grocery store, she frowned as she swore she spotted a familiar face. Looking again, she realised she had. It was a man who was shopping. He had dark hair cut short and was classically handsome. He hadn't seen her yet, but she realised he seemed always to be shopping at the same hours as her. She wondered if he would recognise her just like she did him.

She didn't have to wait long as the man looked up, recognition crossing his face. Sydney gave him a small wave, that he returned with a smile. She smiled back, looking for some fresh vegetables for the week. She jumped when she sensed someone beside her. It was the man.

'Oops, sorry if I startled you,' he said, an apologetic look on his face.

'No, it's fine,' she said. She took a breath to calm her heart rate. 'I'm just a little jumpy, that's all.'

'We seem to shop at the same hours,' he said.

'It seems that way,' she agreed.

He held out a hand. 'I'm Marcus. Marcus Connolly.'

Sydney accepted his invitation and shook his hand. 'Sydney Madinah.'

'Like the place?' he asked.

She sighed. She got that a lot. 'Yes, like the city.'

'No, I mean Medina, as in the hotel,' Marcus said. 'The one close to here.'

'Yes,' she said with a nod. She didn't want to give him her work location, so she kept that to herself. 'Like the hotel. Slightly different spelling, though.'

'Right,' Marcus said. He glanced around. 'I'm guessing you finished working late.'

'I did,' she confirmed. 'You the same?'

He nodded. 'I work in security. We work the same hours as most businesses. I tend to avoid the night shift.'

She frowned as she looked at him. He didn't strike her as the security sort. 'You're a bouncer?'

'Oh, no,' he said quickly, shaking his head. 'Electronic security. Cameras and alarms.'

That made more sense. 'I know someone who works that sort of job.'

'I work for a firm,' he said. 'We do security for a lot of different businesses. I can't tell you exactly which ones, of course.'

'Classified,' she guessed.

He nodded. 'How about you? Office worker?'

'Do I look like one?' she asked, looking down at herself.

'You do dress the part, and you don't strike me as someone who works in retail,' he answered.

'I work at a hotel,' she said.

He raised a brow. 'Maid?'

'A… bit higher than that,' she said. She didn't wish to give too much away. She didn't know this man from Adam, and, with the things she knew, she couldn't be giving away information to just anyone.

'Ah. Desk clerk,' he guessed.

She didn't answer, instead just shrugging.

'Don't worry, I will not ask which hotel,' he said with his own shrug. 'Confidentiality, right?'

'Right,' she agreed.

'Anyway, I'll let you go back to shopping,' he said. 'I have a show that starts soon, and I wouldn't dare miss it.'

'Have a good night,' she said to him.

As he moved away, she frowned after him. She had a feeling that would not be the last she saw of Marcus.

* * * * *

'At least it isn't raining,' Jake said as they walked along Swanston Street early on Saturday morning. The high-rise city skyline did an adequate job blocking the morning sun, leaving the air chill.

'It's not that cold,' Raymond teased, shoving his hands into the pockets of his woollen coat.

'It's colder than it would be back home,' Jake countered.

'I thought you'd be used to it, given you go swimming and surfing early in the morning,' Raymond said. 'Wouldn't the water be cold?'

'That's different,' Jake said. 'The physical activity that comes with swimming and surfing keeps me warm. Walking… doesn't.'

'We're not far away,' Raymond assured him. 'I told you to bring a thicker jacket.'

'It'd be fine if the sun could reach here,' Jake said. 'Damned cities.'

Raymond chuckled. 'So what do you make of Sydney?'

'She seems nice enough,' Jake said. 'She's good at her job. Should have seen her handle a problematic guest the other day. She deescalated the situation and had the guest thinking they got their way when they didn't.'

'She certainly seems to fit in,' Raymond observed.

'The team like her,' Jake agreed. 'She's not too strict, but she's also not one to let things slide. She runs a tight ship. Rita certainly picked the right replacement for Nicholas.'

'On the other hand, Nicholas knew better than to chase a thief down into a restricted area,' Raymond countered.

'True.' Jake frowned. 'Mind you, I think Nicholas knew more than he let on.'

'That wouldn't surprise me,' Raymond said.

'Not that he tried to find out,' Jake continued. 'He didn't get too involved. I think he had enough going on in his life.'

'Sydney didn't mean to get involved,' Raymond said. 'She certainly didn't expect a man to disintegrate right in front of her, given the look on her face.'

'I never asked you how the meeting with her went,' Jake said.

'It went fine. We answered what we could, and she seems to have grasped that it's not something to be discussed openly.'

'Good to know.' Jake looked up at the elegant mixed stone building they were approaching. 'That's it, isn't it?'

'It is,' Raymond said. 'Better try not to look too touristy, like Rita said.'

'Plan of action?' Jake asked.

'Wait until Mass starts, then go inside.'

They stopped on the corner, watching as more and more people gathered for Mass. As they waited, Raymond and Jake made small talk, discussing the changes to Melbourne, their favourite band, and various other subjects. It was past eight when they finally ventured over to the building, making their way up the front steps and inside the iconic church.

'Same thing as last time?' Jake whispered.

'Yeap,' Raymond confirmed. 'Shouldn't be too hard to spot.'

They stepped inside the entrance and began searching the walls for the marks that indicated where the key would be located. They found they weren't the only ones just inside the doorway, with several tourists standing around and taking photos of the impressive structure even as Mass continued. Jake was the first to spot the marks and grabbed Raymond's arm, pointing to a low stone hidden behind a table.

Raymond kept his eye on the tourists as he pressed himself into the small space, carefully feeling around the brick until he found a groove, and with a hard push of two fingers, it sprang free. He fished inside the hole, his fingers finding the cold brass of a key that he carefully pulled out and pocketed before replacing the little door and stepping away.

'Got it,' he whispered to Jake.

'Should we take Rita's suggestion and go inside?' Jake asked.

'Can't hurt,' Raymond agreed. 'Warmer in here anyway.'

'I thought you were used to the cold,' Jake accused.

Raymond shrugged it off, leading the way into the main room and the two of them finding a seat at the back where they could observe the Mass.

* * * * *

Kingston looked up as he heard the knock on his door, pausing him in his pacing. He hurried over, opening the door and seeming to deflate when he spotted Rita and Sydney.

'Don't get so excited to see us,' Rita said dryly as they entered.

'You just weren't who I was expecting,' Kingston said.

'Take it they're not back yet, then.'

'Not yet.' Kingston moved over to the kitchenette. 'Coffee?'

'Yes, please,' Sydney said.

'I didn't think Raymond knocked anymore anyway,' Rita said, pulling out the chair from her desk and dropping into it.

'Why do you say that?' Kingston asked.

'No reason,' Rita said innocently.

Kingston eyed her as he poured two cups of coffee, bringing them over to the women. 'They shouldn't be too far away.'

'Depends on if they stay for the whole Mass,' Rita said.

They paused as they heard faint footsteps outside, only for them to stop short of the room and go into one of the neighbouring rooms at the hotel.

'So, how long have the two of you been here?' Kingston asked.

'Just got here,' Rita said. 'We ran into each other just outside.'

'Couldn't sleep,' Sydney admitted.

Kingston's phone rang before he could reply; Kingston quickly fished it out of his pocket and hit 'accept'. 'How did it go?' He was silent for a second, nodding. 'We'll meet you down there.'

'They found it then,' Rita guessed, as Kingston pocketed his phone again.

'They did,' Kingston replied, crossing over towards the doorway. 'They're almost back. We're to meet them down at the portals.'

Rita and Sydney followed Kingston out of the room and down into the Vaults, the three moving in silence, each lost in their thoughts. Kingston himself couldn't help but feel a flutter in his gut at the idea they'd located another key, and he hoped against hope that this one would work. The keys they had found prior had all been… disappointing. He hoped that it would be third time lucky.

They reached the portal room without incident, cramming into the small space and locking the door behind them. It was a brief wait before the entrance to Melbourne opened, Raymond and Jake joining them in the room. Raymond held up the key to Kingston, the old brass dull in the dim light. Kingston took it without a word, turning towards the second doorway. He opened and closed it once to ensure it was deactivated, then placed the key in the lock and turned it.

There was a noticeable shift in the air, the light from under the doorway shining brighter.

'That's new,' Rita commented.

Kingston glanced at her quickly before turning the handle on the door, noticing that it was slightly warmer than it had been a moment ago.

The storage room behind the door was gone. Instead, they saw a long corridor. They could hear distance chatter and an organ, the air heavy with the smell of melted wax, dust, old brick and the other telltale fragrances that shouted 'church'.

'It worked,' Raymond said softly.

'It did,' Kingston agreed. 'The question being, where are we?'

'It looks familiar,' Raymond said. He gently pushed Kingston aside and stepped through the doorway and into the corridor.

'Raymond,' Kingston hissed.

Raymond raised a hand, gesturing to give him a minute before disappearing around a corner. They held their breath, waiting for him to return. After what felt like forever, he stepped back around the corner, ducking back through the doorway and closing it.

'St Paul's Cathedral,' he said.

'You mean we could have taken a shortcut?' Jake asked.

'You'd have had to check every door in the building to find the right one,' Kingston reminded him.

Jake conceded the point.

'So wait,' Rita said. 'They hid the key that opens the portal to St Paul's Cathedral *in* St Paul's Cathedral.'

'Makes logical sense,' Kingston said. 'Although I wouldn't be surprised if Redmond has more than one key there, given the size of the building.'

'Does this mean all the keys are hidden in their portal buildings?' Jake asked.

'I highly doubt it. Some of them are supposed to lead overseas,' Kingston replied.

'Would be too obvious,' Raymond agreed. 'It would make it far too easy to break the code.'

'Do you have any more leads?' Kingston asked.

Raymond shook his head. 'That was the last one for now. I need to go through Redmond's journals some more.'

'Keep at it,' Kingston told him. He glanced around. 'I'm surprised your mother isn't here.'

'Oh,' Raymond winced slightly. 'I didn't tell her we had a lead.'

'She is going to kill you,' Rita observed.

'Verbally lambaste me, yes,' Raymond said. 'Kill me, no. She's been busy lately with work, and I didn't want to get her hopes up for another disappointment. Figured I'd tell her once we'd retrieved the key.'

'Wait,' Sydney said. 'I thought she lived in the apartment under the library.'

'Yes and no,' Raymond said. 'We have an apartment in the CBD. Mother spends most nights there these days. I guess I had better tell her.'

'Need backup?' Kingston asked.

'I'll be fine,' Raymond said, only to pause. 'This might be a great opportunity for Sydney to meet my mother formerly.'

Sydney blinked. 'Me?'

'So you *do* need backup,' Rita teased.

Raymond gave her a measured look but said nothing.

6

The Barry apartment proved only to be a short walk from the State Library and was in one of the nearby residential towers. Sydney couldn't help but feel a slight flutter in her stomach as she rode the elevator next to Raymond. It almost felt like being the girlfriend about to be introduced to the parents. Sydney glanced at the man next to her and saw his face was still fixed in an unreadable blank look, although she could see in his eyes that he was rehearsing what he was going to say to his mother.

'I should warn you,' Raymond said, breaking the silence. 'My mother likes to ask a lot of questions.'

'Okay,' Sydney said. 'Anything else I should know?'

'She tends to get information from people they don't intend to give,' Raymond said. 'You could say that interrogation is her speciality.'

'Sounds like she should be a journalist,' Sydney said.

'She wanted to be when she was younger,' Raymond admitted. 'Her choice of occupation was made for her, just as it was for me.'

Sydney frowned, looking at him. 'Wait, you didn't get to choose what you wanted to be?'

Raymond gave her a tight smile, and Sydney could tell it was a sore point. She made a note to ask Jake about it later, given that he and Raymond seemed to be good friends, and Sydney wasn't comfortable enough with Rita and Kingston yet to ask such probing questions. The elevator doors opened, ending all further discussion, and Sydney found herself on an open, clean floor. Raymond led the way to one doorway, opening it with a key card.

'Mother,' he called as he entered the apartment. 'You awake?'

'Of course I'm awake,' came the matter-of-fact reply. 'I'm in the living room.'

Raymond held the door open for Sydney to enter before following her in, closing and locking the door. 'We have a guest.'

Sydney heard a shuffling further down the hallway and soon spotted Lucille Barry. The woman was lean and of moderate height, with short grey hair that Sydney wondered if Lucille artificially dyed the colour to hide the greying process. She had blue eyes like her son, and there was a definite resemblance between the two, particularly around the eyes. She was well dressed in a blouse and slacks, with a set of wire-frame reading glasses on the end of her nose that she took off as she approached.

'Sydney Madinah,' the older woman said, extending a hand. 'It's nice to meet you under better circumstances. Lucille Barry.'

Sydney took the hand extended towards her, finding that Lucille's handshake was firm and warm. 'It's nice to meet you too.'

Lucille turned and moved deeper into the apartment without giving Raymond a cursory glance. Raymond rolled his eyes and sighed before gesturing for Sydney to go ahead. The corridor opened into a modestly sized dining and kitchen area, with a carpeted lounge at the far end that looked to open to a balcony. It was a far larger apartment than the one that Sydney herself lived in, and she felt a small bout of jealousy.

'I'm surprised you're awake,' Lucille said, finally addressing her son.

'I'll have you know I've been to Mass,' he replied.

Lucille stopped dead, spinning towards him with wide eyes. 'You located another key.'

He gave a slight nod. 'Yes.'

Lucille was in front of him in two long steps, staring up at him. 'And?'

'We found it, Jake and I,' he said.

'And?'

'And this one worked.'

Lucille made a slight noise of satisfaction at the back of her throat, her eyes narrowing. 'You mentioned nothing about finding the location of a key last night.'

'I didn't want you to be disappointed again,' Raymond said.

'This isn't a game, Raymond,' Lucille said. 'I want to be informed at all times of what is going on.'

'Then you'd be very bored,' he said, stepping around her and making his way over to the couch so that he could sit down. 'And before you ask, no, I have no more key locations.'

Lucille watched him go. 'Were you followed?'

'No,' he said. 'Really, Mother, this paranoia of yours–'

'It isn't paranoia,' she cut in. 'We are being watched, Raymond. It will do you well to remember that.'

'Yes, Mother.'

Sydney felt like a third wheel, slightly surprised when Lucille turned towards her abruptly. 'My apologies. Would you like a coffee, Miss Madinah?'

'Please call me Sydney,' Sydney said. 'And yes, please, Mrs Barry.'

'It's Ms, and call me Lucille,' Lucille said, moving over to the kitchen. 'How do you like it?'

'Milk and one sugar,' Sydney replied.

'Can I ask: are you from Sydney?' Lucille asked as she went about making the coffee.

'Brisbane originally,' Sydney replied. 'My family is still there. I've spent the last few years in America, though.'

'Oh? Which city?'

'New York.'

'I keep meaning to go there one day,' Lucille said, bringing Sydney her coffee. 'Work, however, doesn't allow for vacation time.'

Raymond made a slight sound of disagreement, causing Lucille to glare at him.

'Day trips and afternoons off are not vacations,' Lucille stated.

'But they eat into your vacation time,' he countered.

An old argument, Sydney observed. It made her wonder about the relationship between Lucille and Raymond. His use of 'mother' seemed almost a distancing tactic. They displayed all the hallmarks of a strained relationship. Yet also that they spent a lot of time together and knew each other well enough.

'Do you have a boyfriend?' Lucille asked Sydney point-blank.

'Mother!' Raymond exclaimed, although Sydney had been half expecting the question.

'No,' she replied, feeling herself blush. Raymond was attractive and she did like him, but his mother asking about her relationship status was off-putting. 'I haven't been here long enough to get to know anyone yet.'

Lucille gave Raymond a look with one eyebrow raised, only to receive a glare in response.

'Forgive her,' Raymond said, a thinly veiled warning in his voice. 'She asks every girl I introduce her to that question.'

'It's a fair question,' Lucille said, picking up her coffee. 'You know so few people, and Sydney is only the third girl you've ever introduced me to. Tanya is married to Andrew, and you and Rita squabble like siblings more than anything.'

'That's because she's worked out how to get under my skin,' Raymond said. 'Just as I've worked out how to get under hers.'

'You're the new hotel manager, correct?' Lucille asked, returning her attention to Sydney.

'I am,' she replied. 'And you work at the library.'

'I'm one of their senior archivists,' Lucille replied. 'Raymond here works under me.'

'Unfortunately,' he muttered.

'Would you rather one of the other senior archivists burdened you with so much work you couldn't work on finding the Keys?' Lucille asked.

'Who just stacked my calendar for the next three months?' he asked. 'I must pull overtime to get through the work you gave me.'

'Maybe if you spent less time with Kingston, you'd get through your work faster,' Lucille said.

'I don't spend that much time with him,' Raymond said. 'Besides, I spend some of that time with Jake and Rita.'

It sounded like another old argument, Sydney thought. Raymond wasn't lying either, although he spent a lot of time with Kingston from what she had observed. She'd put it down to their roles as the Keeper and Protector, though, and Raymond had broken the code to the keys.

'So,' Lucille said. 'Our theory for locating the keys was correct.'

'You mean my theory,' Raymond clarified.

'Did Kingston ever come up with a theory as to why the key from the Pilgrim Church didn't work?'

'He believes that the portal on the other end must have been destroyed.'

Lucille frowned thoughtfully for a moment. 'So both ends of the portal need to be present for it to work?'

'Seems that way.' Raymond shrugged. 'I suppose it's logical. A doorway needs to have two sides.'

'It does.' Lucille sighed, leaning back in her seat. 'It makes you wonder how many other keys no longer work.'

'There are supposedly a lot of keys,' Raymond reminded her. 'There are bound to be others that work.'

'But first, we need to find the keys,' Lucille said, eyeing her son. 'So you will need to spend less time off with Andrew and Tanya and more time working.'

Raymond's eye twitched slightly. 'I only go out with Andrew and Tanya every other weekend, as you well know. I am allowed to have a social life.'

'I never said that you can't have a social life. I think you spend too much time with those two.'

'They're my friends,' Raymond reminded her. 'My first real friends. I didn't have time to meet anyone until I went to Uni because you ensured that.'

'You made other friends,' Lucille reminded him. 'There were other people at the University.'

'Yeah, but Andrew and Tanya were my best friends.' Raymond set his jaw. 'And I intend to stay friends with them.'

'Yes, Tanya.' Lucille sipped her coffee, scowling. 'They only married because of the baby.'

'They married because they were in love,' Raymond said, glaring at her. 'Olivia had nothing to do with it.'

'It had everything to do with it.' Lucille narrowed her eyes. 'If he'd bothered to keep a condom on, then the child would never have been subjected to the scrutiny it received for being born out of wedlock.'

Sydney's eyebrows rose at the comment, surprised to hear it given she was in the room. It was an old argument, given how Raymond sighed heavily. She could tell he was biting his tongue and carefully choosing his words.

'It's the twenty-first century, Mother. Olivia being born out of wedlock isn't that unusual.'

'It is still bad for the child,' Lucille said, meeting his eye. 'Don't let me ever hear of you doing such a thing.'

Raymond glared at her, taking his glasses off and wiping them on a cloth. Sydney couldn't help but wonder if it was a distraction to keep him from looking at his mother. Sydney had to admit Raymond was equally handsome without his glasses, but they suited him.

Lucille watched him, sipping on her coffee and glancing at Sydney before she sighed almost dramatically, and she sent a sideways look towards her son, one he didn't miss. 'It would be nice to have a grandchild.'

Raymond rolled his eyes. 'Mother...'

'To have a strong woman keeping you out of trouble,' Lucille raised a finger when he went to reply. 'You should be married by now, Raymond. You must marry and have a child to be the next Keeper.'

'I am not interested in getting married,' Raymond said. 'With the work I have to do, I don't have time to go out and meet some girl. Besides, I doubt you'd ever be happy with anyone I chose to be my life partner.'

'Don't be stupid,' Lucille said. 'Someone like Rita–'

'Oh god.' Ray pulled a face. 'Rita? Are you kidding me?'

'She's a nice girl,' Lucille rebutted. 'She's intelligent, well mannered, has a good sense of style, doesn't take crap from anyone and is strong-willed.'

'Mother, if it's escaped your notice, Rita and I don't get along very well.' Raymond frowned. 'And she's always polite to you, but you should see her on a normal day. There's a reason the people who work at the hotel don't like her very much.'

'They simply misunderstand her,' Lucille said.

'Oh, they understand her. She makes sure of it.'

'Or perhaps you're simply blinded by your disinterest in women.'

Raymond paused, looking across at her. 'Disinterest it women?'

'As far as I can tell, you haven't been on a date since university,' Lucille said. 'All you seem to do is work, go out with Andrew, or you spend all your time with Kingston.'

Raymond seemed to carefully choose his words. 'Just because I haven't taken one out on a date recently does not mean I am disinterested in women. And if I recall, you're the one who has pressured me to work more.'

Sydney sat quietly, listening to them. Their conversation seemed to go in circles. She wondered if this was normal for them. It particularly bothered her they were doing it in front of her. She wondered if she should say something, but remained silent and just drank her coffee. She had a feeling she didn't want to be in the middle of their argument.

'I have not been pressuring you to work,' Lucille said, frowning.

'Between all the meetings in Adelaide and my duties in the Library, I don't have time to do much of anything,' Raymond said.

'You have plenty of time to go out with Andrew and Tanya,' Lucille reminded him.

'Time I set aside,' Raymond said, scowling. 'Look, Mother, I'm happy to update you on what's going on in Adelaide, but let's leave out all the rest, okay? We have a guest.'

'Yes, we do.' Lucille turned back to Sydney. 'I'm sorry you had to hear all that, Sydney. We can get quite carried away.'

'No, it's fine,' Sydney said. 'I have similar conversations with my parents.'

'See, it's all normal chatter,' Lucille said to Raymond. She looked at Sydney. 'Perhaps our next meeting will be in better company.'

'She means without me here,' Raymond clarified. 'So she can interrogate you a bit more freely.'

Lucille gave him a pointed look but didn't reply.

* * * * *

As they headed back down the elevator, Raymond turned to Sydney. 'I apologise for my mother. She's a little obsessed with my having an heir. I probably should have warned you about that.'

'It's okay,' Sydney said. 'I think it's normal for mothers. My parents always ask me when I will settle down and get married.'

Raymond smiled tightly. 'I doubt they'd have been so upfront about it in front of friends of the opposite sex, though.'

'You have me there,' Sydney said. She still couldn't get over how upfront and direct Lucille had been. She was almost surprised that Lucille hadn't proposed point-blank on behalf of her son. 'Your mother seems very concerned about you.'

'There's a difference between concerned and… whatever that is.' Raymond scowled. 'She has very high expectations. I think she's trying to live the life she wanted through me.'

'What do you mean?'

'The role of Keeper skips generations,' Raymond said as they exited the elevator. 'My great-grandfather was the Keeper, meaning my mother was the next in line and they had groomed her to be such. Then my great-grandparents died and my grandfather had to step into the role, meaning that the next heir to the role became me.'

'You think she's jealous?' Sydney asked as they stepped out onto the street.

'I'm not sure it's jealousy,' Raymond said. 'I think there's a bit of envy. She expects me to be everything she is herself, and she's a workaholic perfectionist. Mother has a full social life to keep herself preoccupied, but doesn't want me to have one. She thinks if she were Keeper she would throw herself into the role completely, so she expects the same of me.'

'That's not exactly fair,' Sydney said, feeling sympathy. 'You've got your own life, your own friends.'

'And she hates it,' Raymond said. 'I was home-schooled, you know, until I went to university. There, I made friends, and I'm still friends with those people.'

'Tanya and Andrew,' Sydney guessed.

He nodded. 'We were joint at the hip for a long time. Then they moved to Geelong, and I became the Keeper. Now basically all of my friends are in Adelaide.'

'Jake, Kingston and Rita,' she said.

'Jake mostly,' he said. 'We've got a similar taste in music, so we often go to concerts together. There's one coming up. Rita's more like a sister to me, and Kingston…' Raymond sighed. 'Kingston is Kingston.'

'There's me,' Sydney said, touching his arm gently. She stepped closer, hoping he got the message that she was there for him.

'I hope so,' Raymond smiled at her. 'I'm not exactly the easiest person to get along with.'

'You don't seem so bad,' she said. 'A bit of a workaholic and a perfectionist, perhaps.'

He laughed. 'I am that.' He checked his watch. 'Well, there's still a lot of day left. I hope you have a good rest of the weekend. Don't worry yourself too much about the whole portal thing.'

'It is hard,' she admitted. 'I'm still taking a lot in.'

'It'll all become old hat,' he assured her. 'Just wait.'

* * * * *

Sydney found herself not quite ready to go home after her encounter with Lucille, so she wandered around Adelaide. She wondered if she might have asked Jake to give her the tour, but she didn't have his private number, and Sydney hadn't wanted to disturb Kingston given everyone said he was a private person. So instead, Sydney had taken herself on a self-guided tour using a map she had downloaded off the internet.

She found the city to be breathtaking. It had just the right mix of buildings and the air here was much clearer than the air in New York. There was also a lot less traffic and a lot more green space. It was also somewhat pedestrian-friendly. She found the market that Dorothy and Elizabeth seemed to enjoy so much and had browsed its wares, although nothing had caught her eye, and there were a few historic buildings that had Sydney wondering if perhaps there were keys inside.

She still didn't quite understand why Kingston and Raymond needed to find the keys. If they were so dangerous, it seemed like it would be better to keep them hidden. She could see their reasoning. They needed to know where they were and hide them somewhere new before they were lost. The second portal didn't work without its keys. Sydney wondered just how many buildings the keys led to and how important those buildings were.

As she passed a cafe, she frowned as she spotted a familiar man. Deciding to go up to him, she wandered over. 'Hello, Marcus.'

He looked up from his coffee and half-eaten muffin. 'Oh, Sydney!'

'I promise I'm not stalking you,' she said.

'Please, sit down,' he said, gesturing for her to take a seat. 'I didn't see you on Friday.'

'I was a little later than normal,' she said, sliding into the seat across from him. She looked into the cafe. 'Is the coffee here good?'

'I enjoy it,' he said, smiling. 'They grind their beans fresh.'

'I'll have to try it,' she said. She looked around. 'Do you live nearby?'

'I do,' he confirmed, taking a sip from his drink. 'Do you?'

'Yes,' she said with a nod. She didn't want to go into too much detail, however. She still didn't know him well enough, although she wasn't getting a bad feeling about him. She wasn't getting any real reading off him, and she could normally read people. That was what made her so good at her job. 'I've been exploring the city.'

'So you're new to the area,' he guessed. She wondered if it was that obvious.

She nodded. 'I've only been here a few weeks.'

'I noticed your slight accent,' he said. 'American.'

'New York,' she said. She frowned. 'You have one too.'

'Irish,' he confirmed. 'I lived there when I was younger. I've been in Australia for some time now.'

'Which explains why it's so faint,' she said. She looked down at his coffee and cake. 'So, is this a routine thing coming here?'

'No,' he said, shaking his head. 'I felt like it today. I needed to get out of the apartment for a while.'

'I understand that completely,' she said. 'I was feeling restless, so I explored.'

'Big morning?' he asked.

'You could say that,' she agreed. Of course, she would not go into detail. She hoped he didn't poke any further because she wasn't a fan of lying. Then again, lying was almost part of her job description. Telling someone who had been rude to 'have a nice day' was a lie. But this was outside of work.

Mercifully, he didn't pry. 'Have you been to the zoo yet? It's definitely worth a day out.'

'Not yet,' she admitted. 'I've never really been big on zoos.'

'Perhaps Rundle Mall then,' he said. 'Or maybe the markets.'

'I've been to the market,' she confirmed. 'I need a bigger purse before I go there.'

'Some people do all their shopping at the market,' he said. 'I've never really seen the appeal of it. It's a lot of noise and foot traffic when simply going to a supermarket will suffice. Everything is within easy access there and you don't need to haggle over the prices.'

'Some people enjoy the experience of it,' she said. She was getting the feeling he wasn't a people person. 'They make whole days out of it. They travel all the way in from the outer suburbs to go.'

'That I find even more curious,' he said, prodding his muffin with a finger. 'I suppose for some people it's the only excitement they get in life.'

Sydney had to admit she didn't want to be one of those people. That was one of the reasons she enjoyed working at hotels. She liked not knowing what the next day was going to bring. She preferred it when there was nothing much going on. A routine day was a good day in her books. There was much less paperwork to fill out for a start, and the worst days usually involved the authorities having to get involved. Luckily, she hadn't experienced that yet at the hotel. Hopefully, she didn't.

'I should probably leave you to your food,' she said, looking down at his half-eaten muffin. 'It was good seeing you.'

'And I you,' he replied with a smile. 'Have a good day. No doubt I will see you next Friday when you shop.'

'No doubt,' she replied as she slid out of her seat. It was a little creepy that he would say that, making her think again that maybe he was stalking her. But she had been the one to find him this time, so it couldn't be. With one last smile, she stepped away and began the trek back home.

7

IT SEEMED LIKE Monday morning took forever to come around. Sydney was riding high on the success of the group's mission for the key, even though she still didn't fully understand what was happening. Coming to work had felt exciting, more so than usual, because she never knew what the day would bring. However, the morning had passed without incident, and Sydney thought the afternoon would as well.

'Good afternoon, Miss Madinah.'

Sydney glanced up from her screen, returning Kingston's smile as he leaned against the reception desk. 'Good afternoon. I was told not to expect to see you this early in the day.'

'I'm a man of many surprises,' he said, giving her a wink before turning towards the foyer. 'Rita's meeting seems to be going well.'

'Who is she meeting?' Sydney asked. 'She intercepted them before they could get to me.'

'Something to do with the management systems. I didn't bother her for the details. She'll fill me in when she's done.'

Sydney frowned for a moment. 'Technically, shouldn't you be in the meeting? You are one of the–'

Kingston raised a finger, silencing her. 'Nobody outside our group and a select few others know that.'

'But your name...'

'People believe it to be a coincidence,' he said, meeting her eye. 'I intend for it to remain that way.'

'I understand,' Sydney said, glancing back at her work. She wanted to ask why it was such a secret, but something in Kingston's tone stopped her. She made a mental note to ask one of the others about it later. The more she learned about Kingston, the more questions she had; she was sure this would not be an exception.

'How long has that been going on?'

She glanced up at Kingston's voice, spotting him looking off to the side. She didn't have to follow his gaze to know what he was looking at. 'He's been there since shortly after the meeting started,' she replied.

'Hm.' She saw Kingston's brow furrowed in thought. 'Has he been working or just pretending while watching?'

'Hard to tell from here,' she replied. 'Jake can be a hard one to read.'

She looked over the desk towards where Jake was reclined in an armchair in the foyer, across the room from where Rita was meeting with the three gentlemen. She knew that from casual observation, it would seem he was fixated on something on the laptop screen resting on his knee, but from this angle, she could see him looking through his sunglasses across at the meeting.

'Is there something going on between them?' Sydney asked.

Kingston turned back towards her and made to answer, only to be interrupted by a voice to the side.

'Jake wishes.'

A smile sprang to her lips when she saw Raymond. She'd notice that she always seemed more at ease when he was around. She couldn't focus on why, but his good looks added to it.

'Good afternoon Miss Madinah,' Raymond said, his smile causing her stomach to twist ever so slightly.

'Mr Barry,' she acknowledged, suddenly feeling very self-conscious. 'I didn't expect to see you so early.'

'Indeed.' Kingston's tone made Sydney look up. It was impossible to miss the faint worry on his features as he regarded Raymond. 'The only times you come across this early is because you found something or if something is wrong.'

Raymond gave them a reassuring smile, but a niggling feeling told Sydney that it wasn't entirely genuine. 'Everything's fine, Kingston. I have a matter I wish to speak with Jake about.'

'One that couldn't wait until after you finished work,' Kingston pointed out.

Raymond didn't miss a beat. 'Everything is fine, Kingston, I assure you.' He looked across the foyer from one side to the other. 'She knows he's there.'

'She always knows,' Kingston said. 'Rita doesn't miss a thing.'

'Unfortunately,' Raymond said, frowning slightly. 'I'm guessing that's a meeting you should be at,' he said, nodding towards Rita as he looked pointedly at Kingston.

'You know she forbids me from attending unless necessary,' Kingston reminded him.

Raymond raised an eyebrow. 'Who is whose boss again?'

'She has far better people skills,' Kingston said. 'As charming as I am, business meetings aren't my thing.'

Raymond huffed, the corner of his lips twitching up. 'You overestimate your abilities.'

'You don't seem to have a problem with them,' Kingston said, leaning closer into Raymond's personal space, the other man not giving an inch.

Sydney flicked her gaze between them, adding another piece of the puzzle of exactly what the nature of the relationship between them was and decided to ask Jake and Rita about it. Kingston and Raymond were comfortable getting into one another's space. She thought it was rather cute.

'I better go speak to Jake,' Raymond said, keeping his eyes locked with Kingston's. Kingston nodded, straightening and giving him room. Raymond stepped around him, Sydney catching herself admiring his assets from behind. Hearing a chuckle, she looked up and realised Kingston had seen her.

Kingston winked at her as he slid from the desk and towards the cafe. Glancing at her watch, Sydney sighed, settling herself quickly back into her chair. She swore that there was something about Kingston that electrified the room. That man had a presence unlike any she'd encountered before, but it wasn't bad.

She dragged her eyes from his, retreating into her work. One thing was for sure, working here – there was never a dull moment.

* * * * *

Jake glanced up at him briefly as Raymond joined him, dropping into the next armchair. 'Rarely see you at this hour.'

'Came to see you,' Raymond admitted. He frowned. 'You know Rita knows you're watching.'

'I know she knows,' Jake said, pushing his sunglasses back up his nose from where they had slid down. 'And I know she knows I know she knows.'

'Knowception,' Raymond said without missing a beat.

'Exactly.' Jake glanced back at his screen, cycling through the tabs of the various cameras in the hotel. 'She asked me to monitor things.'

'Really?' Raymond was genuinely surprised.

'See Mr Handsy over there?'

Raymond looked towards the meeting, spotting the man Jake was referring to. He was an older gentleman, hair thinning slightly and his suit cut so well it had to be tailored. When he spoke, he emphasised each point with broad gestures with his hands, but there was an abruptness to it that showed this was a man who was used to getting what he wanted.

'I see him,' Raymond said.

'Well, Mr Handsy has a reputation for being just that: handsy,' Jake said, glancing sideways at Raymond. 'Especially with women.'

'Oh.' Raymond frowned, watching the man. 'How do you know?'

'Surveillance is only effective if you don't stare at the person you're watching,' Jake chastised him.

Raymond instantly averted his eyes. 'Sorry.'

'Rita found it when she was running background on the guy before the meeting,' Jake answered, cycling through the feeds again. 'He has at least a half dozen sexual assault cases that he's settled, and too many sexual harassment accusations to count. He keeps a few lawyers on retainer just for it and at least one PR person to keep things swept under the rug.'

'How is he still in business?' Raymond asked.

Jake gave him a look and raised his eyebrow.

Raymond nodded. He understood. 'Money.'

'His grandfather made it big in the banking sector, so his family is loaded. The business he works for is his own startup and has been doing well. Most of the larger regional hotels have some sort of partnership with them, so Rita thought it made sense to chat with them and see what they offered.'

'And the owner goes personally to meetings?'

'His thing, apparently. He likes to sign off on all deals himself.' Jake glanced at Raymond. 'Mind you; the company sends him out with babysitters.'

'That'd be the other two guys,' Raymond said. 'And why they're so quiet while he's doing all the talking.'

'It's the exact opposite of Kingston and Rita,' Jake said. 'She is a lot better at this sort of thing than Kingston.'

'Kingston does like his privacy,' Raymond said.

'Tell me about it,' Jake muttered. 'You know I ran a background search on him, and I can't find a thing before he moved here. Even his bank accounts weren't opened until he settled in, and the funds that went into them were untraceable. And nothing has his first name on it.'

Raymond frowned. 'You ran a background check on Kingston?'

'Of course I did,' Jake said. 'I wanted to make sure I wasn't working for a criminal. I'm still not sure that I'm not.'

'I thought his secrecy would be obvious given his role as Protector,' Raymond said. 'I'm sure you wouldn't find much if you ran a trace on me, either.'

'You at least have a birth certificate,' Jake said.

Raymond paused. 'Hang on, you *have* run a trace on me?'

'I've run a trace on everyone,' Jake said. 'Just finished one on Miss Madinah over there last night. I've already given the info to Kingston. She's got a clean record and doesn't have so much as a parking ticket to her name. From what I could tell, she's trustworthy, so I doubt we have to worry about her.'

'Good to know.' Raymond gazed over the meeting group on the other side of the foyer, then out towards the street. One figure caused him to pause. 'Kian's still here?'

'Yeap,' Jake typed a quick message on his computer before looking up towards the older gentleman sitting at a table with a clear view into the foyer. 'He went to leave at his usual time, but stopped when he saw Mr Handsy walk in. I'm guessing he knows of his reputation and decided to keep his eye on things.'

'Huh.'

'So why are you here, Raymond?' Jake asked. 'It's still within work hours for you, so I'm guessing you're not just here for a chat.'

'No, I'm not.' Raymond reached into an inside pocket of his jacket and pulled free an envelope, holding it out to Jake. 'I'm here because of this.'

Jake took the envelope and opened it, sliding out the white sheet of paper. He unfolded it and took in the words. 'A piece of brass can open a door but also take a life. Which one is more important to you: the piece of brass or your life.' Jake looked up at Raymond sharply. 'Where did you get this?'

'Mailbox to our apartment in La Trobe St,' Raymond said. 'Mother found it when she returned from lunch. She said it wasn't there this morning.'

'This was delivered personally,' Jake said, sliding the note back into the envelope and studying the single name 'Barry' on the front. 'This is a death threat, Raymond.'

'We know.' Raymond took off his glasses, polishing them absently with the corner of his shirt.

'I can try to backtrack your security footage,' Jake said, 'but you know that won't do me much good, as it only shows who comes and goes in the building, nothing of the interior.'

'I know that too,' Raymond pushed his glasses back onto his nose. 'I just thought I'd let you know.'

Jake leaned towards him, a serious expression on his face. 'You need to tell Kingston.'

'No,' Raymond snapped. 'You know how he'll react. Rather, he'll over-react.'

'He's the Protector, Raymond,' Jake reminded him. 'It's his job to, you know, protect.'

'You know what his 'protection' can get like,' Raymond said. 'I'm not getting locked in my home, not again.'

'Okay. For now,' Jake warned. 'But if this gets worse, I'm telling him.'

'Thank you,' Raymond said with relief.

'Now I've got to get back to work,' Jake said. 'So scram.'

Raymond chuckled as he stood, smoothing out his shirt before he walked away.

* * * * *

'So,' Kingston said as Raymond rejoined them at the front desk, Kingston sipping a fresh cup of coffee from the cafe. 'What was that about?'

'Nothing important,' Raymond said, shrugging it off. 'Just finalising some plans to see a concert next week, that's all.'

'That's all, hm?' Kingston narrowed his eyes, clearly not sure that he believed him.

'Why? Don't you trust me?' Raymond asked, eyes searching Kingston's face.

'No, I trust you,' Kingston said. He looked over towards where Rita was having her meeting. 'Just an odd time of day for you to come across.'

Sydney looked from Kingston to Raymond, waiting for a reply. Raymond seemed to regard Kingston for a moment before following his gaze towards the meeting. 'So, is Mr Handsy behaving?'

'I'll have you know that's a very important businessman,' Kingston chastised. 'But yes, he is. I think he is aware of all the eyes on him.'

'Hope the meeting goes well then,' Raymond said, reaching out to clap Kingston on the shoulder in a farewell. He nodded towards Sydney. 'Miss Madinah.'

'Mr Barry,' Sydney replied. She watched as he disappeared through the doorway leading towards the basement-level staircase. She turned back to Kingston, noting that he was watching Raymond out the corner of his eye with a slight crease of concern on his forehead. 'You realise he was lying,' she said softly.

'I'm aware,' Kingston said. He sighed. 'Something has worried him, but he doesn't want me to know about it just yet.'

'Any reason?'

'He's worried about how I'd react,' Kingston said. 'So whatever it is, it is serious.'

Sydney searched his face for some clue about what he was thinking, but came up with nothing. Kingston was a hard man to read. 'Are you going to ask Jake?'

'Jake won't tell me,' Kingston said, shaking his head. 'That man is good at keeping secrets. I'm sure, in time, we'll find out what it is.'

Sydney nodded in silent agreement. She was still learning about the group, but one thing was sure – they all had their secrets. Given what she had observed, she didn't expect Raymond and Kingston to keep anything from each other. It made her wonder just how Raymond expected Kingston to react. There was an element of danger to the older man that he kept well hidden, but Kingston couldn't mask it completely. Sydney wondered if perhaps she could get Jake to tell her what was going on. It was worth a shot.

Right now, however, Sydney had to finish preparations for a wedding party scheduled for that weekend. She left Kingston to his business and got back to work.

8

Knocking on the door frame, Sydney poked her head inside. The room was cast in an eerie blue from all the security monitors. Jake looked up at her, a smile crossing his lips. 'Need something?'

'I was hoping you could show me around a bit,' Sydney said. 'I know you get off soon, and Rita didn't exactly look to be in the best mood right now…'

'Sure, I can do that,' Jake gave her a thumbs-up. 'Just let me take care of the changeover, and I'll meet you out front.'

Sydney nodded, stepping back out of the room. She quickly went about handing over to the night manager, cleaning up her office, logging off her computer, and grabbing her jacket. As soon as she was finished, she made her way to the lobby, seating herself in the seat that Jake had occupied earlier that day. She didn't have long to wait until Jake came out to join her, running a hand through his blond hair before straightening his jacket.

'Anywhere, in particular, you want to go?' He asked.

Sydney shook her head. 'Just give me a local's insight,' she said.

'I'm not that local,' he warned her as they made their way out the front doors and into the street. 'I'm a beach kid. Most of the time, I surf.'

'Really?' That explained the tan, Sydney thought to herself. 'Do you still live with your parents?'

'Heck no,' Jake chuckled. 'I have a flat. It's small, but it's big enough for me.'

'I know what you mean,' Sydney said, thinking of her tiny apartment. 'You know a lot more about Adelaide than I do, though,' Sydney said, gesturing around them. 'Some of the local cafes, restaurants and things.'

'Oh yeah, I know that,' Jake nodded. 'Simon does the best coffee, though. Don't tell him I said that.'

Sydney laughed.

'Now, where to begin?' Jake said, stopping and looking around. He clasped his hands together, thinking.

'Better start with the touristy places,' Sydney said. 'The sort of thing a hotel manager will need to know.'

'Got it,' Jake said. 'Let's start the tour.'

⋆ ⋆ ⋆ ⋆ ⋆

With a sigh, Raymond closed the door on the filing cabinet, carefully slipping off his white gloves. He cast a small smile at the portrait on the wall, his ancestor, the great Redmond Barry, maintaining his serious expression as he gazed out from the frame with an almost scrutinising frown. Paying him no mind, Raymond made about returning his tools to their appropriate places, shuffling his notes back into order and slipping them into their folder. Hearing a step behind him, he didn't turn as a shadow cast itself against the light coming through the doorway. 'Are you done for the day?'

'I am.' Raymond glanced over towards the door. 'I have a couple of errands tonight, Mother. I promise to be back before dark and all the evil, bad men come out.'

'I think there's more in here than out there.' Lucille gave him a measuring look. 'Don't forget the note we got this morning.'

'Hard to,' Raymond said, giving her a reassuring smile.

'Keep your wits about you,' Lucille said, stepping away from the door. 'Be careful.'

Smiling, Raymond switched off the lamp above his desk and gathered up his things, pulling his jacket on. Making sure he had his keys, he made his way to the door, switching off the room's main light as he exited and locked the office behind him. He moved through the off-limits area of the library and into the main area. The people moving around barely noticed him as they chatted and awaited the nearby elevator.

Raymond shoved his hands deep into his pockets as he headed through the Domed Reading Room, the long familiar feeling of smallness washing over him as he glanced up quickly at the impossibly high roof above him. Around him were the sounds of quiet talk, turning pages and the tapping of keyboards as people used the library's Wi-Fi internet.

He nodded to the man on security just outside the reading room exit as the man checked the size of a student bag, others heading straight for the locker room as they entered the building proper. Raymond passed them without a second glance, moving around and out the automatic doors into the sunshine.

The smell of cigarettes greeted him. Raymond glanced at the small group just outside standing around smoking without caring for those entering and exiting the historic building. Moving down the steps, he paid no mind to the students from the neighbouring RMIT University that lounged around on the grass incline, textbooks and notepads spread out around them.

The ground trembled slightly as the tram stopped in Swanston St; more students exited the overladen vehicle, and others boarded to head for Melbourne University up the road. Raymond joined the gathering group on the corner, waiting for the traffic lights to change and briefly casting his gaze to the scrolling red letters advertising the cinema inside the building.

The tram moved off, passing through the intersection despite the light having turned red, causing Raymond to roll his eyes and silently curse tram drivers even as he stepped off the curb with the surrounding people. He dodged the oncoming foot traffic, moving through them easily and veering slightly left as he neared the opposite curb.

Raymond stepped around the small newsstand, a busker, and a homeless man begging for change as he moved down Swanston St to the entrance to Melbourne Central, turning right down into the tunnel and giving the newsagent wares a cursory glance before focusing ahead, moving with the crowd.

At the end of the tunnel he again felt the almost overwhelming sense of smallness as the roof disappeared into the high glass cone, the Coop's Shot Tower standing proudly inside. Raymond glanced at his watch again as the oversized stopwatch clock attached to the following level's balcony began to play its tune of Waltzing Matilda, the different animated elements dropping out and causing tourists to halt in their path directly in front of him.

Sighing, Raymond moved around them and dodged through the crowd that veered right down the escalators towards the underground railway station. Once he had moved out of their stream, he found his path clear and the sense of urgency had faded. Smoothing his jacket, Raymond moved along the shop fronts and into the bookstore, greeted by the smell of new books and coffee.

Smiling to himself and feeling a sense of comfort return at the sight of the novelisations and magazines spread out before him, Raymond drifted casually down the main path, turning only when he reached the magazines and began searching their display, snagging the Star Trek one Jake had been looking for and tucking it under his arm and continuing to browse.

He never let on that he knew he was being watched.

* * * * *

Sydney sighed as she dropped her keys onto the counter inside her flat. She gazed around the dark apartment's interior, not wanting to turn the harsh lights on. She needed to get herself one of those night lights that plugged into the socket so that she had some light when she got home from work. Something gentle on the eyes.

While the tour with Jake had been insightful, it hadn't been productive. She tried various ways to weasel the information about Raymond's meeting with him that day, but every avenue she had pursued had come up blank. Jake gave her the same answer Kingston had gotten from Raymond – that it was about a concert they were attending next week. She'd gotten the name of the band – The Runaway Boys – so she would look it up later, but that was as far as she had gotten in that course of questioning. Jake had shut her down every time she had tried to press further.

She had garnered some interesting information, though. Sydney was sure that Jake had a crush on Rita. It was about how he had talked about her, not to mention the look in his eyes when he spoke about her. Sydney also knew roughly how long Rita and Jake had worked at the hotel and that Kingston and Raymond had been there before Jake had gotten the job. She'd also learned that Kingston had had a hand in recruiting both Rita and Jake, and that Jake had found the portal by accident while scouting the hotel. Kingston had accidentally left the door to his storeroom open. That was something that couldn't happen anymore, given they had since installed a self-closing and locking mechanism on the door.

Rita had been more formally introduced to the portals. Kingston himself had shown her them, and according to Kingston, she'd taken the whole thing in her stride. Jake claimed he'd been the same, but Sydney had detected an element of untruthfulness in his words. Jake had assured her she'd get used to the idea of the portals in time and that even he hadn't gotten his head around how they worked. His theory was they were some sort of alien tech. Rita accepted they existed, and Sydney had to pause when questioned. She wasn't one to believe in aliens, but there was nothing like the portals anywhere. Unless people like the CIA had them. It wouldn't surprise her if that were the case.

One thing was sure, though – Sydney would not get any more out of Jake. Kingston was correct in saying that the man kept secrets well. Every word he said was calculated and measured, and he never gave up more information than he had to. He was happy to answer her questions about the portals and their situation, at least to his knowledge. She got the impression that even Jake didn't know everything.

Dropping onto her coach, Sydney ran a hand over her face, calculating her next move. She didn't like not knowing something, and wondered if perhaps she could get Raymond himself to open up about what was going on. There was only one way to find out.

* * * * *

Raymond spotted the other's reflection in a shop window, strolling a couple of metres behind him, trying to seem like a simple window shopper. Raymond would have paid no mind to someone following him a few feet behind. Still, the man had been following him for the better part of ten minutes, even after Raymond had taken an escalator randomly down and then taken the following one back up, confirming that he was indeed being tailed.

He frowned, tucking the bag tighter under his arm and reaching into his pocket, tugging out his mobile and raising it as if he were checking his messages. He switched the phone to the front-facing camera and pointed it over his shoulder, taking in the image on the screen.

The other was there, back just past the escalator, watching him in the reflection of a shop window. Raymond snapped the phone case shut, pocketing it and moving towards the stairs beside the Shot Tower. He picked up his pace, pushing his way down through the shoppers and tourists milling around, and as he reached the bottom, he glanced back upward, spotting the other man as he roughly shoved his way through the crowd. Raymond paused briefly as he caught the dagger flash on the other man's belt.

Frowning, Raymond turned back into the crowd, pushing his way through the throng and ignoring the insults and threats of violent retribution that followed in his wake. He reached the escalator, catching hold of the handrail for balance as he stepped onto it and hurried down the right-hand side past the other shoppers.

He heard a crash behind him as he stepped off, and as he hurried across to the next set of escalators, he glanced up and spotted the man coming down after him, knocking bags from hands as he moved. Without another look, Raymond widened his step, clutching his bag tighter as he pushed past a couple of shoppers and rushed down the next escalator.

Raymond fished into his pocket, cutting across the people to the front of the group milling around the barrier that separated the shopping centre from the train station. He waved his card over the machine to make the gates part and rushed through, heading for the closest escalator.

He briefly considered attempting to slide down the rail, but decided against it as he pushed his way down the right-hand side of the escalator, muttering his apologies as he went. Hearing the slide of fabric on rubber, he swore under his breath, throwing himself to the side as the man tried to grab him. The move caused the other man to lose his balance, the man being sent sprawling and sliding with no control towards the bottom, knocking others over on the way down. His dagger fell with a clatter from his belt onto the floor tiles.

Raymond jumped the last couple of steps, using the momentum to keep him moving as he stepped around the fallen people, some panicking at the sight of the dagger. Raymond made a point of kicking further away. The stranger made a grab for him, catching the edge of Raymond's pants and causing him to stumble. Raymond swore, tugging away and making a tight left turn, away from the gathering crowd at the foot of the escalators.

He ran out along the edge of the platform until he reached the end, hearing the announcement behind him about the approaching train. He felt the breeze whip up from the tunnel above as he crouched, planting his free hand onto the platform and using it to drop him down onto the line.

He heard someone yell out behind him as he raced down tracks, feet slipping slightly on the slope between the tracks. Before him he could see the approaching light, and pushing himself, he raced towards an alcove just ahead, dark against the light on the tunnel's edge as the whistle sounded. The train's brakes screeched to an emergency stop as he grabbed the wall.

He glimpsed the driver's shocked face, and looking back down the tunnel; he saw the equally stunned look of his pursuer before the train blocked Raymond's sight. He heard the sickening thump and the screams of onlookers still on the platform. Raymond sighed and moved back to the platform, pulling himself up and heading back up the escalator before anyone could stop him.

9

Sydney paused for a moment after stepping through the portal to take the room in. The last time she had been here, she hadn't looked around. It was strange stepping from the long brick corridors of the Adelaide Treasury Vaults into what had every appearance of being an average home. The room on the other side of the portal looked like a typical dining room/kitchen combination, with the portal situated where a back door to a home would typically be. Directly in front of her was a long corridor with rooms branching out from it, most of the doors closed. At the far end, she could make out the staircase they had gone up when Raymond and Kingston had taken her above ground to the streets of Melbourne.

There was something cosy about the living space, and it wasn't just the fact there were no windows to speak of. The walls were painted brick – an off-white colour. The doors were a deep burgundy, and there were a surprising number of plants around the room. Nearing one, it surprised Sydney to find that they weren't artificial. They must be a shade plant, given there was no sunlight for them.

The room was furnished in a way that told her that Raymond and Lucille must live here. The smell of freshly made coffee was in the air, and there was no hint of dampness or dust she would have expected for somewhere so deep below ground. Instead, the air was warm and clean, with a homely feel. The dining room table was large enough to seat six, and the kitchen was more significant than Sydney's one in her flat. This was a full-sized home hidden beneath the Victorian State Library, of that much she was sure.

Wondering if anyone was home, Sydney took a deep breath and called out into the space just loud enough that she knew they could hear her from the rest of the home. 'Mr Barry?'

There was a brief pause before she heard an answer. 'First door on your left.'

Sydney spotted the open door, just past the opening of the corridor, and headed towards it.

Raymond smiled faintly as he spotted Sydney standing in the doorway. 'Good afternoon, Miss Madinah. Is there something I can help you with?'

'No, no, just…' She laughed nervously, pointing back over her shoulder towards the corridor. 'I'm still getting used to the whole…'

'Yes, the portal.' Raymond reached across and switched off the small lantern above his desk and stood, tugging off the white gloves as he moved past her, gesturing with his head for her to follow him into the corridor. 'They take some getting used to.'

'But you're used to them.' Sydney followed him, eyes taking in her surroundings. 'You were probably wandering back and forth through it when you were a baby.'

'No, actually. I only went through the portal five years ago.' He led her back into the dining room, smiling at Sydney's hesitance as she hovered in the doorway. He gestured her in as he picked up his mug, looking back at her. 'Coffee?'

'Yes, please.' She came to join him, her eyes studying him in the warm light. 'Did you find it as I did? Just… stumbled on it?'

'No.' He handed her a mug, pouring his own. 'I went through to meet Kingston. It was my last test in becoming the Keeper. Milk?'

'Yes, please.' She held the mug as he poured it in, then added a single sugar. She sipped from the mug, blowing on it gently before taking a long drink. It was the good stuff, not just the cheap instant they had in the break room of the hotel. She took a moment to savour it before continuing. 'Did it take you long to get used to it?'

'Not long.' Raymond moved to sit on one of the dining room chairs, watching her as she sat beside him rather than opposite him, causing him to frown slightly. 'Still having issues, are you?'

She nodded. 'Jake told me that three people stepped through the portal, and all that was left on the other side was dust. Like that guy when I first came through.'

'We're not sure exactly how it works,' Raymond watched her, cupping his mug between his hands. 'I remember asking Kingston about it, and he told me that certain people possess a quality that allows them to use the portal, something unique that sets them apart from the rest of humanity. He wouldn't be any more specific, but if anyone who doesn't possess the quality walks through, their atoms don't reconstruct from one portal to the other, leaving only dust.'

Sydney frowned. 'So if I hadn't had that quality…'

'You'd be dust,' Raymond said, blowing gently on his coffee and taking a sip. 'You got lucky.'

Sydney shivered, cupping her mug tightly as she frowned. 'If it's so dangerous, why is it so easy to get to?'

Raymond frowned, shaking his head. 'It's not. In the five years I've been a Keeper, only two people have found it by accident. Usually they get spotted on the CCTV before they get this far.'

'What happened to the other person?'

Raymond's eyebrows rose slightly as he smiled faintly. 'Mother bitched about cleaning up the dust for over a month. She still brings it up now and again.'

'Oh.' Sydney blinked, staring down into her coffee. 'So… to go through the portal, you move through it quickly, right?'

'No, you can stop right in the middle, one foot on either side of the door frame.' Raymond tilted his head slightly. 'To us, it's just like every other doorway. The difference is that walking through it you end up in another city, not just another room.'

Sydney frowned. 'Have you done that?'

Raymond nodded. 'Once or twice.'

'I'm not sure I'm game too.' Sydney sipped again from her coffee, wincing as it burned her tongue mildly. 'Did it take you long before you did that?'

'Not that long.' Raymond smiled and shrugged. 'It just becomes natural after a while. You don't think about it. If you keep going back and forth, you'll stop worrying.'

'Is that what you did?' Sydney looked up at him. 'Did you keep going back and forth until you were used to it?'

Raymond frowned slightly, shifting in his seat and looking up towards the portal at the sound of approaching footsteps. There was a moment's pause before they approached the doorway. Rita stepped in without hesitation and let her gaze drop on them.

'Should have known.' She frowned, looking from the coffee cups in their hands and back up. 'In here, having yet another coffee break while the rest of us are working.'

'It's hard to work when you're in the wrong city, 728km from your job,' Raymond pointed out without batting an eyelid, instead calmly sipping his coffee.

Rita narrowed her eyes. 'Only you'd be anal enough to know that, Ray-Ray.'

Raymond's jaw set as he looked up at her through narrowed eyes, leaning back in his seat. 'Something you'd know all about if you realise I wasn't guessing, Margarita.'

Rita's eyes flashed as she glared at him, the two staring each other down. Sydney shuffled uncomfortably, looking from one to the other. She cleared her throat, drawing their attention back to her as she smiled at Rita.

'Did you want to see one of us, Rita?'

Rita shot Raymond another look before returning her gaze to Sydney. 'Simon's looking for you. He wanted to go over the catering for the wedding on the weekend. I think Kingston also wanted a certain arsehole to go over something.'

'As charming as ever, Rita.' Raymond set his mug down on the table, glaring at her as he stood and moved past her. 'It's little wonder you haven't got a boyfriend.'

'And you're such an expert, Mr Sad and Single.' Rita glared after him before looking back at Sydney. 'Coming? I'm sure Raymond won't care if you brought your coffee with you, just so long as you get the cup back before Lucille notices and cuts his balls off.'

Sydney chuckled, standing and making sure not to spill her coffee. 'Are you sure? She does seem rather keen on an heir.'

'Lucille's clever.' Rita smiled and winked. 'She'd find a way.'

* * * * *

Kingston stopped to catch his breath as he finished another set of laps of the pool. Spotting movement out the top of his eye, he looked up, smiling as he spotted Raymond leaning against a pillar, watching him from the other end of the pool. Pushing himself off the wall, Kingston swam the short distance to the other end and pushed himself out of the water.

Raymond held his towel out to him, Kingston taking it. 'You know you're welcome to join me,' Kingston said.

'I don't own a bathing suit,' Raymond said, moving to pick up Kingston's robe from one of the deck chairs and holding it up for him.

'Who says you need one?' Kingston said without missing a beat, allowing Raymond to help him into his robe.

'I'm sure Jake would love that,' Raymond replied. 'Probably scar him for life.'

'Then he should learn to appreciate the human body,' Kingston said as they started walking towards the pool exit.

'Jake knows how to appreciate the human body,' Raymond said, allowing Kingston to hold the door open for him and nodding his thanks. 'He just prefers female ones.'

'Rita's in particular,' Kingston said, and was rewarded with a laugh from Raymond. 'I am serious, though – you are welcome to join me for my swim.' Hearing no reply, Kingston glanced towards the man walking beside him and saw a slight frown creasing Raymond's forehead. 'You do know how to swim?'

Raymond shook his head as they reached the stairs, climbing them together. 'I never really had the time to learn.'

Kingston frowned. 'So you're a dead shot with a gun, a master of throwing knives, know two forms of martial arts, have an eclectic knowledge of every book in Victorian State Libraries catalogue, can tell exactly what category a book can be found in from its number and vice versa, and yet you don't know how to swim?'

'Like I said,' Raymond said, shrugging it off. 'I never really had the time.'

'Your friends live in Geelong, do they not?' Kingston said, thinking back to a previous conversation. 'Couldn't they teach you?'

'They… don't know,' Raymond said. 'It's never really come up.'

'It's something you should learn, Raymond,' Kingston said as they reached the door of his room. 'Ask Jake. If I recall, he holds a bronze medallion in lifesaving.'

'I'll think about it,' Raymond said as Kingston unlocked his door, letting them into the room. 'Just… don't tell Rita.'

'She'll tease you, but I think you'll find she will agree with me about asking Jake,' Kingston said as he closed the door, flicking the lock. He turned to regard Raymond. 'Rita found you then.'

'She did,' Raymond said. 'She's as snarky as ever, I should add.'

'Yes, she is in a good mood today,' Kingston said with a chuckle. 'So, what do you have?'

'I found another one,' Raymond confirmed.

Kingston couldn't help but feel the slight flutter of excitement in his chest at the news. 'Where?'

'Flinders Street Station.'

'I told you there would be one there.' Kingston crossed towards his desk and dropped into his seat, watching as Raymond settled into the chair across from him.

'I think there may be more than one,' Raymond said. 'At least that's what I can gather from the journal. But I only have one definitive location.'

There was something in how Raymond said it that caused an

alarm bell to ring at the back of Kingston's mind. 'How hard is it going to be to get it?'

'Hard,' Raymond confirmed. 'It's in the ballroom.'

'Which is closed off.' Kingston sighed, resting his elbows on the desk as he thought. 'On a positive note, once we gain access, no one will interfere.'

'*Once* we gain access,' Raymond reminded him. 'As far as I recall, all the doors are locked or alarmed, or you must go through an area that is staffed.'

'We'll have to talk it over with Jake,' Kingston said. He smiled at Raymond. 'Good work.'

10

'So,' Jake said as he sidled into Kingston's room, glancing at the others before fixing his gaze on Kingston himself. 'Do you want the good news or the bad news?'

'The good,' Kingston said from behind his desk. It was now early evening, Sydney and Rita having formerly clocked off for the day when Kingston had called them all into his office to let them know about the new key location.

'The good news is I've found a way into the ballroom, and it should be fairly easy to slip past the security.' Jake dropped onto the couch next to Sydney. Kingston had given him a heads up earlier that day to let him know about the location, and he'd spent the better part of the afternoon researching between his duties.

'And the bad news?' Rita asked.

Jake glanced over at her. 'In my research, I found a news article that featured a recent photo of the ballroom interior. Apparently, it's been stripped completely bare.'

'How bare?' Raymond asked.

'To the foundations bare,' Jake said with a sigh. 'They even took the ceiling out. They were meant to be restoring it, but they stripped it down to the brickwork.'

'Any sign that they disturbed the brickwork?' Kingston asked.

'Couldn't tell from the photo, but it doesn't look good in terms of finding a key there,' Jake said, shrugging. 'Sorry.'

'It might still be there,' Sydney said, looking over at Kingston. 'I mean, if there's a chance, right?'

'I will not risk it on the "chance",' Kingston said, rubbing a hand over his face. He turned to Raymond. 'You said there might be more keys there.'

'I think, but I haven't narrowed down the location,' Raymond admitted. 'They could be anywhere, and that place has been renovated many times.'

'What about other locations?' Kingston asked. 'Other keys?'

'Oh, I found several,' Raymond said. 'The Menzie's Hotel for one.'

'We could try there,' Sydney said hopefully.

'Demolished in 1969,' Raymond said.

'Any others?' Kingston asked.

'The Finks Building,' Raymond answered.

'Let me guess: demolished,' Rita said.

Raymond nodded. 'In 1967.'

'Any more?' Kingston asked, resignation creeping into his voice.

'The Scott's Hotel,' Raymond answered. 'And yes, it's demolished. 1961.'

'Are there any that aren't demolished?' Sydney asked.

'Not that I've found yet,' Raymond answered. 'They took most of the heritage buildings down in the sixties. There was a major demolition and construction boom during that era. They wanted to modernise Melbourne, so everything old had to go.'

'Which doesn't bode well for us,' Kingston said, sighing heavily. 'Therefore, it was important to find the keys back then.'

'Did the Keeper back then try?' Sydney asked.

'Yes,' Raymond said softly. 'They broke the code back then. Found about a dozen keys before…'

'Before what?'

'Before the Keeper died,' Kingston said. 'Before he and his wife were killed.'

Sydney blinked. 'Wait… killed?'

'That's how my grandfather became the Keeper,' Raymond said. 'It usually skips a generation, so my mother was in line to be the next Keeper, but they killed my great-grandparents when they were trying to find a key in Werribee, meaning my grandfather had to step in. He tried for decades to break the code but couldn't.'

'And then you did,' Sydney finished.

Raymond nodded. 'I did, yes.'

'What happened to the Protector back then?' Rita asked. 'Did he die too?'

'No, he didn't,' Kingston said, a haunted look on his face. 'He tried his best, but… things happened. He never forgave himself.'

'I'm sure he did his best,' Sydney said.

'They wouldn't have died if he had,' Kingston replied softly.

Raymond narrowed his eyes at the way Kingston said that. It was almost as if Kingston had been there. 'It's ancient history now,' Raymond said. 'As Mother says, "you can't change the past."'

'No, you can't,' Kingston said. He paused for a long while before looking back over at Jake. 'You're certain that there is nothing left.'

'I'm sure,' Jake said. 'Sorry.'

'Saves us the trouble of finding out the hard way,' Kingston said. He sighed. 'I guess that leaves us back at square one.'

'Hang on,' Rita frowned. 'All the locations you mentioned were in Melbourne. What about Adelaide?'

'The Black Eagle Hotel,' Raymond said. 'Demolished in 1983.'

'Wait, that's the Aurora,' Kingston said. 'We got that key.'

Raymond blinked. 'You did?'

Kingston nodded.

'Did it work?'

'Surprisingly, yes,' Kingston said. 'The portal led right back to the Aurora.'

'So it doesn't work anymore,' Rita said.

'No, it wouldn't,' Kingston said. 'The portal would have been destroyed, along with the hotel.'

'How many keys are there?' Sydney asked.

Raymond and Kingston looked at each other, Raymond eventually shrugging.

'We don't know,' Kingston answered.

'A few,' Raymond guessed. 'Redmond wrote quite a few journals with the locations hidden in the pages. It's just a matter of finding the locations.'

'But why were they hidden in the first place?' Sydney asked.

'To stop people from abusing the portals,' Kingston answered. 'The keys were never meant to be lost like this.'

'No,' Raymond agreed. 'Redmond died before he could pass on the knowledge of his code to the next Keeper. That knowledge was supposed to be passed down through the family, but the Keepers that break the code keep… well, dying.'

'Because someone keeps killing them,' Jake said, eyes on Raymond. 'Which is why it's important to keep the Keeper safe.'

'Which is my job,' Kingston continued. 'Which I can't do if I don't know anything is going on.'

'What makes you think anything is going on?' Raymond asked.

'Call it instinct,' Kingston said.

'Instincts can be wrong,' Raymond pointed out.

'Occasionally,' Kingston agreed, never breaking his gaze.

Sydney cleared her throat after a few moments' silence, breaking the tension in the air. 'So right now, we don't have any leads.'

'No, I have leads,' Raymond said, finally breaking Kingston's gaze. 'I just don't have anything solid right now.'

'Guess you better hit the books then, Ray-Ray,' Rita said.

The corner of Raymond's eye twitched as he threw her a glare.

'She's right,' Kingston said. 'Hopefully you will soon find somewhere that hasn't been demolished.'

* * * * *

'I want you working this weekend,' Lucille said as Raymond stepped back through the portal and into their dining room.

Raymond fought to keep from sighing. 'And what makes you say that, Mother?'

'We need to stay one step ahead of these people,' Lucille said, raising her hand to reveal the letter in her hand. 'The sooner we find all the keys, the better.'

Raymond shrugged it off. 'I can't work this weekend.'

Lucille shot him a look. 'Why?'

'I have plans already.'

'Well, cancel them.'

'No.' Raymond frowned. 'I've had these plans for a while. Two weeks in a row, I've been working hard. I need a break.'

'A break.' Lucille huffed. 'You are the Keeper. Your job is important.'

'I'm fully aware of that.' Raymond shook his head. 'Two days ago, you told me off because I don't go out enough, and now when I have plans, you want me to stay in?'

'You don't go out enough, but when you do, it should be when there is nothing important to do. Right now, you have something important to do.'

'As far as you're concerned, there's always something important to do, and I'd never get to go anywhere.' He narrowed his eyes. 'Then again, I should be used to that, shouldn't I?'

'Don't start.' Lucille glared at him, setting her jaw. 'I know full well what you're doing this weekend. You're meeting up with Andrew, Tanya and that kid of theirs and taking off again.'

'And what's wrong with that?' Raymond asked. 'What's wrong with me going out with my best friends to the footy or fishing?'

'You have a responsibility–'

'And I do my job.' Raymond returned her glare. 'You just don't like that I have friends, because the Lord knows you never had any.'

He registered the pain before seeing her move, his face stinging where the blow had landed, leaving his glasses slightly askew. He set his jaw, fighting back the reflexive tears as he reached up to straighten his frames, making a note to keep his breathing even not to alert her to his pain.

'You listen to me, Raymond,' Lucille hissed, voice dropping into a low, reprimanding tone. 'You seem to fail to realise just how important your mission is. You need to be here at all times to protect not only the secrets and archives, but Kingston. You can't go gallivanting off with your worthless friends every other weekend simply because you choose to. That was fine when you were at university or training, but you are the Keeper now.

'You have a job to do, a job that is 24/7, 365 days a year. A job that, if you screw up, could ruin things forever. Raymond, you won't be the only one to pay the price of your failure. And need I remind you what happened when the Barry family first deserted the Kingston family?'

'Redmond. Died. First.' Raymond let out a steadying breath, keeping his gaze locked on hers. 'And Kingston can defend himself. He's the one who told me to take the weekend off.'

'Kingston is getting too comfortable. We can't afford to do the same.' Lucille's eyes narrowed. 'You and he are the last of your lines, because you are both too foolish to find women to marry and have children with. I have urged you several times to find yourself a girl, but you waste all your time with Andrew, Tanya and their kid.' Lucille spun on her heel and stalked back down the corridor towards the staircase. 'I'll see you at the weekend.'

Raymond let out the breath he had been holding as Lucille stalked away, reaching up to rub the still stinging pain away from his cheek. As she disappeared around the corner, he turned his head slightly. 'How long have you been standing there?'

'For all of it.' Kingston stepped through the portal, pulling his hands out of his pockets and looking after Lucille. 'She takes her job very seriously.'

'Too seriously.'

'Can be handy at times.' He reached out, dropping a hand onto Raymond's shoulder and squeezing gently. 'Maybe she's right; you should get yourself a girlfriend. Give your mother an heir, and she might leave you alone. She'd be too preoccupied with training your child to care about what you do on weekends.'

Raymond gave him a measured look, shrugging the hand from his shoulder as he moved towards the office door. 'That's what I'm afraid of.'

11

Weddings were exhausting affairs. Sydney decided that if she ever got married, she would make sure it was a small one. Marrying at the registry office and having a quiet brunch at a cafe for the reception would do her just fine. She sighed, placing the papers back in order and sliding them into their folder. It didn't help that the groom of this wedding was a groomzilla. The bride seemed happy that the wedding was happening, but the groom wanted every 'i' to be dotted and 't' to be crossed.

Feeling eyes on the back of her neck, she looked up and spotted Jake peering at her from across the lobby. He gave her a quick thumbs-up before disappearing down the corridor towards the security office, barely giving her enough time to wave a quick 'hello' back in his direction. Deciding she needed a break, Sydney slipped the folder into the drawer, standing up from her seat and heading towards the cafe.

'Miss Sydney, come join us,' Dorothy said as soon as she arrived.

'You've been working so hard,' Elizabeth added, sliding a plate full of cupcakes towards her. 'Have one. Simon says they're fresh out of the oven.'

'Thank you,' Sydney said, graciously taking one. She bit into it as she sat at their table, looking around at the other people in the cafe. It was over half full, Simon busy serving coffee from behind the counter. Sydney spotted Kian at his usual table, typing away on his small laptop and occasionally sipping from his drink. 'Busy today.'

'Market day,' Dorothy said.

'Pension day,' Elizabeth expanded.

Sydney chuckled. 'So normal for a Friday.'

The two women nodded.

'Would you like some tea?' Dorothy asked. 'We can have Simon bring over another cup.'

'No, it's fine, thank you,' Sydney said. 'Thank you for the cupcake.'

'You look like you could do with the sugar,' Elizabeth said. 'I'm guessing you're run-off your feet preparing for the wedding this weekend.'

Sydney didn't even want to know how they knew that. She instead just nodded her agreement. 'Weddings are a lot of work.'

'I remember my wedding,' Elizabeth said. 'We married out on my parents' farm. Nothing fancy, with just the family attending. My mother baked the wedding cake herself, and we used flowers from the garden.'

'I got married at the local church,' Dorothy said. 'Reception in the church hall. Everyone brought something to share on a plate. None of this fancy catering that they have these days.'

'If things were like that today, Simon and I would be out of a job,' Sydney joked.

The two ladies chuckled, Elizabeth leaning towards her. 'So, how are you finding things? Settling in?'

'I'm getting to know the place better,' Sydney said. 'Jake took me on tour the other day.'

'Did he now?' Dorothy said, also leaning in her direction. 'And how is young Jake? Still single?'

Sydney had to give them credit for the forwardness. 'Jake seems fine, and I'm not sure of his relationship status. It's never really come up.'

'Poor man works himself to the bone,' Elizabeth said. 'It's nice to hear that he could show you around.'

'Speaking of people overworking themselves,' Dorothy held up a hand to hide the finger she was pointing in Kian's direction from him.

'Nothing new there,' Elizabeth said. 'Although he has been a lot more earnest than usual.'

'I know you're discussing me, ladies,' Kian said from over at his table.

'It's rude to listen in on conversations,' Dorothy said.

'One might say it's rude to gossip,' Kian countered.

'But it's such fun,' Elizabeth said. 'Don't say you don't enjoy our conversations. Otherwise, you wouldn't be listening in on them.'

'It's hard not to,' Kian said, looking up from his computer. 'When you're so loud.'

'We're not loud,' Elizabeth said as Dorothy huffed. Elizabeth looked at Sydney. 'Would you say we are loud, Miss Sydney?'

'Not 'loud',' Sydney said, trying to think of how to phrase things so as not to insult them. 'More boisterous.'

The hint of a smile cracked at Kian's lips.

'Well, we are that,' Elizabeth had to concede.

'How boring would life be without some fun now and again?' Dorothy said, taking a sip of her tea. 'Especially when you have so much going on in your life.'

'Tell us, Miss Sydney, what do you do for fun?' Elizabeth asked.

Sydney had to admit the question stumped her. Most of her life revolved around her job. The only thing that didn't was the whole portal thing, which in a way, was fun. Thinking for a moment, Sydney eventually answered. 'I guess I watch a lot of movies.'

'Nothing like a good movie to take your mind off things,' Dorothy said with approval.

'How long has it been since we saw a movie, Dot?' Elizabeth asked. 'It's been over a month, hasn't it?'

'We need to go again,' Dorothy answered. 'I'm not sure what's even playing right now. We'll have to look it up next time we come to town.'

'What about you, Kian?' Sydney asked, looking over at the man. 'Seen any good movies lately.'

'Real life provides enough drama for me,' Kian said, returning his attention to his computer.

'Sour puss,' Elizabeth scolded. 'Some people just don't know how to have any fun.'

'Indeed,' Dorothy agreed.

* * * * *

Stepping through the underground, Rita couldn't help but feel a sense of claustrophobia. She'd never liked it down here. It always felt too enclosed and airless, even though it was appropriately ventilated. She put it down to the lack of windows and the walls being too close for her taste. The exposed red brick didn't help, and she couldn't fathom why anyone would want to hold a wedding reception in a place like this.

Bypassing the more public areas of the vaults, Rita made her way towards Kingston's security door, swiping her key card and stepping through. She paused briefly outside the Melbourne door, knocking on it twice before opening it. It was someone's home after all, and unlike Kingston and Jake, she didn't like just barging through. It was more polite to announce her arrival, even though she knew she was expected.

The home of the Barry's still gave her claustrophobia, but it wasn't as bad as the vaults in Adelaide. She linked it to the painted white walls, and the space felt like a home. The lack of windows was still off-putting to her, and she was glad that she wasn't the one who had to live here. Little wonder that the Barry's had an alternative apartment in a high-rise with a view of the city, with big bay windows and a balcony. It was a stark contrast to the home beneath the library, even though Rita knew that Raymond still spent most of his time down here when he wasn't working in the library or at the state archives.

'Good, you made it.'

Raymond poked his head out of his office, giving her a half-smile as he came out to join her. Rita closed the portal door and stepped further into the living area.

'I got your message,' she said, casually regarding him and noting that he looked like he hadn't been sleeping well. It was something she'd have to quiz him on later. After all, she was the team doctor, even though very few people knew of her medical degree. 'What did you want?'

'A favour,' Raymond said. 'One at short notice, too.'

'Really,' Rita said. It must be important if Raymond was coming to her for a favour. 'What mess do you need me to clean up?'

'Nothing like that,' he said, shaking his head. 'I hoped you might accompany me to a ball this Saturday.'

'A ball.' Rita blinked, surprised. That was the last thing she had expected. 'What kind of ball?'

'Charity ball. Formal. And the others can't know about it.'

Interesting. Rita wondered just what he was playing at. 'Business or pleasure?'

'Business,' Raymond said without hesitation.

The pieces of the puzzle snapped together in her mind. 'You found another key,' she accused.

'I did,' he confirmed. 'I was hoping you would come with me to get it.'

'Yet you don't want the others to know.' She narrowed her eyes. 'Exactly where is this ball?'

Raymond took off his glasses, cleaning them with the edge of his shirt to avoid her eye. 'Werribee Park Mansion.'

Rita felt as if someone had dropped a ton of bricks on her at those words. 'Oh no. No. Kingston will have a fit.'

'Which is why we will not tell him,' Raymond countered, sliding his glasses back on. 'Come on, Rita, I know exactly where the key is. We go, we get it, we get out of there. It shouldn't take more than a couple of hours.'

'Does your mother know about this ball?' Rita asked.

'Of course not. She thinks I'm spending the weekend with my

friends in Geelong.' Raymond widened his eyes in a look like a hurt puppy. 'You know I wouldn't ask if it wasn't important.'

'Why not ask Sydney?' Rita asked. 'I'm sure she'd be happy to go with you.'

'She's still getting her head around the portal. Besides, you're a better lookout.' He shrugged. 'You also know me better, so it would be more believable if you came along as my date.'

'This is definitely not a date,' Rita countered.

Raymond shrugged it off. 'Other people don't know that. It also won't look suspicious if we sneak off alone somewhere.'

'You realise what people are going to think,' she accused. Seeing the look on his face, she knew he knew exactly what they would think, and he didn't care. 'How do you plan on getting there?'

'As I said, Mother thinks I'm going to Geelong for the weekend and took the car,' Raymond answered.

There was a plus side to the whole thing. Rita loved the Barry's car, and riding in it would be a perk. 'You realise I only have a day to prepare?'

'I know,' Raymond answered. 'I warned it was short notice.'

'Extremely short notice,' Rita said. 'I have to get a dress, then organise to get my hair and makeup done. And what makes you think I had nothing on this weekend, anyway?'

'There's a wedding at the hotel,' Raymond said. 'You keep your schedule clear in case there is a disaster.'

'Yes, there is a wedding. Which I have to keep my schedule clear for.'

'Sydney will have it covered,' Raymond assured her. 'There's a key at stake here, Rita. After all the disappointments lately, we need a win.'

He wasn't wrong. Rita sighed, running everything through her head. She knew that if Kingston found out he'd flip out, but if they came back with a key – and if that key worked – then he might be more likely to forgive them. Raymond was also right in that they only had to stay for as long as required to get the key, and then they could leave. They'd probably be in and out before anything had the chance of actually happening.

'Okay,' she said. 'I'll go with you to the ball. I take it you have tickets.'

'Technically, they were sent to Mother, but yes, I do.' Raymond gave her a relieved smile. 'It's an afternoon event, so we'll be needing to leave here at about twelve Melbourne time.'

'I guess I'll meet you here then,' Rita said. 'You better be sure about this.'

'I'm sure,' Raymond said. 'I triple-checked the location. So long as we can get to the staircase, it should be a breeze.'

'Famous last words,' she warned.

'Not mine,' he said firmly.

12

'You realise we never discussed payment,' Rita said, breaking the silence in the car.

Raymond glanced at her. 'Well, this is a charity event.'

'Ha ha,' Rita said, smoothing her hand down her dress to work out a few of the creases.

'Okay then, name your price.'

'Dinner. At Enoteca Cucina.' Rita said without hesitation.

'Okay,' Raymond said, taking the turn into the park. 'That all?'

'I want reimbursement for the dress and the hair,' she continued.

'I can do that,' he said. He steered the Nissan GT-R up the long driveway, following the car park attendant's directions into a free car space.

The two of them exited the car, following the signs towards the entrance to the Park. Raymond showed their tickets at the gate, the attendant pointing the direction up along the dirt driveway towards where they could hear music. Raymond offered Rita his arm, Rita hesitating a moment before taking it. She had worn sensible shoes, so she didn't find it hard to walk on the loose gravel, unlike a couple of other ball attendees walking just ahead.

Rita had to admit that Raymond dressed up nicely. He was

dressed in a well-fitted suit that looked tailored; his hair slicked back without a strand out of place. Rita's dress was a dark emerald that set off her red hair, and she'd found a dress she could move around in easily just in case they needed to make a fast getaway. The last thing she needed was to be hobbled by her dress and shoes should this whole thing go south.

The mansion stood proudly at the end of the driveway, the sandstone shining in the sun. The tower overlooked all, and the arches made them feel small. They had barely joined the crowd of people near some large tents placed out on the lawn in front of the mansion when someone called Raymond's name.

'Crap,' she heard him mutter as a woman roughly the age of Lucile came toward her with her arms outstretched.

'Raymond, it is so good to see you,' the woman said, gripping his arms and pulling him forward so she could kiss him on the cheek. 'You grow more and more handsome every day.'

'Good to see you too, Jennifer,' Raymond answered politely. 'I didn't know you were attending.'

'Oh, I never miss a party,' Jennifer said. Rita gave her the once over, taking in the woman's sparkling gown and extravagant jewellery. Clearly, a woman who loved to be the centre of attention. 'Have you seen Sally yet? I'm sure she'd be overjoyed to see you.'

'We just arrived,' Raymond said, with a slight emphasis on the 'we'.

It didn't escape Jennifer's attention. 'Who's this?' She asked, her eyes finally turning to Rita. There was barely masked disdain in her voice and a disapproving look in her eye.

'This is Rita Taylor,' Raymond said. 'Rita, I'd like you to meet Jennifer Smith. We work together at the archives.'

'A pleasure to meet you,' Rita said, offering her hand. Jennifer took it reluctantly.

Rita could tell from the tightness in Raymond's arm that he wanted to get away from the situation fast. Thinking for a moment, Rita turned toward Raymond. 'Honey, didn't you say we would find drinks?'

'Yes, dear, we were,' Raymond said, playing along.

Jennifer's eyes seemed to widen at the pleasantries they

exchanged, but she didn't say a word. She smiled tightly, turning her attention entirely to Raymond. 'I'll let Sally know you are here. Enjoy your evening.'

'You too,' Raymond said, hastening away.

'You owe me two dinners,' Rita hissed at him as soon as they were out of earshot.

'Okay, okay,' Raymond said, leading her toward the drinks table. He glanced back quickly to make sure that Jennifer hadn't followed them before he relinquished Rita's arm. 'I had no idea that bitch was coming.'

'Let me guess,' Rita said. 'She's trying to set you up with her daughter.'

'She's been trying since the first day I started working at the archives,' Raymond confirmed. 'I've known her for longer than that, though. She's a quasi-friend of my mother's.'

'"Quasi" friend?'

'They make out like friends,' Raymond said. 'It's more competition than anything. Right now, they're competing over whose child will get married first.'

'Your mother is out of luck,' Rita said with a chuckle.

'So's Jennifer,' said Raymond. 'See, Sally and I are both in on what is happening. Sally is a lovely lady, but she's not my type, and I'm not hers. Sally has no interest in being in a relationship, but her mother drags her around to parties to meet potential suitors. She hates it.'

'I can't blame her,' Rita said as they reached the drinks tent. Rita took a glass of champagne and handed one to Raymond. 'I'm guessing that you and this Sally spend time together at events like this just to protect each other.'

'We do,' Raymond admitted. 'Downside is that now Jennifer is going to talk to Mother about how I was at this ball.'

'Which means she's going to find out you are in Werribee,' Rita continued. 'You're never going to hear the end of it.'

'No, I'm not,' Raymond said with a sigh. 'Mother will no doubt try to ground me.'

Rita snorted. 'I'd like to see her try.'

'You will,' Raymond said. 'Jennifer will also mention that you were with me to see if Mother knows you.'

'Oh.' Rita hadn't thought about that. 'Your mother won't think we're dating, will she?'

'Don't worry; I won't let her think that,' Raymond said, sipping from his champagne. 'It probably won't stop her from dropping hints, though.'

'Great,' Rita said dejectedly. She remembered the first time she met Lucille and the hints the woman had dropped about her son being single. 'No offence, Raymond, but you aren't my type.'

'No offence taken; you're not mine either,' Raymond said. He took another drink, gazing around the crowd before focusing on the Mansion itself. 'So, when should we try for the key?'

'The sooner, the better,' Rita said. 'Just in case we run into any more of your mother's "friends".'

'Agreed.'

* * * * *

Sneaking into the Mansion proved to be a simple enough task as the Mansion itself was open for tours. After entering the large stone building, Rita and Raymond separated from their tour group, stepping around the main staircase. Their shoes tapped on the intricately tiled floor, the furnishings looking to be original as busts observed their moves. Rita took lookout as Raymond inspected the wooden panels, sliding his fingers along the groves. Hearing the next tour group nearing, Rita stepped closer to Raymond.

'I thought you said you knew where it was,' she hissed.

'I know where it is,' Raymond answered back. 'I just don't know *exactly* where it is.'

'Great,' Rita said. 'You've got maybe five minutes before the next group comes in.'

'Wait, wait.' Raymond's fingers found an impression, and a panel slipped open with a pop. Raymond reached into the space, fingers finding cold metal. 'It's actually here.'

'Really?' Rita glanced over at him quickly, then up again at the sound of nearing voices. 'Quickly.'

Raymond slipped the brass key into his pocket, snapping the panel back into place before rejoining Rita. 'Okay, I've got it.'

'Which means we can get out of here,' Rita said.

'You're not going anywhere.'

They both looked up at the voice, spotting two men standing a few feet away. They were dressed in formal attire, which told them they were attendees of the gala, not security. The men were built well and fit; from their posture, they were ready for a fight.

'Can we help you?' Raymond asked, half stepping in front of Rita.

'As a matter-of-fact, you can,' the shorter of the two men said. He outstretched his hand. 'How about you hand over that key you just found?'

'What key?' Raymond asked.

'We're not here to play,' the man said. 'Hand it over, Barry.'

'I'm not handing anything to you,' Raymond said, feeling Rita grip the back of his jacket tightly.

'I will not ask again,' the man said. 'Just hand over the key and walk away.'

'I don't think you heard me,' Raymond said, a growl creeping into his voice. 'I'm not handing you anything.'

The two men exchanged a look, the taller cracking his knuckles while the shorter took half a step forward. 'So you want to do this the hard way, then?'

'I suggest you walk away,' Raymond said. 'Before someone gets hurt.'

The two men laughed at that.

'Raymond,' Rita said softly in a warning. In a louder voice, she directed the two men. 'Come any closer, and I'll start screaming.'

'Go ahead,' the shorter man said. 'It'll only take me a second to finish this.'

He flicked his wrist, a knife slipping out of his jacket sleeve. Rita slipped further behind Raymond, who reached inside his jacket.

His fingers closed around his switchblade, Raymond bringing it out and flicking it open. The other man seemed genuinely surprised to see that he was armed, before he slipped into a fighter pose alongside his companion. Raymond stepped fully in front of Rita, keeping himself between her and the two men.

'We don't care about Miss Taylor,' the man said. 'It's you we want, Barry.'

'You seem to know who we are,' Raymond said. 'Be rude not to introduce yourselves.'

The two men laughed, the shorter shaking his head. 'Yeah, that's not going to happen.'

Raymond widened his step, slipping into a fighting stance. He sized the two men up. He could tell by their posture that this wouldn't be their first fight, and that both of them were fit. Raymond could take down the shorter one first and use his speed to take out the taller one. It was clear that he needed to separate them. Two against one was not a good position to be in, and he had Rita to consider. He hoped she kept her promise of screaming, as that would be the only thing that would get him out of this alive.

The sound of the front door opening broke the silence, Raymond snapping his blade closed and palming it to hide it from view. He saw the other man push his blade back up his sleeve and turn around to face the tour group that had entered from behind him. Using the distraction, Raymond took a long step back, catching hold of Rita's hand and tugging her in the general direction of a side doorway.

The tour group assembled in the foyer, the tour guide going over the home's features. Raymond and Rita waited until they came closer before slipping in among them, then out the back of the group and out through the main door. They didn't stop until they reached the main gala, mingling among the bodies. They then took a moment to glance back, trying to spot the two men and unable to see them among the hundred or so gathered.

'Let's get out of here,' Rita said.

'No arguments here,' Raymond agreed.

The two slipped out of the crowd and made for the car park briskly, not stopping until they reached Raymond's car. He unlocked it, the two sliding in without a word. Backing it up, Raymond spotted the two men coming out of the gate. Raymond carefully navigated the car out of the car park. It surprised the attendant to see someone leaving so early into the event.

Raymond watched in the mirror as the two men ran toward them before Raymond floored it, sending the car sideways slightly on the loose gravel before it gained traction and shot them down the driveway and to a hasty retreat.

13

They were almost halfway back to the city when Rita broke the silence. 'They were waiting for us.'

'Yes, they were,' Raymond agreed.

'And it did not surprise you to see them,' Rita accused.

Raymond bit his lip. 'No, I wasn't.'

'Care to explain?'

'Not really.'

Rita turned toward him. 'Raymond, we were set upon by two men who knew we were there after a key. I deserved an explanation.'

'What's to explain?' Raymond said. 'You just summarised the whole thing.'

'How about starting with who they were?' Rita said.

'I don't know.' Raymond spotted her glare. 'No, seriously, I don't know. They're just a couple of thugs who are interested in the keys.'

'I see.' Rita settled back into her seat. 'What are the odds they're connected with that guy that tried to access the portals. The one from when Sydney found out about everything.'

'Pretty good,' Raymond conceded. 'I mean, it could just be sheer coincidence, but the timing suggests otherwise.'

'Yes, it does.' Rita smoothed a hand down her dress, working out the creases. 'You realise we're going to have to tell Kingston.'

'I am aware,' Raymond said. He patted his pocket. 'At least we have something to show him.'

'True.' Rita looked at the traffic ahead. 'Did you want to tell him, or shall I?'

'We'll cross that river when we get to it,' Raymond said.

They continued to drive in silence, each lost to their thoughts until they arrived back at the car park where the Barry's kept their car. Raymond parked without a word, climbing out of the car and coming around to help Rita. She thanked him, stepping out of the vehicle and smoothing the wrinkles out of her dress as Raymond locked the car.

The walk back to the Library remained in relative silence, the two only commenting on traffic and pedestrians. Raymond led the way through the side door and down the stairs to the catacombs, then off to the locked door that led to the underground. He swiped his key; the door popping open. Raymond offered Rita a hand down the stairs, but she waved him off, instead holding the handrail with one hand and her dress with the other as she led the way down the stairs into the home.

Rita was first through the quiet home, Raymond snapping the lights on as he followed her through the familiar corridor toward the portal door. Rita opened it and stepped through, stopping beside the second portal doorway and looking back toward Raymond.

'Should we try the key?' Rita asked.

'I don't see why not,' Raymond answered.

He slipped the key out of his pocket and into the lock, turning it. There was a noticeable shift in the air, Raymond turning the door handle. The door swung open to reveal a familiar-looking ornate interior, Rita and Raymond stepping through to inspect it.

'This is Werribee Mansion,' Rita observed.

'Yes, it is,' Raymond agreed.

'Typical,' Rita said.

They stepped back through the door, closing it behind them. Raymond pulled the brass key back out of the lock and dropped it into his pocket. Turning toward him, Rita gestured upward.

'We better go tell Kingston.'

Raymond silently agreed, opening the main door back out into the Vaults. The sound of the wedding party echoed through the long corridors. Rita knew a way through the passages to avoid disturbing the group. As they made their way up a rear flight of stairs, they surprised Sydney, who was coming down. She looked from one to the other, a question on her lips.

'We'll explain later,' Rita told her.

'Okay,' Sydney said, passing them and continuing down to go about her business.

The rest of their journey up to Kingston's room was undisturbed. Rita pulled her key card from her purse. She swiped it, opening the door and finding that the room appeared empty. Raymond followed her in, casting his gaze around.

'Kingston?' Raymond called.

There was no answer.

'Strange,' Rita said, dropping her bag onto her desk. 'He's usually here on the weekend.'

'I know,' Raymond agreed, a note of relief in his voice. He stepped past Rita and over to Kingston's desk, taking the key from his pocket and placing it in the middle of the space. 'I guess we'll have to catch up with him later.'

'You know he's going to flip out,' Rita said, sitting on the couch.

'I know.' Raymond dropped onto the seat next to her, letting out a long breath. 'What a day.'

'It definitely could have gone better,' Rita agreed with him. 'It was a success, though.'

'True,' Raymond said. 'I think I owe you three dinners.'

'Oh, you definitely owe me three dinners,' Rita said. 'Next time, ask Jake to go with you.'

'I'm sure Jennifer would have loved that,' Raymond joked. 'Two eligible bachelors to hook her daughter up with.'

'What was with that woman?' Rita said. 'The look on her face when she saw me. If looks could kill.'

'I'm sorry about that,' Raymond said. 'I should have realised that Jennifer would be there. She goes to all the charity events connected to the Library.'

'She certainly pounced the moment you walked in,' Rita observed.

'She was probably watching the gate to see who came in,' Raymond answered.

'One of those, is she?' Rita shook her head sadly. 'I can't stand people like that.'

'Try working with one,' Raymond answered. 'Thankfully, she's more in my mother's department than mine, so I don't get to see her as often as I could.'

'I feel sorry for her daughter,' Rita said.

They both looked up and stood as the door opened, Kingston stepping into the room. He paused as he saw them, swapping his grocery bag to his other hand as he closed the door behind him. 'Hope I'm not interrupting anything.'

'Just some gossip,' Rita assured him.

'You're very dressed up to be just gossiping,' Kingston said, looking over them. 'I didn't realise they invited you to the wedding.'

'We weren't,' Raymond told him. 'We had… something else on.'

'I see.' Kingston placed his bag down on his desk, stiffening as he spotted the key on his desk. 'What's this?'

Raymond swallowed. 'A key.'

'Where did you get the key?' Kingston asked.

Rita and Raymond exchanged a quick look.

'Where?' Kingston repeated more slowly, an element of menace in his voice. 'Did. You. Get. The. Key?'

Raymond looked back at him, meeting his eye. 'Werribee Park Mansion.'

There was a long silence, causing even Rita to fidget slightly. Kingston turned away from them, leaving them unable to see his expression.

'Werribee,' he said, dread in his voice. 'You went to Werribee.'

'Yes,' Rita said softly after Raymond didn't answer.

'Did you have any trouble?'

Raymond and Rita exchanged another look, Raymond shaking his head at her. Rita swallowed hard, knowing this was her boss. Not only that, but he was the Protector, and she didn't like the idea of keeping things about Raymond's safety from him. 'A little,' she answered. 'There were… a couple of men. They tried to get the key, but we were able to escape them.'

'I see.' Kingston still didn't turn back toward them, but it was clear from the set of his shoulders and tightness of his back and neck that he was angry. 'That all?'

'That's all,' Rita confirmed.

After an awkward silence, Kingston raised a hand. 'Miss Taylor, I need you to leave now.'

Rita nodded. 'Yes, sir.' Before she opened the door, she gave Raymond a sympathetic look. She cast one last look toward Kingston, but he remained with his back toward her. She glanced at Raymond and saw a set to his jaw, knowing he was expecting a fight. Stepping out of the room, Rita closed the door, leaving the thick tension behind her.

* * * * *

'Raymond,' Kingston said, breaking the long silence. The warning was thick in his voice, but he still didn't turn back.

'I knew if I told you, you would have refused to go after the key,' Raymond said. 'That's why I didn't tell you.'

Kingston finally turned back around; mixed emotions etched into his face. The anger was there, but so was sadness, regret, worry, and exasperation. He shook his head. 'It was Werribee,' he said, his voice wavering slightly on the name. 'You know the history of Werribee.'

'It was over fifty years ago,' Raymond reminded him. 'We can't let it get in the way of doing our job.'

'Our job?' Kingston came toward him, clenching and unclenching his fists as he came. 'How can I do my job if you refuse to tell me what's going on?'

'Nothing happened, Kingston,' Raymond told him. 'Nothing I couldn't handle.'

'But you didn't know that going into it,' Kingston said. 'You expected something to happen, that's why you took Rita with you.'

'I needed a lookout,' Raymond replied. 'Sydney's too green, and it would have looked odd if I took Jake with me to a ball. Rita was the most logical option.'

Kingston nodded, running a hand over his jaw. Raymond spotted a tremble in his fingers. 'These men… they were expecting you?'

'It seemed that way,' Raymond admitted. 'They confronted us after we found the key and demanded we hand it over. We distracted them long enough for us to get out of there.'

'How public was the area where this confrontation happened?'

'Public enough,' Raymond said. 'Rita threatened to scream. We would have been heard if she had.'

'I see,' Kingston nodded again, sighing heavily as he refused to make eye contact with Raymond. 'And what would have happened if that hadn't been the case?'

'Kingston, *nothing happened*,' Raymond emphasised. 'Could'ves, would'ves don't matter.'

'Dammit, Raymond,' Kingston reached out, grabbing Raymond by the shoulders. 'I could have lost you today.'

'Calm down,' Raymond soothed, catching hold of Kingston's arms in a light grip. 'I'm a trained martial artist, remember? I know how to use weapons. And Rita's no slouch either when it comes to these things. Besides, we got the key, and we made it home. That's what matters.'

'No, it's not,' Kingston said. 'What matters is keeping you alive. You know how much risk you are under. There are people out there who will kill you without a second thought. Rita would have been collateral to them. You know this. Why do you keep taking risks?'

'Everything is a risk, Kingston,' Raymond assured him, reaching up to loosen the grip from his shoulders. 'Look, trust me. I know what I'm doing.'

'You're getting far too cocky,' Kingston chastised him.

'Maybe,' Raymond confessed. 'Or maybe I'm better at assessing the risks. Tell me, Kingston, would you have allowed us to go after this key if you'd known about it beforehand?'

'No,' Kingston said without hesitation.

'Why?'

'You know why.'

'Because of something that happened fifty years ago,' Raymond said. 'What happened to my great-grandparents was a tragedy. I do not deny that. But you can't let something like that paralyse you.'

Kingston sighed, finally relaxing his grip and letting his hands fall to his sides. 'You're right. You're right.'

'We successfully got a new key,' Raymond continued. 'Can't we celebrate that?'

'Yes, we should,' Kingston said. 'Did you try it yet?'

Raymond nodded. 'Leads right back to Werribee Mansion.'

'It's amazing how many of the keys seem to lead back to the location where they're found,' Kingston said.

'I know, right?' Raymond clapped Kingston on the shoulder, giving it a light squeeze in reassurance. 'Come on, don't you think this deserves a drink?'

'I guess it does,' Kingston said. 'Scotch or Whisky?'

'Whichever is closer,' Raymond answered.

* * * * *

Sydney was exhausted after the wedding finally wound down for the night. She had tried to keep herself focused on what was happening, but her mind kept turning back to Rita and Raymond. They had been dressed better than some of the wedding guests, making Sydney wonder just what they had been up to. She would have to search on social media to find some clues, but with nothing to go with, she had a feeling she would find nothing.

The groomzilla had kept her on her toes the entire day. She had hoped he'd settle down once the wedding was over and the reception was in full swing, but he hadn't. The wine and champagne hadn't been chilled enough to his liking, and he didn't like how the food had been arranged on the plates. Even the decorations were wrong despite his signing off on them days beforehand. His bride had kept him in check, which meant no outbursts. Sydney had a feeling that without that, it would have been a mess.

Needing a drink, she gravitated to one of the local pubs that Jake had shown her during his tour. She had missed it herself when she had been wandering. Jake told her that sometimes the group of them would come there for a drink after a long day. Rita rarely went with them, and sometimes Kingston would excuse himself, so often it was just Raymond and Jake. Sydney wondered if that's why the two of them seemed to be so close.

The pub atmosphere was relaxed and comfortable, with a few people sitting around in booths. Sydney headed for the bar, ordered herself a drink, and then found a nice, quiet corner. Most people here seemed to be there with someone, but the occasional person was there alone. Sydney just hoped that no one approached her to hit on her. She wasn't in the mood to let anyone down slowly. Not to mention she knew some people didn't like being let down.

She sipped her drink and pulled out her phone. She scanned the local event pages and found nothing that jumped out at her that would explain Raymond and Rita's attire. On a haunch, she looked up at Melbourne and again found herself at a dead end. She needed something to go with to aid her in her search. She was flying blind here. All she knew was that it had required formal attire. She figured it must have something to do with the keys, and she felt left out that she knew nothing about it. Heck, even Jake had mentioned nothing. She wondered if he knew. He had to have known – he was their security, after all.

She took a long gulp of her drink and slid her phone back into her pocket in defeat. There was no way she would work out just what Rita and Raymond had been up to. She had to admit, they'd looked good. Rita, beautiful in her green gown, and Raymond had been more devastatingly handsome than normal in his suit, with no hair out of place. Not that they usually didn't look good, but they both dressed exceptionally well. Sydney couldn't help but feel a little jealous.

Sure, her blond hair could go well with nearly any outfit, but there was just something about red hair and the colour green that went together well, and Rita's dress had been precisely the right shade of green to compliment her. And Raymond's suit had matched Rita's dress very well. She wondered if they had coordinated. It looked like they had. She hadn't thought they had that sort of relationship. They always acted more like siblings than anything. Then again, it was probably professional what they were doing, not a date. She wondered if she'd find out on Monday just what had happened.

Feeling eyes on her, Sydney looked up, and it surprised her to see Marcus stepping through the bar toward her. Had he followed her? She clutched her drink, watching as he approached. He was smiling, which eased her nerves a little. She glanced around, but no one seemed to pay them any mind.

'Hello, Sydney,' Marcus said as he joined her. 'I saw you on the security camera and thought I'd come to say hello.'

'Security camera?' She looked around and spotted one looking in her direction, which meant that Marcus must have been in the security room. 'You're working?'

'I am,' he confirmed. 'The security system is malfunctioning, yet I can't seem to find what is wrong.'

'So you're on a call-out,' Sydney realised.

'Yes,' he said with a nod. 'I was the closest person, so I looked into it personally.'

Sydney realised he must have people who work under him. He must be more than just a grunt in his business. 'So, shouldn't you be dealing with it?' she asked.

'We're now waiting for an actual technician to come out. They're about fifteen minutes away,' he told her.

'I see,' she said, looking back at the camera. 'You know, I was wondering if you were stalking me.'

He chuckled. 'No, it just seems to be a small world,' he said. 'Although I could ask you the same question.'

'I didn't even know your business did security here,' she said, sipping her drink. 'Let alone you did call-outs this late.'

'The problem with security is that you have to be on call at all times,' he said with a tight smile. 'You look like you just got off work yourself. Overtime?'

'You could say that,' she said. She didn't want to go into details lest he work out what hotel she worked for.

'Secret stuff, hm?' he asked with a knowing look.

'Secret enough,' she confirmed. 'Very busy though, and very demanding.'

'I think all jobs are demanding in their own way,' he said. 'Lucky for some, they are restricted to normal business hours.'

'I envy those people,' she said with a chuckle. 'I don't think they realise how good they have it.'

'I think some do,' he said. His phone pinged; Marcus pulled it out of his pocket. He frowned down at it before sliding it back away. 'So, anything exciting happen today?'

'Just my secret business,' she answered. 'That was exciting enough.'

'So, nothing unusual?' he asked.

She wondered what he was prying at. He was fishing for some information. 'I wouldn't call it unusual,' she answered.

'Not even something with your friends?' he asked.

Okay, that was out of the blue. How did he even know she had friends? 'I haven't been here long enough to call anyone a 'friend',' she admitted. 'I have some co-workers I get along well with, but we're still more acquaintances than anything.'

'I see,' he said, his phone pinging again.

'You look busy,' Sydney said. His mind was in two places at once as he rechecked his phone.

'Just an update on that technician,' Marcus said. 'They're on their way.'

'So you'll be able to resolve the security issue soon,' Sydney said.

'That is the plan,' he said, putting his phone away again. 'I should leave you to your drink and go back to see if I can work out the issue.'

'Good luck,' she told him.

'Thank you,' he said, stepping away. 'Have a good evening.'

She watched as he left, heading back in the direction he had come, and vanished around a corner. Sydney frowned after him. He had been prying at something. Perhaps he was trying to work out where she worked. That was the most logical conclusion she could come to. Still, mentioning her 'friends' left her wondering just what his deal was.

Sydney decided she didn't want to hang around any longer than she needed. Finishing her drink, she slipped out of her seat. As she headed out, she passed a man coming in with a bag and figured it was probably the technician. She cast one last look up at the security cameras and wondered if Marcus was watching her. The thought caused the back of her neck to prickle. The sooner she got home, the better.

14

SOMETHING HAD GONE down over the weekend; that much was clear. There was tension in the air between Kingston and Rita, and Sydney had to guess at Raymond as well. The wedding had gone without a hitch, but whatever Raymond and Rita had done had not. Sydney kept herself busy at the front desk, but she slipped into the security office when it was time for a lunch break.

'Hey,' she said as she spotted Jake coming out.

'Hey,' he answered. 'Do you have any idea what's going on?'

'I was about to ask you that,' Sydney said as they headed toward the cafe. 'I know Raymond and Rita were dressed to the hilt on the weekend.'

'Really?' Jake asked. 'What were they wearing?'

'Raymond was in a suit, and Rita was in this beautiful green dress with her hair done up.'

'Wish I could have seen that.'

They'd almost reached the cafe when Rita caught them. 'Meeting,' she said, and without another word, she disappeared back the way she came.

'Maybe we can get some answers,' Jake said.

'Hopefully,' Sydney said.

Rita was just ahead of them as they headed up the stairs. They followed her into Kingston's rooms, Rita holding the door for them as they entered. They noted Raymond was absent, but Kingston was sitting behind his desk.

'I'm pleased you made it,' Kingston said, tapping his fingers together with a furrowed frown upon his brow.

'Everything all right?' Jake asked.

Rita looked away.

'I don't know,' Kingston said, watching as the two of them sat down. 'You tell me, Jake.'

Jake blinked. 'I don't know what you mean.'

'I think you do,' Kingston said. He picked up something on his desk, revealing a key.

Sydney gasped. 'Is that a new one?'

'It is,' Kingston said, setting it back on his desk. 'I want to know who knew about Raymond's plans to get it this weekend?'

'He told me last minute,' Rita said, not meeting Kingston's eye. 'I barely had enough time to get ready.'

'I had no idea at all,' Jake said. 'I wish he had told me.'

'Nobody told me anything,' Sydney said, shaking her head. 'I saw Raymond and Rita on the weekend after they returned from wherever they went.'

'Werribee Park Mansion,' Kingston said.

Jake sucked in a breath. 'Shit.'

'Indeed,' Kingston confirmed, levelling his gaze on Jake. 'So your little meeting last week had nothing to do with his findings?'

'No, it didn't,' Jake said, shaking his head. 'It was about something else.'

'So I'm to say that the only person who knew about this was Rita.'

Rita shifted in her seat. 'I should have told you,' she said softly.

'Yes, you should have.' Kingston drummed his fingers on the top of his desk. 'Raymond is getting cocky. This will not end well if he continues on this path.'

'So what is this, an intervention?' Jake asked.

'In a manner of speaking,' Kingston confirmed. 'From this point on, if Raymond has any plans, I want to know about it.'

'We've got a concert in a couple of nights' time,' Jake said. 'We've had it planned for weeks.'

'He owes me dinner,' Rita said. 'We haven't got any finalised plans, though.'

'I don't have any plans with him at all,' Sydney said, feeling a little left out.

They paused as there came a knock on the door. Rita stood and opened the door. Lucille stepped in, glancing over at each of them before she turned to face Kingston.

'I got your message,' she said. 'You said it was urgent.'

'Urgent enough.' Kingston narrowed his eyes. 'Do you know where your son was on the weekend?'

'Geelong,' Lucille answered, an element of disdain in her voice. 'With those friends of his.'

'No,' Kingston shook his head. 'He was here. Getting this.' He held up the key. 'In Werribee.'

All the blood drained from Lucille's face as she faltered. 'Werribee?'

'Werribee,' Kingston confirmed.

'I'm going to kill him,' Lucille said. 'I'm going to ground him into his next life.'

'You can ground him?' Sydney asked.

'You watch,' Lucille said.

'So I take it you did not know his plans,' Kingston said, placing the key back on the table.

'If I had, he wouldn't have gone,' Lucille said as a matter-of-fact. She looked over at Kingston. 'Did he get into trouble?'

'Some,' Kingston replied.

'We handled it,' Rita assured her.

"We'?' Lucille shot her an accusing look. 'You went with him, did you? Despite knowing the history of Werribee.'

'We had a plan,' Rita countered. 'And we stuck to the plan. We got the key.'

'In Werribee,' Lucille hissed. 'It was that ball, wasn't it? You went to that charity ball as a cover. No wonder Jennifer has been giving me the stink eye all day.'

'We did,' Rita confirmed.

'The details don't matter,' Kingston said, tenting his fingers. 'What matters is what we do going forward. And from now on, if Raymond so much as breathes, I want to know about it.' He turned to Jake. 'I want you to stick to him like glue when you go to this concert.'

'I would have anyway,' Jake assured him.

'Good,' Kingston said. He turned to Lucille. 'Think you can keep him busy?'

'He'll have so much work he'll be pulling overtime,' Lucille said, scowling. 'He won't even have time to look for any keys.'

'You needn't go that far,' Kingston said. 'But do monitor him.' He looked around the room. 'Let's call this meeting closed. Remember to look out for each other.'

* * * * *

Raymond noticed the silence as he stepped into the flat. He frowned, noting that the lights were on but surprised by the lack of a television or radio. Usually, when he came home, his mother would be watching the news or clattering around the apartment. Instead, he was greeted with deathly silence.

Closing and locking the door behind him, Raymond let his jacket fall from his shoulders, hanging it up on the hook inside the doorway. He stepped further into the flat, finally spotting his mother seated on the couch in the main living area. She was staring at the dark screen of the television, a look of pure impassiveness on her face. That was never a good look.

'Mother?' Raymond asked.

'How was your weekend?' Lucille asked.

'Good,' he answered.

'And how are Tanya and Andrew?'

'They're fine.'

'And little Olivia?'

'She's fine too.'

Lucille stood up, moving over to face him straight on. She smiled at him, Raymond feeling a sense of nervousness wash over him. She was altogether far too calm. Then, as if a switch had been thrown, her face became one of rage, an open hand striking him across the side of the head.

'Werribee!' she shrieked. 'You were in Werribee?!'

'Who told?' Raymond asked, ducking out of the way of the next blow.

'It doesn't matter who told. What the hell were you doing in Werribee?!'

'I found a key,' Raymond said, slinking off to the side of the room to put some distance between himself and his mother. 'I knew you'd never approve, which is why I didn't tell you about it.'

'Of course, I'd never approve. You know what Werribee is to this family.' Lucille's voice cracked at that. 'Your great-grandparents died in that evil place.'

'That was over fifty years ago,' Raymond countered.

'It doesn't matter,' Lucille shot back. 'And then there is the fact you know we're being watched. There are people after you, and you still went to the godforsaken place.'

'Yes, I still went because I would not let the past haunt my future,' Raymond said. 'I found a key. I went and located that key. That key works. Case closed.'

'No, it is not.' Lucille clenched her fists. 'You are getting far too reckless. I don't think you fully understand the seriousness of the situation.'

'I know how serious it is, Mother,' Raymond said, straightening his glasses. 'But I also know that if we "play it safe", we'll never find any keys. Sometimes you have to take risks to reap the rewards.'

'Those risks are your life,' Lucille reminded him.

'I'm aware of that.' Raymond held his hands up, palms outward. 'Don't worry; I'm not trying to get killed. I'm just trying to do my job.'

Lucille sighed, letting out a frustrated growl. 'At least let Kingston know what you're doing.'

'Okay,' Raymond said. 'I can do that.'

'You had better,' Lucille said. 'I want you to let him know where you are at all times.'

'Isn't that a bit extreme?' Raymond asked.

'You went to Werribee,' Lucille hissed.

'Okay, okay, I get it.' Raymond waved her down. 'I'll text him if I'm going anywhere.'

'You do that.' Lucille stepped back, still clenching and unclenching her fists. 'How can he do his job as Protector if you don't let him?'

'Okay, I get the point.' Raymond sighed heavily. He moved toward the door.

'Where are you going?' Lucille accused.

'I think I'll spend the night in the bunker,' Raymond said, picking his jacket up and pulling it on. 'Let you cool down a bit.'

'Just let Kingston know where you are,' Lucille reminded him.

'I will. I promise.'

Without another word, he exited the flat.

15

It surprised Sydney to find Rita and Jake having lunch together in the cafe. She cast her gaze around the otherwise empty space, noting that Elizabeth and Dorothy were absent, which was unusual, and then remembered that there had been a problem with the buses running that day. Kian was in his usual spot, deeply engrossed in the day's newspaper, with his laptop sitting closed on the table in front of him.

'Coffee?' Simon asked when she entered.

'Yes, please,' she said.

Wandering over to the table of the others, she gestured toward one of the empty chairs. 'Mind if I join you?'

'Go ahead,' Jake said.

'We were just discussing recent events,' Rita filled her in.

'You mean the intervention?' Sydney asked as she sat.

They nodded. They glanced up as Simon brought Sydney her coffee before heading back toward the counter.

'Has anything like this ever happened before?' Sydney asked.

They shook their head. 'Not to this degree,' Rita answered. 'Raymond has always been a cocky little shit, though.'

'That's putting it mildly,' Jake said. He looked at Sydney. 'Raymond's had self-defence training, so he thinks he's covered it.'

'You don't think he does,' Sydney guessed.

Jake shook his head. 'Something is going on that's bigger than all of us. These guys want the…' he glanced at Kian, who didn't seem to be listening but lowered his voice anyway. 'They want the you-know-whats, and they will do whatever is in their power to get them.'

'They knew who we were,' Rita said. 'But they said they were only interested in Raymond.'

'You're sure you've never seen them before?' Jake asked.

Rita shook her head. 'I'd have recognised them if I had.'

Sydney couldn't even imagine what it would have been like to have been in Rita's place and was glad it hadn't been her that Raymond had asked to the gala. She had been busy with the wedding as it was.

'Do you think they're after the… you-know-whats or the information on how to locate them?' Sydney asked.

'Both probably,' Jake answered. 'Which means they probably want the journals, too. We're going to have to double the security in the bunker.'

'How?' Rita asked. 'You said that you couldn't add any more security.'

'There's always more,' Jake assured her. 'For a start, having someone in the bunker for as much time as possible.'

'The Barry's are going to love that,' Rita said sarcastically.

'Tough shit, it's what we're going to have to do,' Jake said. 'They're also going to have to limit how much time they go out alone. Especially Raymond.'

'That shouldn't be hard,' Rita said. 'Not like he has much of a social life.'

Jake conceded the point.

'But why are people so interested in the you-know-whats?' Sydney asked.

'Power,' Jake guessed.

'Money,' Rita added. She leaned forward. 'Imagine having control over something like that. You have doors into an untold number of buildings, full of riches and power. Imagine what you could use something like that for.'

'Not good,' Sydney said, the puzzle pieces falling into place. It felt like something out of a movie, with the bad guys trying to gain access to the portals. 'Maybe it would be better if the you-know-whats stayed hidden. If Raymond just destroyed the journals.'

'We've had discussions about that,' Rita said, Jake nodding his agreement. 'Kingston and Raymond won't have it.'

'They argue their ancestors died to protect those things, so they must keep up with the "tradition",' Jake said, making air quotes around the latter word.

Sydney nodded, guessing she could understand that. If people had died to protect the portals, it would make sense to keep the tradition alive. Still, it made more sense to her to destroy the things, especially given how much trouble the Barry's and Kingston's had gone to hide the keys. Their location wasn't supposed to be so secret, but it would be safer for everyone if they did away with the evidence and walked away from it all.

Something occurred to Sydney when she glanced between Jake and Rita, causing her to clear her throat. 'I'm guessing now is an appropriate time to mention someone has been hovering around the hotel?'

'Someone is always hovering around the hotel,' Jake said in a hushed voice, nodding his head toward Kian.

'Not Kian,' Sydney said. 'There's been a man lately. He sits across the road on a bench watching who has been coming and going.'

'Really,' Jake said, frowning. 'How long has he been there?'

'About a week now,' Sydney said. 'I'm surprised you haven't seen him. He has an overcoat and a hat.'

'I haven't seen him either,' Rita confessed, frowning. 'I'll have to keep an eye out.'

'Same,' Jake said.

Seeing a movement out of the corner of their eye, they looked up and spotted Kingston and Raymond stepping out into the courtyard. It genuinely surprised Sydney to see Raymond, not expecting to have seen him in Adelaide so soon. She ran her eyes over him, and other than looking a little tired, he seemed perfectly fine. She had to admit that she was slightly relieved, given everything going on. He was as handsome as always.

'Look what the cat dragged in,' Jake said, giving Raymond a wave. 'It's actually good to see you.'

'I doubt that,' Raymond said as he and Kingston joined them at the table. 'You can't talk about me now.'

'What makes you think we were talking about you?' Rita asked.

'My ears were burning,' Raymond replied. 'Also, Jake and Sydney had guilty looks on their faces.'

Sydney felt her cheeks burn in embarrassment. She averted her eyes.

'So, what were we discussing?' Kingston asked, pulling up a chair.

'Things,' Jake replied. 'Including an apparent new stalker who sits across the road from the hotel.'

'That so?' Kingston asked, looking around the table. Sydney nodded when his eyes fell on her. 'We'll have to keep as close an eye on this stalker as they do on us then.'

'I'm on it,' Jake said, giving a mock salute.

'Speaking of, Ray-Ray,' Rita said, Sydney spotting Raymond's eye twitch at the name, 'aren't you and Jake going to a concert tomorrow night?'

'Yes, we are, Margarita,' Raymond said. 'The Runaway Boys.'

'Is it really such a good idea to go with… everything?' Sydney asked.

'It'll be fine,' Raymond assured her. 'Besides, Jake will be with me.'

'That's right,' Jake said, leaning back in his chair and flashing Sydney a grin. 'We've had this thing planned for months. We both love the band, so there is no way we're going to miss it.'

'Sydney is correct,' Kingston said. 'You need to be on guard. You don't know who could be watching.'

'Kingston, I'm always on guard,' Raymond told him. 'Nothing is going to happen. Don't worry.'

'Famous last words,' Rita muttered under her breath.

'No, they're not,' Raymond said.

'I recall you saying last weekend that it would be simple too,' Rita challenged. 'It wasn't.'

'It would have been if those guys hadn't shown up,' Raymond countered.

'But they did show up,' Kingston said. 'That's what matters, and that's what we have to avoid in the future.'

'We'll stick together,' Jake said. 'We won't let each other out of each other's sight.'

'What he said,' Raymond said. 'Now I have to go get back to work. Mother has somehow managed to get me assigned to a rather large project that will consume a lot of my time over the next few weeks, so my breaks are shorter than usual.'

'Funny how that happened,' Kingston said.

'Indeed.' Raymond deadpanned, giving Kingston a dark look.

'Have a good rest of the day,' Sydney said, trying to break the tension in the air.

'I'll certainly try,' Raymond said, standing and leaving the table.

They watched him go, Kingston waiting until he was out of sight before turning back to Jake. 'Not out of your sight, not even for a second.'

'I promise,' Jake said, crossing his heart. 'I'll stick to him like glue.'

* * * * *

Sydney kept a good eye on the man across the street. She had thought little of him until they had mentioned it. He seemed to be watching people; in return, she watched him without making it obvious. She knew Jake was looking into him as well as he had asked her to point the man out before heading back to the security office.

The man wasn't doing much of anything. He sat on a bench, watching everyone coming and going from the hotel. At first, Sydney had wondered if maybe it was Marcus, but a closer look at the guy told her the man was the wrong shape and build to be Marcus, even under the oversized coat and hat. Besides, Marcus had a job, so he wouldn't have time to sit outside a hotel. He probably didn't even know where she worked, and she intended to keep it that way.

As she headed out to get her shopping, she absently wondered if she would see Marcus again today. It was strange how he kept turning up. The city might not be the size of New York, but it was not that small. She wondered if she was being paranoid about everything. She brushed it off as her just being worried about the keys and the fact she now knew people were after Raymond.

Speaking of Raymond, she indeed was worried about the man. She half wanted to tell Jake that they should forget about the concert and that it was too risky for them to go out. She didn't want to seem like the overbearing, paranoid person in the group. Sydney had a feeling Kingston was also worried, which just added to her worry. Kingston's job was to protect Raymond and the portals, after all. If he was concerned, then she was right to be worried.

Sydney stepped into the supermarket and grabbed a small trolley to do her shopping. As she wandered the aisles picking up what she needed, she let her mind wander. She still thought it was a bad idea for them to be hunting for the keys and that it would be safer for everyone if they just left them hidden and lost to time. The problem was, the word was no doubt out now that Raymond had broken the code, which was why people were after him. She wondered just how many people out there knew about the portals and wanted to use them. She had never heard of them before working at the hotel, and they were a secret even there.

As she reached the fresh produce area of the supermarket, she felt eyes on her, and without even having to look up, she knew it was Marcus. She grabbed some potatoes, and it wasn't until after she had put them in her trolley she finally raised her eyes. Sure enough, she saw Marcus further down the way, near the meat section. He gave her a wave, but he didn't approach her. She was a little glad. She decided not to approach him either, so as not to appear some sort of stalker.

She finished gathering her fruit and vegetables before moving toward the meat aisle and finding that Marcus had already gone when she reached it. She wondered about him. His attentions seemed innocent enough. They were just two strangers that kept bumping into each other. After all, it wasn't like he designed the security problem at the pub she went to. And she had been the one to approach him at the cafe. If anyone appeared like a crazy stalker, it was her, not him.

That thought made her relax a bit. She wished she could talk to someone about everything. That was the big problem with secrets – there was no one she could talk to. She wondered if maybe she should approach Kingston and ask him about it. He always seemed like he was busy. He was doing what exactly she didn't know. It was like he didn't have an actual job other than being a silent partner in the hotel. The fact he lived there told her he had money. She wondered where he had gotten it from.

There was a lot Sydney still didn't know about the group, and it just made her feel even more like an outsider. Maybe she should start a conversation with Marcus the next time she sees him. It would probably do her good to have a friend outside of all the crazy stuff connected to her work life. And the group hadn't invited her out for drinks or anything. She wasn't sure she could consider them friends. She needed a friend in this city, so why not Marcus?

She didn't see Marcus as she finished her shopping. He had no doubt already checked out ahead of her and gone home. She made a mental note to approach him the next time they saw each other. Maybe even go somewhere for coffee. He might even tell her a few things about the city that could help her with her job.

Yes, that was a plan. She was going to make a friend out of Marcus.

16

'Seriously, man,' Jake said, gesturing back over his shoulder. 'If you're going to play a gig, ensure you have proper security to keep the arseholes from throwing beer on the speaker.'

'They designed most speakers to withstand it,' Raymond pointed out.

'No, they're not. The good ones maybe, but not those.' Jake shoved his hands into the pockets, frowning into the night. 'And what was with those guys trying to kill each other? It's almost as bad as Hindley St on a Friday night.'

'It was Southbank,' Raymond checked his watch, 'and just after midnight. It's probably worse.'

Jake snorted. 'I wouldn't put money on that.'

Raymond smiled tightly. 'You should try the pub we were at on the fight night.'

'I'll pass, thanks.' Jake glanced to the side, a thin line creasing his forehead as Raymond watched him set his jaw. 'How long are these guys going to follow us, anyway?'

Raymond blinked. 'I'm not sure what you mean.'

'Don't bullshit me, Raymond,' Jake shot him a look out of the corner of his eye. 'You know they're there. You've been watching them watching us all night.'

Raymond's thumb played over the handle of the switchblade in his pocket. He looked to the side, noting Jake's hard look and knowing there was no kidding around here. 'They've been following us since we passed City Square on the way to the pub.'

Jake nodded, looking forward again. 'This isn't the first time, is it?'

'It's not important.'

'Yes, it is.' Jake no doubt caught the reflection of the three men not far behind them and closing the distance. 'We'll deal with these three, and then we'll talk.'

Raymond scowled. 'Jake–'

'And don't be a stubborn arsehole about it.'

Raymond nodded just ahead of them. 'There's a street just ahead. Flinders Lane. We can duck down there. Coppers are just across the street if it gets nasty.'

Jake nodded, widening his step and forcing Raymond to widen his own to keep up with the younger man. They could hear the footsteps of the men behind them as they quickened their own pace to keep up, Raymond overtaking Jake and turning sharply into the laneway, quiet in the absence of the daytime foot traffic and hurrying along it and into the entryway of the underground parking of the building, pausing as Jake joined him. The two men leaned against the wall as they waited.

They didn't have to wait long. The footsteps grew closer, the three men turning the corner briskly, no doubt afraid that they were about to lose sight of their prey. They stopped dead when they saw Jake and Raymond waiting for them.

Beside him, Jake stood with clenched fists, ready to strike should they make any move against them. Raymond knew Jake was good at one-on-one combat – he'd seen him fight on over one occasion, not to mention remove problem patrons from the hotel.

Fingering his switchblade, Raymond watched the three men as they hesitated, clearly surprised by the move he and Jake had made.

Then one seemed to gather himself, moving forward and quickly chasing the shocked look from his face as he glared at them.

'Problem, guys?' Jake asked, setting his jaw. 'You seemed to be rather interested in following us. Are you having that slow a night?'

'We've got no interest in you, Peterson,' the frontman said, nodding toward Raymond. 'It's Barry we want to talk to.'

'Well, I'm listening,' Raymond said, sizing them up. 'You have three minutes.'

The man scoffed. 'You think you're in charge here?'

'We are in charge,' Raymond said, giving them a tight smile that he saw threw them slightly. 'We chose the place and the time and already have a plan. What do you have?'

He saw Jake smirk.

'Alright,' the leader said, nodding but not happy. 'I'll give you that.'

'You now have two minutes and thirty seconds, gentleman,' Raymond said, glancing at his watch. 'You better start talking.'

'This is the only chance you're going to get,' Jake added.

'We know what you do,' the leader said, moving closer but stopping when Jake took a step forward. He threw Jake a weary look before looking back at Raymond. 'We know what you protect.'

Raymond smiled. 'I'm not the Protector.'

'No,' the man agreed, narrowing his eyes. 'That's Kingston. You're the Keeper.'

Raymond kept his expression neutral. 'Is that supposed to impress me?'

'We want your key card,' the man said, not faltering. 'Your access, all your codes. We want into the Library.'

'The Library is open every day to everyone. The best part is it's free.'

The man stepped closer, this time ignoring the look he got from Jake. 'We want access to the portal. To all your records.'

Raymond raised an eyebrow. 'And you've chosen now to do it?'

'We know you've found a way of finding the keys,' the man continued. 'Our boss has been waiting for a Barry to be smart enough to work it out.'

'Your boss have a name?' Jake asked.

The man laughed, shaking his head and throwing Jake a bemused look. 'Nah. You're not getting that out of us. Just know he's been watching you for a long time.' He gestured to Raymond. 'Especially this one. He had a feeling about this one. Said he felt different.'

Raymond narrowed his eyes. 'I don't like it when people 'feel' me.'

The man returned his attention to him, moving closer to use his more considerable height to his advantage. 'Got no problem with Kingston being so close.'

Raymond set his jaw, not flinching as he drew his switchblade out and flicked it open. 'One step closer, and you will find yourself lacking a certain part of your anatomy.'

The man glanced down, spotting the blade and stepping back, gesturing for his two men to stand down as they went for their knives. He sized Raymond up, then Jake, before moving back further. 'We're going to gain access to the Library. To the portals.'

'The portals are no good to you,' Raymond said. 'You can't use them.'

'Nah, but our boss can. Said he'd reward us.'

Raymond eyed him, then glanced at his watch. 'Oh, look, time's up. As much as I've enjoyed our little chat, gentleman, it is time for you to move on.'

The man shot him a stern glare and gave Jake a measured look before backing off further. 'Okay. Yeah, we'll go. But we'll be back. You haven't heard the last from us.'

'God, I hate that line,' Jake muttered. 'You need better catchphrases.'

The man shot Jake a glare as Raymond smirked. He moved back, gesturing to his companions to follow as they headed around the corner. Across the road, two police officers were watching them go, looking back at Jake and Raymond with suspicious looks. Raymond pocketed his switchblade and waved across at them, one of them recognising him and giving a quick wave back before turning to his partner and seeming to reassure him that everything was fine.

As they headed back into the street and glanced after the three men heading back toward Flinders Station, Jake shot Raymond a stern look. 'And now we talk.'

'When we get back to the bunker,' Raymond said. 'Then we'll talk.'

* * * * *

Jake closed the door to Raymond's room and watched as the other man dragged the cot out of the corner, unfolding it and the mattress before snagging the blankets and pillows and dumping them onto the bed. It wasn't unusual for Jake to crash at Raymond's place after a night in Melbourne, so Raymond had kept the cot handy.

Jake leaned against the doorway, watching as Raymond quickly set up the cot before tugging off his jacket, throwing it over the back of the lone chair and kicking off his shoes. Raymond allowed himself to drop back onto the bed without a word, the springs squeaking in protest at the sudden weight.

Jake walked over toward the cot, crossing his arms over his chest as he leaned back against the door of Raymond's wardrobe, scrutinising the man on the bed. The bed was almost too short for him, but Jake knew two people could lie in that bed.

'Staring is rude, you know,' Raymond said, not bothering to open his eyes.

'So is keeping things from your colleagues,' Jake countered.

'That sort of thing happens all the time,' Raymond said, shrugging. 'You tell people what they need to know.'

'And I need to know if someone is stalking you.' Jake narrowed his eyes. 'So is there?'

'It's not important, Jake.'

'Yes, it is.' Jake took three steps forward, dropping onto the edge of the bed and glaring down at the other man, who had cracked his eyes to watch him. 'I'm head of security.'

'In Adelaide.' Raymond pushed himself up to lean back against the headboard, watching him. 'We're in Melbourne.'

'I'm not just in charge of the hotel's security, and you know it.

I'm in charge of security for the team.' Jake met his eye and held Raymond's gaze. 'Is someone stalking you?'

'I wouldn't say stalking,' Raymond said, giving a dismissive wave. 'Just following. Both myself and Mother. Have been for about a month now.'

'That's stalking,' Jake said, frowning as a thought occurred to him. Something he'd spotted on the news. 'That report on the news a while back. Two guys running through Melbourne Central, one that gets hit by a train–'

'Jake,' Raymond warned.

'That was you!' Jake punched him in the side of the leg. 'I knew I recognised the gait. I was going to analyse that security footage, but Sydney arriving distracted me.'

'Or Rita's new low-necked shirt,' Raymond said with a smile.

'Leave it.' Jake gave him a warning look. 'Those guys tonight were armed. What about the others?'

'Normally, they just watch.' Raymond pulled the switchblade from his pocket, setting it down on the bedside table. 'They've only really come after me four times.'

'What happened?'

'Three you know about,' Raymond said. 'The first time was when I was on the train between Flagstaff and Melbourne Central. Guy grabbed me and told me I was to go with him when we got off the train. I winded and shoved him out the door when we got to the station, then got off myself at Parliament Station.'

'How many were armed?' Jake asked.

'Just this last lot and the guy before that.' Raymond shrugged it off. 'Look, Jake, I've been trained for this. You don't need to worry yourself about it.'

'Like hell.' Jake glared at him. 'Kingston would kill me if something happened to you. And if your mother gets to me first, they'd never find the body. You're the key member of this team. Kingston may be the leader, but you're the brains.'

Raymond scoffed. 'Don't let Rita hear you say that.'

'I don't care what Rita says.' Jake paused, realising what he had said even as he spotted Raymond's raised eyebrow. 'Okay, maybe I do care, but that's beside the point. I am in charge of keeping you safe, and if someone is after you and Lucille, I need to know about it.'

'Mother hasn't even noticed,' Raymond said, tugging off his watch and dropping it beside the blade. 'I can handle it, Jake.'

'I don't want to take any chances,' Jake said. 'You're the Keeper. Without you, we're screwed. Besides, I'm not about to let a friend get killed when I could prevent it.'

Raymond frowned. 'I'm not going to get killed.'

Jake gestured upward and out toward where Swanston Street was. 'If you'd been alone tonight, you may have been.'

'More likely, I would have killed them.' Raymond shrugged it off, hitting the switch for the lamp beside the bed, then climbing off the bed to go switch off the main lights, allowing the smaller light's warm glow to fill the room. In this light, Jake could see how tired Raymond looked, although he knew the other man would never admit it. 'Focus yourself on protecting Kingston and the portals. Without either of them, we're screwed.'

'They want access to the portals from here,' Jake reminded him, watching as Raymond began undressing. Jake headed for the cot. 'In the morning, I'll start upgrading your security system here.'

He saw Raymond frown. 'Jake…'

Jake tugged off his shirt, dropping it onto the end of the cot. 'And I'm telling Kingston.'

Raymond whipped around to stare at him. 'Don't you dare!'

'Don't argue with me on this.' Jake gave him a pointed look. 'I'm telling him, and I don't care what you say or how you try to talk your way out of it. He needs to know, Raymond. He's our leader, and we can't keep stuff like this from him. Leaders cannot do their job properly if they don't know everything.'

'I've kept it from him for a reason,' Raymond hissed.

'I know,' Jake said softly. 'He's protective of the Barry family, but I doubt he'll lock you and Lucille down here to make sure nothing happens. But he's going to be pissed, that's for sure.' Jake tugged at the blankets on the cot and climbed between the sheets, ignoring the burning on his back where Raymond glared at him. 'Look, let's deal with it in the morning. Goodnight, Raymond.'

17

MUCH TO RAYMOND'S dismay, Kingston called a meeting for the very next day. He'd gotten the text while at work and had been dreading it. Raymond asked his mother about it when he'd seen her during lunch and found that she hadn't been called, so he could only assume that Jake hadn't yet told Kingston about what had occurred the night before. He spent the entire day with his thoughts, watching the clock until it was time to head across to Adelaide.

Stepping through the portal, he made his way through the Vaults to a rear staircase, taking it slowly until he reached Kingston's door. He knocked once before opening it with a key card that Kingston had given him over a year beforehand. Stepping into the room, he greeted Rita.

'How was the concert?' she asked.

'Good,' he replied. 'Would have been better without the drunken brawl at the show's end, though.'

'There's always someone that ruins it,' she observed.

He nodded his agreement, heading over to the couch and dropping onto it. He glanced up at Kingston, noting that the man was staring at his computer screen with a furrow on his brow. Something had his full attention. Deciding not to interrupt, Raymond kept his mouth shut, instead pulling out his phone and flipping through the latest news headlines.

Hearing a knock on the door, he looked up as Rita opened it, admitting Sydney and Jake into the room. Jake caught his eye, giving him a measured look. Raymond returned one of warning as the two new arrivals exchanged pleasantries with Rita.

'Good, you're all here,' Kingston said, looking up from his computer. 'We can begin.'

Kingston stood, coming around the side of his desk so that he could sit on it, facing them. 'Jake, did you look into our new observer?'

'Sydney was right,' Jake said. 'I found him. He's sitting on the bench across the road at the park, just watching.'

'So I wasn't seeing things,' Sydney said, relief in her voice.

Jake shook his head. 'I went back through some security footage, and the guy has been there for about a week now.'

'Well, that's disturbing,' Kingston said, frowning. 'Try to monitor him. Even if he isn't connected to anything related to the portals, he might still be a threat to the hotel itself.'

'I've told my team to watch him,' Jake confirmed. 'They'll let me know if he comes into the hotel.'

'Good,' Kingston said. 'We should all keep an eye out for anything strange around the hotel, especially considering recent events.' He glanced at Raymond before looking over the group. 'Does anyone have anything new to report?'

Raymond felt himself sink a little into the couch as he shot a look at Jake. He found Jake was staring at him with a dark look on his face, Raymond shaking his head. Jake narrowed his eyes before he looked up at Kingston. 'I do.'

Kingston turned to him expectantly.

Jake met his eye. 'Someone's after the Barry's.'

Raymond shot him a glare as the others in the room straightened. The smile evaporated from Kingston's face as he turned his head to look at the man in question, his voice dropping into a serious tone. 'Raymond?'

'It's no big deal,' Raymond said. 'Just a couple of guys, that's all.'

'More than a couple,' Jake said. 'There were three the last night.'

'Nothing I can't handle.'

'They were armed.'

'I've dealt with worse.' Raymond straightened, leaning toward Jake as he glared daggers at him. 'Look, I told you to leave it alone, Jake. I have the situation covered.'

'Yeah, right.' Jake returned the glare. 'You've already killed one of them.'

Rita gave Raymond a sharp look. 'When was this?'

'Remember that article I showed you on the news about the chase in Melbourne and a guy getting hit by a train?' Rita and Sydney nodded as Jake pointed at Raymond. 'He did that. He was the other guy in that vid.'

'As I said – I can handle it.' Raymond lowered his voice. 'You need to learn to leave things alo–'

'Raymond.'

Raymond cut himself off and looked sharply at where Kingston was giving him a firm glare. 'It's not your problem, Kingston.'

'You know that it is.' Kingston narrowed his eyes. 'You also know I don't like it when you keep things from me.'

Raymond met his eye. 'I knew how you'd react.'

'You mean by having Jake increase your security,' Kingston said, 'and by putting you and Lucille under surveillance.'

Raymond scoffed. 'It's bad enough that they're watching me without you watching me, too. What is this, Big Brother? Since when did my life have to become a George Orwell novel?'

'Don't be so dramatic.' Kingston leaned back in his seat. 'Need I remind you about how important you are to the team–'

'I know. I'm the Keeper, and I'm important and all that crap. My mother makes me hear it all the time. She uses it as her excuse to keep me under her thumb.' Raymond met Kingston's glare with his own. 'I just never expected you to sprout that shit.'

'It's not 'shit', Raymond.' Kingston's voice dropped into a calm growl. 'You're only the second Keeper ever to find out how the code works to find us the keys, which makes you important. We're not ready to lose you yet.'

'Oh, I see. It's because you can use me. Brilliant.' Raymond pushed himself up. 'Well, don't think I'm about to let you–'

'Sit down!'

Jake, Rita and Sydney jumped and winced at the command, Raymond stopping dead where he was on his way toward the door. He looked back, spotting the flash in Kingston's eyes. Something flickered over Raymond's features, an almost knowing and cautious look as he moved back to his seat, sitting down but never taking his cool glare off Kingston.

'You will listen to me and do as I say,' Kingston said, eyes burning with a barely checked anger. 'You have two choices. Either let Jake increase your security, or I will have you locked up where I know exactly where you are until we've sorted this out. What will it be?'

Raymond set his jaw, nodding slowly. 'Okay. Fine. Let Jake increase the security. But expect nothing from me.'

'I'm not going to,' Kingston reassured him.

The two men continued to glare at each other, the other three looking between the two men wearily, almost seeming to sense the silent argument between them. His eyes narrowing, Kingston tossed his notepad onto his desk and stood abruptly.

'I think that's all for today,' he said, moving toward the bedroom door. 'Dismissed.'

All but Raymond jumped as he slammed the door closed behind him. Raymond muttered under his breath in Latin, Rita wincing slightly. Raymond got up without a word, snatching up a book from the side table and throwing it hard at Jake, who cursed as it hit him.

'Raymond,' Sydney said quietly, the man ignoring her as he stalked out the door, slamming it behind him and causing them to cringe.

'Well,' Rita said, shooting Jake a look. 'I hope that went the way you hoped.'

Jake gave her a dark look.

* * * * *

'This is ridiculous,' Lucille said as she watched Jake put up the security devices. 'Nobody is going to get into the bunker.'

'This is just a precaution,' Jake said.

'Overkill, more like it,' Raymond called from the lounge.

'It's just a temporary measure for when you aren't in the bunker,' Jake said. 'In case someone tries to get in.'

'They can "try",' Raymond said. 'How about you put up lasers to disintegrate them while you're at it?'

'Stop being a moron,' Jake said, screwing the last screw into the camera. 'This is for your protection.'

'We don't need protection,' Lucille countered. 'We are more than capable of looking after ourselves.'

'You've had death threats and people coming after you,' Jake reminded them. 'It's only going to get worse.'

'You don't know that,' Lucille said.

'Jake,' Raymond said, leaning against the door frame. 'Mother is right. We don't need all this extra protection. And if I recall, all the previous security breaches have been from your end, not ours.'

'It's only a matter of time,' Jake said, climbing down off the stepladder. 'Look, Kingston gave the order; I'm just following through. Take it up with him.'

'I intend to,' Raymond said, scowling. 'You know what he gets like. Why the hell did you have to say anything?'

'Would you rather his option B?' Jake asked. 'And I had to because it's his job. He's the Protector. He's just trying to protect you.'

'Stifling us more like it,' Lucille growled. 'He doesn't trust us.'

'I doubt that,' Jake said. 'He's just taking precautions.'

'I fail to see how this system will work anyway,' Lucille said. 'How can you monitor it from Adelaide?'

'It's a Wi-Fi-based system,' Jake told her. 'I can monitor it from my phone.'

'No good if you don't have service,' Raymond said. 'Like… say… now.'

'I don't need to monitor it right now, do I,' Jake fired back.

'Kingston just wants to spy on us,' Lucille said. 'Don't think I don't know about his request for Raymond to spend more time in the bunker.'

'That's also for security reasons,' Jake said. 'First, that way someone can guard the bunker, and second, it makes it harder for anyone to come after Raymond.'

'And what if they go after Mother?' Raymond asked.

Lucille shot him a look. 'Don't give him any ideas.'

'I'm sure once things settle down, it can all go back to normal,' Jake said, folding up the stepladder.

'They had better,' Lucille said. 'I don't know how much of this my nerves can take.'

18

It surprised Sydney to find Kingston standing by her desk when she returned from lunch. It had been a relatively uneventful day, with only a minor mishap with one room that had been taken care of quickly. Sydney rarely expected to see Kingston during the day, especially alone. Usually, when he made an appearance, it was when Raymond was with him, yet here he was standing alone.

'Miss Madinah,' Kingston said as she joined him.

'Mr Kingston.' Sydney stepped behind her desk, checking to ensure all her papers were in place and order. 'Something I can help you with?'

'Perhaps,' Kingston said. 'I was wondering if you were available for dinner this evening.'

Sydney looked up, surprised. 'Tonight?'

'I know it is short notice,' Kingston said with an apologetic smile. 'But Raymond and I were hoping you might join us.'

So Raymond was coming as well. She should have expected as much, given how they seemed to be joined at the hip. 'I have nothing planned,' she told him.

'Excellent,' he said, his smile broadening. 'We'll meet you tonight when you finish work.'

Without another word, he was gone, leaving Sydney to her thoughts.

* * * * *

'I HATE THIS,' Raymond muttered as he followed his mother along La Trobe St toward their apartment. 'It feels like we've been grounded and under constant surveillance.'

'You *are* grounded,' Lucille reminded him. 'But I have to agree. The whole situation is Orwellian.'

'Problem is, I don't think it's going to get any better,' Raymond said. 'It's going to get worse.'

'Especially if those men continue to stalk you,' his mother agreed. 'I think you need to sit down with Kingston tonight during dinner and discuss how much he is overreacting.'

'I can try,' Raymond said. 'You know how stubborn Kingston is. Once he gets his mind set on something, it's near impossible to change it.'

'Just like you,' Lucille said, a flicker of a smile on her lips.

They reached the entryway of the apartment complex, stepping inside. After checking their mail, they went to the elevator in relative silence, not speaking again until the doors closed.

'Jennifer has been horrible since your adventure in Werribee,' Lucille told him. 'All I've had is questions about Rita.'

'Really?' Raymond raised an eyebrow. 'What have you been telling her?'

'I've told her that what you do is none of my business,' Lucille said. 'But you know how persistent that lady is.'

'I know,' Raymond said, giving his mother a sympathetic look. 'I didn't even think that Jennifer might have been at the gala.'

'You were focused on the key,' Lucille guessed as the elevator doors opened. 'You can be very single-minded with these things.'

'I wouldn't go that far,' Raymond countered.

Lucille gave him a measured look, swiping her key, unlocking the apartment door, and switching on the light. She had barely stepped inside when Raymond reached out and caught her arm.

'Mother, wait.'

He gestured toward the ground, Lucille spotting a folded sheet of paper inside the doorway. She bent down, picked it up and unfolded it. The page was blank, other than a single line of words. 'Time is running out. Tick tock.'

'This is a threat,' Lucille observed.

'You think?' Raymond said sarcastically. He stepped further into the apartment, one hand in his pocket with his fingers closed around his switchblade. He checked every room of the flat, and when it satisfied him it was empty, he returned to where his mother was still waiting by the door. 'It's clear.'

'This had to have been delivered personally,' Lucille said, closing the door to the apartment. 'Raymond, maybe it isn't such a good idea for you to go out tonight.'

'If we restrict ourselves, we let them win,' Raymond said, scowling. 'Besides, one of us is supposed to stay in the bunker, remember?'

'Hard to forget,' Lucille said, folding up the paper and placing it on the table. 'Stay vigilant tonight.'

'I'm always vigilant.' He spotted the look his mother was giving him and raised his hands reassuringly. 'I'll be extra careful. I promise.'

'Good.' Lucille approached the fridge. 'Now, let me give you a list of things I'd like to discuss with Kingston tonight.'

* * * * *

Sydney found Raymond and Kingston waiting for her when it was time to clock off. She said goodbye to her colleagues and followed the two men out of the hotel. It was only a short distance to the restaurant they had chosen for the evening, and the weather was pleasant, so they walked the streets of Adelaide. Upon arrival, Kingston gave his name, the three of them being led to a back table reserved for them and sitting. Sydney sat on one side of the table, Kingston and Raymond facing her.

'I'm not in trouble or anything?' Sydney asked, breaking their silence.

'Should you be?' Kingston joked, then shook his head. 'No, there's no problem.'

Sydney felt relief wash over her. She's spent the afternoon wondering if she'd done something wrong, running over everything that had happened up until this point but unable to come up with anything.

'We're just looking to touch base,' Raymond told her. 'Check and see how you are going.'

'You've been thrown into the proverbial deep end,' Kingston said. 'Especially with everything that has been going on of late.'

'I'm fine,' Sydney assured them. 'It's taken a lot to get my head around it, and I still have many questions, but I'm fine.'

'That's good to hear,' Kingston said. 'We can try to answer some of those questions if you like.'

'I'm not sure you can,' Sydney said.

'Try us,' Raymond said.

'Well, for one, how do the portals work?'

Kingston frowned. 'I believe we explained that.'

'No, I mean, *how do they work?* She gestured with her hand. 'Specifically. They look like regular doorways. What is it that sets them apart?'

Kingston and Raymond exchanged a look, Raymond shrugging. Kingston narrowed his eyes and turned back to Sydney.

'I don't know the specifics of that myself,' he said. 'If I had to hazard a guess, it's something to do with the construction of the doorways themselves. Perhaps it's the material that they're made of. They did not brief me on the technology behind the portals.'

That was a fair enough answer, but it proved to Sydney that the two men didn't know everything. 'So it's not in the journals?' She asked Raymond.

'No, it's not,' Raymond said. 'The journals are more like diaries outlining Redmond's day-to-day activities. He hid the location of the keys in the journals, but he didn't mention anything about the portals there. Believe me; I've looked.'

'What about these people that are after you?' she asked. 'How do they know about the portals?'

'It seems to be one person, in particular, that does,' Raymond told her. 'The men we've seen refer to them as their 'boss' and claim that he can use the portals himself. No doubt his ancestors have a connection to the portals, and he wants access to them.'

'For nefarious reasons, no doubt,' Kingston added.

'No doubt,' Raymond agreed.

'Has anyone been after you before?' Sydney asked.

'Not since the day Kingston and I met,' Raymond admitted, seeming to catch the look Kingston was giving him at that question. 'These new people didn't show until we started locating keys.'

'Which means they were watching,' Kingston pointed out. 'They may not have been coming after you, but they were still watching.'

'They could also have been watching you,' Raymond said.

'Or both of you,' Sydney said. 'After all, that guy is watching the hotel.'

'An excellent observation,' Kingston praised her. 'Even Jake missed him, and Jake doesn't miss much.'

'Any other questions?' Raymond asked her.

'A few,' Sydney said. 'Did Nicholas know about the portals?'

Kingston and Raymond glanced at each other. 'We don't know,' Raymond said.

'If he did, he never said anything,' Kingston said. 'He knew I had a private room in the Vaults, and he kept to himself for the most part.'

Sydney nodded. She looked from one man to the other. 'I understand why the two of you are involved with all this, but what about Jake and Rita? How did they get involved in everything?'

'I recruited them,' Kingston answered. 'Rita, I poached from a medical office. She may not have mentioned it yet, but she's a qualified nurse, and in our line of work, you never know if someone will get hurt. Jake, I recruited straight out of university. He came in for a job interview and impressed me so much that I hired him.' He smiled. 'Of course, it helps that both of them can access the portals. That played a large part in their hiring.'

'How did they react to finding out?' Sydney asked.

'The entire thing fascinated Jake,' Kingston said. 'He spent the next month studying the portals to figure out how they work.'

'And Rita?'

'Barely reacted,' Raymond admitted. 'She just took it in her stride. If she had any other reaction, she never let it on.'

That sounded like Jake and Rita, all right, Sydney thought, at least from what she had observed of them. 'I have to admit, I'm still trying to get my head around the whole thing,' she said.

'Take your time,' Kingston assured her. 'There's no rush.'

'Speaking of rushing,' Raymond said, glancing at his watch before turning to face Kingston. 'Don't you think you're rushing this whole 'security' thing?'

'I don't see what you mean,' Kingston said. 'There are men after you, Raymond, who want access to the portals. Extra security is justified.'

'There's extra security, and then there's putting constant surveillance on my mother and I,' Raymond pointed out. 'Have you ever heard of 'a right to privacy'?'

'As I said, there are people after you.' A serious look flickered over Kingston's face and into his voice. 'If you really want my opinion, I'd prefer it if you and your mother were restricted to the bunker until the threat has passed.'

'And what if it doesn't pass?' Raymond asked. 'You'd just keep us locked up forever?'

'If necessary,' Kingston said.

'Isn't that extreme?' Sydney asked. 'They are people, after all, and it's their lives.'

'Thank you,' Raymond mouthed over toward her.

'You must understand the gravity of the situation,' Kingston said. 'These people will not stop. They didn't stop last time, and the Keeper was killed. I'm not about to let that happen again.'

'That was a different time,' Raymond reminded him. 'And it

happened when they were out locating a key. If you want to avoid it happening again, then perhaps I should stop looking for the keys.'

A conflicted look passed over Kingston's face. He set his jaw, scowling. 'No. We need to find the keys.'

'Then there's nothing to stop it from happening,' Raymond told him. 'That's where the vulnerability is. So all this extra security is useless.'

'It's not useless, Raymond,' Kingston said. 'It's peace of mind.'

'For you, maybe,' Raymond said. 'For Mother and myself, it's infringing on our day-to-day activities. Mother has already had to cancel two events she was supposed to attend, and I can't even run errands without knowing that Jake is probably tracking my every move to report to you.'

'It's not that bad,' Kingston said.

'It feels like it.'

'Is the threat really that severe?' Sydney asked.

'Yes,' Kingston said as Raymond said 'no'.

'Yes,' Kingston reiterated. 'The threat is that serious. These men have been armed. They mean you harm, Raymond.'

'What good would it do them to hurt me?' Raymond asked. 'They could torture me for all I care. I will not give them what they want.'

'Don't talk like that,' Kingston said. 'No one is going to torture you.'

Sydney shuddered at the thought, her movement catching Kingston's eye.

'Look, let's change the subject,' Kingston said. 'How are you finding the hotel, Miss Madinah?'

* * * * *

The rest of the dinner went on without a hitch, the three sticking to more pleasant avenues of conversation while they ate. After they had finished, Raymond watched as Sydney moved out of the restaurant, disappearing into the night and the wave of never-ending pedestrians. His smile slowly became a frown as he felt the steady gaze on him, and he sighed as he turned back to face Kingston. The other man watched him almost unblinkingly, Raymond raising an eyebrow at the fixation.

'Is there any particular reason why you're staring at me?'

'Do I need a reason?' Kingston smiled tightly, leaning forward. 'What's wrong, Raymond?'

Raymond's frown deepened. 'There's nothing wrong.'

'You're flustered and slightly distracted. Did something happen?'

'Kingston, you know if something happened, I'd tell you.' Raymond shrugged it off, smiling at the other man as he picked up his drink. 'You worry too much.'

'Our line of work isn't exactly safe,' Kingston reminded him. 'And you know I don't like it when people keep things from me.'

'I know.' Raymond drained his glass, setting it down and standing, picking his coat off the back of the chair and pulling it on. 'Veritatem dies aperit.'

'Raymond,' Kingston warned.

'I'll see you later, Kingston.' Raymond slapped Kingston on the back as he stepped past him, smiling. 'Things to do and all that.'

Kingston watched him with narrowed eyes until he vanished into the crowd.

19

On Friday, Sydney found herself once again at the supermarket, buying her groceries. She was a little distracted by everything that had gone on during the week. Sydney had noted that Raymond hadn't visited since the meeting and that Kingston had seemed a little withdrawn. She wondered if it was the lack of Raymond that caused that withdrawal. They seemed to be joined at the hip, and it was rare for her to see one without the other, so it had been strange seeing Kingston alone.

Sydney was wondering about the relationship between the two of them. She had mentioned it to Jake, who had shrugged and admitted that he'd had thoughts himself but wasn't sure. He'd told her that Rita was in the same boat. They speculated that Kingston and Raymond were together, and many agreed, but it had never been confirmed or denied. And no one had been game enough to say anything to their face. Sydney, for sure, would not be the one to ask.

It was a little disappointing, though. Sydney had to admit she had a bit of a crush on Raymond. The whole place seemed to light up when he arrived. He might not be as charismatic as Kingston and came across as more the quiet one, but he was sure of himself.

Maybe a little too sure of himself. That was no doubt the problem. He didn't realise just how much danger he was in, which was why Kingston had resorted to his measures.

Jake had told her about their experience with the three men who had followed them from the concert. And Rita had filled them in on what had happened at Werribee Park Mansion. Sydney knew she would have reacted badly if she had been in their shoes. Once again, it made her wonder exactly what her place was within the team. She was useless as far as she was concerned. There was nothing she could contribute.

She came out of her thoughts as she rounded a corner and almost ran her trolley into Marcus. 'I'm my gosh, I'm sorry,' she said.

'No harm done,' he said with a smile, shifting his trolley to the side to give her room to pass.

'Actually, I was hoping I'd run into you,' she said, pulling her trolley off to the edge of the aisle to give anyone that came past room.

He raised his brows. 'Should I be worried?'

'No,' she assured him. 'I was just hoping to talk.'

'Oh,' he said, relief on his face. 'What about?'

'I was wondering if maybe you wanted to meet somewhere,' Sydney said. 'For coffee, maybe.'

He frowned at that. 'You want to meet up for coffee?'

'If that's okay,' she said, suddenly feeling unsure. Maybe he thought she *was* a crazy stalker.

'No, that would be fine,' he said, the frown disappearing. 'Tomorrow, maybe?'

She hadn't expected him to ask to meet up so soon. She ran through her calendar in her head and realised that it was clear. 'Sounds good.'

'Anywhere in particular?' he asked.

'How about at that cafe where I saw you that one time?' she said. 'You said they have good coffee.'

'They have excellent coffee,' he clarified with a nod. 'Do you have a time in mind?'

'How about 11:30?' she said.

'Before the lunch rush but after they open,' he said. 'That makes sense. I'll see you there.'

'Good,' she said, relieved that he hadn't blanket turned her down. She had been worried he'd reject her outright. A small part of her still kind of wished that he had. She felt a little like a crazy stalker. 'I'll see you then.'

'Have a good evening,' he said with a smile.

She wished him the same, then pushed her trolley away to continue her shopping.

* * * * *

Sydney arrived at the cafe ten minutes early. She worried she would present herself as over-eager and didn't want to give Marcus the wrong impression. After all, she was just after a friend. She hoped he read nothing more into it than that. Sydney found the cafe was reasonably busy despite the early hour, but she held off on ordering until she was sure he would not stand her up. She had spent the night worried that he wouldn't show. That would certainly make the next Friday shopping trip awkward if they ran into each other.

Five minutes before the meeting time, she spotted Marcus making his way down the street. She was relieved that he was coming and glad to see that he hadn't dressed any differently from average. She had made a point of not dressing up herself. Again, not wanting to give the wrong impression. She certainly wasn't currently in the market for a boyfriend, and she was still dealing with her little crush on Raymond.

Not that Marcus was bad to look at. Sydney had to admit that he seemed to have been blessed in the looks department. He still didn't hold a candle to Raymond, Kingston, and even Jake. Sydney frowned as she realised good-looking men surrounded her, and none of them seemed to be available. Jake had a thing for Rita, and Sydney still wasn't sure about the exact nature of Kingston and Raymond's relationship. They were more than comfortable getting into each other's personal space, that was for sure.

'Good morning,' Marcus greeted her as he reached her. 'I'm a little surprised to see you.'

'You thought I'd stand you up?' she asked.

'I did,' he admitted with a shrug. 'You wouldn't be the first.'

'I always keep my plans,' she said, looking into the shop. 'Should we order?'

'We should. They don't look kindly on people who sit in their seats and order nothing,' Marcus said.

'Yes, I know of another cafe that's the same,' she said, thinking of the coffee shop in the hotel. Simon would often move people along if they ordered nothing. Seats were a premium during certain hours, so he only accepted paying customers, although he sometimes allowed exceptions for hotel patrons. Even Sydney had learned she needed to order something to sit down there.

'It seems to be fairly standard practice,' he said.

They entered the cafe, Sydney ordering herself a coffee. She also contemplated getting something to eat, but decided it was too early for lunch and too late for morning tea. Sydney took her coffee in a 'to go' cup and waited until Marcus had ordered his own. She noted he hadn't even looked at the menu before ordering. Clearly, he came here a lot and knew what he wanted. Meanwhile, Sydney had studied the menu for a moment before spotting something she liked.

Marcus led the way to an outside table. The weather was pleasant, and there were fewer people, so Sydney could see the move's appeal. She followed, sitting in the seat opposite him. Once seated, she tried her coffee and found it was rather good. She would even dare say it was better than what they had at the hotel, and that was excellent coffee itself. Freshly ground beans always had a better flavour to them.

'It's good, isn't it?' Marcus said, gesturing to the coffee.

'It is, yes,' she agreed, setting her cup down on the table. 'I'm sorry about the short notice.'

'To be fair, I was thinking of asking you myself,' he said. 'We see each other often enough that I thought we should try to get to know each other.'

'Exactly what I was thinking,' she said with a nod. 'We can't exactly have a lengthy conversation in the middle of a supermarket.'

'We could, but I don't think the other customers would appreciate that very much,' he said.

He was right there. Nothing was more infuriating than navigating the narrow aisles of a supermarket and coming across two people with trolleys blocking the path while they chatted. 'No, they wouldn't,' she agreed.

He smiled and sipped his coffee.

'Did you ever resolve that issue at the pub?' she asked, thinking back to when she had seen him there.

'Yes,' he said with a nod. 'It turned out to be a software error. A system update didn't… work.'

'I know little about computers,' she admitted. 'I mean, I know how to use them, but that's about the extent of it.'

'I'm not much into the technical side myself. I can fix minor issues, but the more technical problems I leave to the experts,' he said.

'So you're more on the business side of the business,' she guessed.

He nodded. 'I handle clients and work out deals. I don't do any of the installations and programming.'

'Well, there's no shortage of people who need security,' she smiled.

'Everyone has it these days,' he agreed. 'Many people have it for their homes as well. Everyone seems to watch everyone.'

'No wonder so many people are paranoid,' she joked. 'There are eyes everywhere.'

'Yes, there are,' he confirmed. 'I can see three on us right now.'

Sydney frowned and looked around. She spotted two cameras connected to the store – one inside and one on the outside, covering the tables. She tried to find the third and couldn't.

'Across the street,' he said, seeming to read her mind. 'There's a camera on a store over there that's pointed this way.'

Looking across, Sydney squinted, trying to see what he was talking about. Eventually, she saw it, half-hidden under the eave of a shop in a little black dome. She couldn't tell which way it was pointed because of the dome itself, but she knew those cameras tended to be able to move. For all she knew, it was pointed this way and watching them. It made little sense to be doing so, but it was possible.

'You pay attention to that?' she asked.

'When you work in a particular field, you become a little hyperaware of things related to it,' he said. 'Checking for cameras is one of the first things I do when entering a new place. Of course, sometimes knowing where the dead zone is helps.'

'Dead zone?' she asked.

'Blind spot,' he clarified. 'A spot that no camera covers.'

'Shouldn't cameras cover all areas?' she asked.

'A good system does,' he said. 'But even good systems have their blind spots. You can't look everywhere at once, even though some systems are getting a lot better with it. You'd be amazed at some of the technology on offer these days. But better systems come with higher price tags, and not everyone will pay for it.'

'I'm guessing most people just go with a standard system,' she said.

He nodded. 'I'm willing to bet that even the hotel you work at has a standard system.'

She became very self-conscious at the mention of her workplace. She still didn't know him well enough to tell him where she worked. Instead, she shrugged the question off. 'Not my area of expertise, but I know the security guys work hard.'

'Did you know,' he said, leaning forward, 'that most security systems have a back door? If you know the key, you can get into them. And with most of them connected to the internet these days, you can get away with anything.'

She knew. Jake had told her about it and how he used it to his advantage. He had become something of an expert in cracking security systems. He had helped cover their search for the keys with his knowledge, and she knew he had also been looking into the security system at the Barry apartment building. 'Is that how criminals get away with things?' she asked.

'Most criminals aren't sophisticated enough,' he said. 'You need to know what you're doing. It's why smart businesses keep their security system offline and on a separate network.'

She nodded. Sydney guessed she could understand that. She wondered if the hotel's network was connected to the internet. She'd have to ask Jake about it when she saw him on Monday. 'Is that what you advise your clients to do?'

'Definitely,' Marcus said. 'Otherwise, tracking someone through the security networks is very easy. You never know who could be watching you.'

That made Sydney worry about the Barrys. With people after them, they might have been being tracked as well. All it would take was someone who knew what they were doing, and they could work out the Barry's entire schedule. That could be why Raymond had people after him – they knew where he would be at certain times. It made Sydney a little paranoid about it all herself.

'I wouldn't worry too much, though,' Marcus said with an easy smile. 'Someone would have to have an excellent reason to want to go through so much effort to track you.'

She nodded, knowing that her worry must have shown on her face. 'I guess so. No one would be interested in someone like me.'

He shrugged, taking a sip of his coffee.

Sydney picked up her drink and took a long sip. The coffee was still hot, but it was just the right temperature now that she didn't scold her tongue. She swallowed, glancing around them and taking in the other patrons.

'Can I ask you something?' Marcus said.

'I believe you just did,' Sydney joked.

He seemed to accept that, but continued. 'Why did you suggest we come for coffee?'

Honestly, she had been expecting that question. 'I guess we see each other a lot, and I wanted to get to know you.'

'So you're looking for a friend,' Marcus guessed. 'You're new to the area and haven't met anyone yet.'

'Exactly,' she agreed. 'There are people at work, but… I guess I don't feel like I fit in.'

He frowned at that. 'How come?'

'They all have established relationships,' she said, trying to work out how to phrase what she was feeling. 'I guess I feel like an add-on. An extra wheel. That I just got shoe horned in.'

'Perhaps it's simply that you haven't found your place yet,' Marcus said. 'You did say you're new.'

'I am,' she confirmed. 'But their relationships go back years. I feel they're just token gestures when they reach out to me. Like they could go on without me, no problem.'

'I'm sure you're more important than that,' Marcus said. 'Do they keep you updated?'

'Yes,' she confirmed. 'When there are meetings, they include me. But sometimes, they go off and do things and don't fill me in. I find out after the fact.'

'So they don't plan ahead,' Marcus said.

'I think they do,' Sydney said. 'I'm just not included.'

'Interesting,' he said. 'They keep you in the loop, but simultaneously, you feel like an outsider.'

'Exactly,' she said. 'And they all have varying degrees of friendship and private jokes that I'm not in on. Sometimes it feels like they're talking past me.'

'Do they care about including you?' he asked.

'They seem to,' she said. 'I mean… when I have questions, they're always willing to answer them. If they can, I mean.'

'You think they're keeping things from you,' he said.

'I do,' she said with a nod. 'I swear two of them are dating, and nobody knows for sure.'

'Is that so?' he said. She had to give him credit – he actually seemed interested in what she was saying. 'So it's a secret relationship?'

'Yeah,' she said. 'I don't know why, though. I don't think anyone would have a problem if they were. It would be nice to know for sure, that's all.'

He narrowed his eyes. 'Sound's to me like you're interested in one of them.'

Was she that obvious? She felt her cheeks warm, staring down at her coffee as she tried to figure out how to respond.

'I could understand why you'd want to know for sure,' he said.

'But why would they keep it a secret? Unless it's a manager and a subordinate.'

'They don't work for each other,' she said, shaking her head. 'I mean, they do, but… they're not in the same department. No one's anyone's boss… although one is kind of a leader. It's complicated,' she finally said.

'Sounds like,' he said. 'I imagine it's frustrating.'

'It is,' she said, taking another long drink from her coffee.

'It must be hard not having someone to vent to,' he said, stirring his drink with a spoon. 'Have you considered an online journal?'

'Probably a bad idea,' she said. 'Privacy reasons.'

'Fair enough,' he said. 'Although you could keep it vague.'

'Still not a good idea,' she said. 'In my industry, there are a lot of secrets. I wouldn't want to let something slip accidentally.'

'It's not like anyone would get killed,' he said, setting down his spoon.

The problem is someone might, but Sydney wasn't about to tell him that. The last thing she needed was to slip up and cue someone in that she was connected to the portals or give any information away that could be used against Kingston and Raymond. She was in a sensitive position. Honestly, she knew that if she hadn't stumbled across the portals by accident, they would probably never have filled her in on them. They trusted her with a lot of information.

'Tell me, Sydney,' Marcus said, looking up. 'Do you ever miss home?'

She blinked. 'Home?'

'Where you're from originally,' he clarified.

'You mean Brisbane?' She considered it for a moment. 'Sometimes, I guess.'

'Do you have family there?' he asked.

'My parents,' she said.

'Are you still in contact?'

'We are,' she answered. 'We talk every other week. It's a lot easier now I'm back in Australia. The time zones between Brisbane and New York made things hard.'

'I can imagine,' he said. 'What would you do if someone prevented you from being able to go back home?'

She thought about that. 'I don't know. No one ever has.' She looked at him. 'Why? Is someone preventing you from doing that?'

'You could say that,' Marcus said.

She frowned at that, wondering just what could prevent him. 'Where were you from before you came here?' she asked.

'Before I came here?' he asked. 'Ireland.'

'So you can't go back to Ireland?' she asked.

'No, I can go to Ireland any time I want,' he said. 'I just… can't go home.'

She wasn't sure that she understood what he was saying. Then again, she had never been in that position, so she wasn't sure she could. She guessed it had something to do with a family fight. 'Are your parents there?'

'My mother is still at home, yes,' he nodded. 'Not my father, though. He's the one who brought me here. He's one of the reasons I can't go home.'

'Are you fighting with him?' she asked.

'I haven't seen or heard from him in a long time,' Marcus said.

'I'm afraid I don't really understand what you're saying,' Sydney admitted. She was trying to wrap her head around it, but failing.

'No, I guess you wouldn't,' he sighed. 'But I would give anything to see my mother again. Do anything.'

That almost sounded like a threat. She felt herself becoming uncomfortable and fidgeted slightly in her chair.

'I'm sorry. I've made you uncomfortable,' he said, a smile crossing his lips. 'Forget I said anything.'

It was hard not to, but she wasn't about to press him any further. It was clearly a sore subject for him. She picked up her coffee and took a long drink. It had cooled a lot now, the water lukewarm. It was still excellent coffee. Some coffees became bitter when they cooled, but this one didn't seem to. That was the hallmark of a perfect coffee.

'So,' Marcus said after drinking from his cup. 'What do you think of Adelaide?'

A WEEK PASSED with no sign of Raymond in Adelaide, which didn't go unnoticed. Sydney commented to Jake about it, who told her he had been checking on Raymond and had found that he had been working more than usual. Jake had spoken to Rita, who took it upon herself to check on the man.

Rita watched the man at the desk as he scrutinised the pages of the book in front of him. She could see just from the way he was sitting the tenseness in his shoulders, the brightness of the light on his desk casting long shadows over what she could see of his face.

He knew she was there. He always knew when someone was watching him. She figured it was part of his training, being ready for fight or flight when the time was right. He was pretty much always in fight mode. She suspected that came from his genetics; Lucille was no different. He was a bit more cunning and a heck of a lot quicker.

'Are you going to stand there and watch me all day, or are you here for something?' he asked, not even bothering to look up from his work. 'And I should tell you I haven't got time to argue with you right now.'

Her eyebrows rose slightly, but she made no move to step further into the room. She was content enough leaning against the door frame, and she'd always found that room to feel claustrophobic. This whole place was.

'You need windows,' she commented.

'So Jake is always telling me.' He turned a page, his frown deepening as he gazed down at the words carefully etched over it. 'Why don't you go pick on him?'

Rita set her jaw, letting her gaze run over the back of his head and noting that he'd probably be getting himself a haircut sometime soon. He seemed to be fixated on keeping it at a certain length. Why he bothered, given the fact it was often dishevelled, was beyond her. 'When was the last time you slept, Raymond?'

'What do you care?' he asked.

'If it's slipped your notice, I'm the team medic.' She shifted around the door frame slightly, closer to him, while keeping one foot in the corridor. 'You've been working yourself ragged since the incident with those men and the fight with Kingston.'

'I'm working the same amount as I always am,' he corrected her, still not turning to her as he scribbled a note onto his pad in that incomprehensible shorthand of his.

'Yes. I can see that.' She narrowed her eyes. 'It's just that you're doing the same amount of work you'd do in a month within a week. The last thing we need is for you to burn yourself out.'

'That's not going to happen.'

'Not to mention that your reflexes are going to slow down, meaning that the next guy that tries to jump you is actually going to do it because you won't see him coming.'

He lowered his pen. 'Rita…'

'And that's just the start of it, Raymond.' She met his eye as he turned his chair slightly so he could look back at her out of the corner of his eye. 'Just because you want to get back on Kingston's good side doesn't mean you have to work yourself into the grave.'

'In case it's slipped your notice,' he said, firing her own words back at her, 'I'm the Keeper. I *am* going to work myself into the grave. My grandfather is one of the few that survived this job. There's a good reason we don't have a retirement plan.' He turned back to his work. 'It is simply our job to get as much done as possible in the short time we are here.'

Rita huffed. 'You sound like your mother.'

Raymond straightened, dropping his pen onto the table and crossing his arms over his chest. 'I already told you I have no time for you to insult me, so just go back to snarking at everyone back in Adelaide like you always do.'

Rita nodded, setting her jaw as she glared at the back of his head. 'Right. While you just sit here being Kingston's good little pet trying to find a bone.'

'I don't give a shit about Kingston right now, okay?'

'Oh, I see.' She shrugged, crossing her arms over her chest. 'Which is why you're working so hard to find a key for him so you can beg his forgiveness.'

'I've already located a key.'

Rita straightened. 'What?'

He picked up a book to the left of the desk in one gloved hand, holding it up for her to see the hastily written and coded writing on the yellowed pages. 'Found it yesterday. Right now, I'm doing work for my real job.' He gestured upward toward the Library, and glancing at the box of books on the desk, Rita recognised the reference number as one from the Library's ordinary archives.

'If you found a key, then why the hell didn't you tell us?' Rita snapped. 'We've been waiting for you to come up with something.'

'Oh yes, waiting on me,' he said, sarcasm so thick in his voice she could almost see it. 'Because I'm the "Chosen One", aren't I.' He turned back to the desk. 'They've been waiting for over a century. I'm sure you can all wait a little longer.'

Rita stared at him, a little warning bell going off at the back of her mind that she made a mental note to look into later. She kept an impassive look on her face as she watched him, mentally running a check on him. 'Raymond, you really should come back over to Adelaide. Kingston's been worried–'

'If he were so worried about me, he would have come over himself instead of sending his bloody secretary.' He shot her a hard glare before his eyes seemed to stare at a spot on the wall. 'All he wants me for are the bloody keys. He'd take no bloody interest whatsoever if it weren't for that.'

'Keep telling yourself that, Raymond.' Rita shook her head as she gave him one last pointed look. 'When you finally collapse with exhaustion, don't say I didn't warn you.'

She heard him huff as he snatched up his pen, immersing himself back into the book he was making notations on. Rolling her eyes, Rita stepped back into the corridor, her heels tapping on the wood floor that oddly didn't echo. She pushed aside her frustration as she headed back toward the portal, mentally preparing herself for what she had to do next.

It was time to talk to Jake.

* * * * *

'He said what?' Jake asked, staring at Rita.

'You heard,' Rita said, gesturing downward toward the Vaults. 'For someone complaining about being locked up, he's certainly doing it to himself.'

'He's definitely spent too much time with his thoughts,' Jake said, shaking his head. 'We need to get him out of there.'

'Good luck with that,' Rita said. 'You know what he can get like.'

'Yeah.' Jake sighed, rubbing the back of his neck. 'Maybe we should send Sydney in.'

Rita frowned. 'What do you mean?'

'She's new to all of this,' Jake said, gesturing to them. 'She's also new to Melbourne.'

'You mean we should get Raymond to give her the tour?' Rita asked, her eyes lighting up at the idea.

'That's exactly what I mean,' Jake said. 'That might take Raymond's mind off everything. Either that or we should try to contact his friends to get him out of the bunker for a while.'

'I'll try to find their contacts,' Rita said. 'Lucille may have them.'

'Start with Sydney, though,' Jake said. 'She can make anyone's day better.'

21

Sydney stepped tentatively through the portal, still unsure how safe it was. Even though Kingston and Raymond had assured her that no harm would come to her for using it, she still couldn't get the image of the man disintegrating before her eyes from her head. She couldn't help but make sure she was still in one piece, knocking on the portal door. When there was no answer, she stepped further into the apartment.

'Hello?' she called, looking toward the office she knew was Raymond's.

When she didn't get a response, she headed toward the office door, knocking on it lightly. It swung open slightly. Sydney spotted the back of Raymond's head over where he sat at the desk.

'Do you want something, Miss Madinah?' Raymond asked, not bothering to turn around.

'Yes, actually,' she said, shuffling on the spot. Working up the nerve, she cleared her throat. 'I was wondering if you might show me around Melbourne.'

There was a long pause, Raymond not looking up from his work. 'Did Rita put you up to this?'

'No,' Sydney lied.

'Jake?'

'I came up with it on my own,' she answered.

Slowly Raymond turned toward her, and Sydney at once saw what Rita had been talking about. The man looked worn down, with dark circles under his eyes and messy hair. His eyes were slightly bloodshot, and he just looked plain tired. She felt a pang of sympathy wash over her, at once deciding that she would help take his mind off everything.

'You're not a very good liar,' Raymond commented after a long pause.

'I'm a hotel manager,' Sydney retorted. 'I'm an excellent liar. But I'm not lying. I really want to get to see Melbourne. I've never been here, and you live here so…'

That wasn't a lie. Ever since she discovered the portal, she wanted to get to know the other city. Jake's tour of Adelaide had been excellent, but she'd be a fool not to use the opportunity to see Melbourne. She had a feeling she could probably ask Jake or Kingston, but given Raymond actually lived in the city, he was the best one to ask.

'Okay,' Raymond said, dropping his pen onto the table and standing. 'Just let me get my jacket.'

Sydney stepped back from the door so that he could pass her, Raymond ducking into the room next to the office. Glancing in the doorway, Sydney could see that it was a bedroom, Raymond scooping his jacket up off the back of a chair. There was nothing remarkable about the bedroom, but Sydney could tell it was lived in.

Raymond led the way out of the home, up the main stairway and out through the Library into the city's streets. It surprised Sydney how busy it was, but she remembered that this was probably one of the city's major streets and one of the central hubs.

'What sort of thing are you interested in?' Raymond asked.

'Anything,' Sydney admitted.

'We've only got a couple of hours of light left, so we won't be able to get much in,' Raymond told her, 'so I can only show you the immediate area. If you want to see more, you'll have to come over earlier.'

'That's okay,' Sydney said. 'Lead the way.'

* * * * *

Rita watched Kingston out of the corner of her eye as he paced the apartment, a troubled look on his face. She tried to focus on what she was doing, but he was making it impossible. Sighing, she eventually gave up, leaning back in her chair and directing her attention toward her boss.

'You're making it hard to work,' she said.

'Hm?' He looked up at her, startled by her presence. 'Sorry.'

'What's on your mind?' She asked.

'Nothing is on my mind,' he said stubbornly.

'Cut the bullshit,' she said. 'Something is on your mind. Is it Raymond?'

'He hasn't called in a week,' Kingston confessed, dropping into his office chair. 'He hasn't visited. He's completely cut me off.'

'You know he wasn't happy about the increased surveillance,' Rita said.

'That's no excuse,' Kingston said. 'I'm supposed to be protecting him, and I can't do it if he won't even talk to me.'

'You realise you could just visit him.'

Kingston shook his head, sighing heavily as he rubbed a hand over his face. 'I'm probably the last person he wants to see.'

'You're as stubborn as each other,' Rita muttered, turning back to her computer. 'Look, I need to finish working on this contract, so I can't have you pacing around the office looking like someone kicked your puppy.'

'I don't…' Kingston complained.

'Sydney is out with Raymond right now,' Rita told him. 'Doing what you should be doing. He's been working himself ragged. Oh, and he found another key, by the way.'

Kingston looked up. 'He did?'

'Yesterday, apparently. But he's sulking like a spoiled brat, so he kept that information to himself.' Rita looked at her document, trying to remember where she was up to. 'Now, are you going to let me work or not?'

'Yes,' Kingston said, pulling the keyboard of his computer toward him. 'I'll let you work. No more pacing.'

'Good.'

* * * * *

Raymond had been right about not having a lot of daylight left, as soon Sydney found that the sun was dipping into the horizon. The peak hour traffic was jamming up the CBD, restricting their ability to move freely. By the time they were heading back in the Library's direction, the sun had disappeared from the sky, a cool breeze threading its way from between the buildings.

'Like I said,' Raymond said, breaking the momentary silence. 'You really need a day to explore the city properly. You'd better come over on the weekend when you have time.'

'I'll have to do that,' Sydney agreed. She cast her gaze around, looking at their reflection in the window and sighing. 'How long has that man been following us for now?'

'Since we left the library,' Raymond shook his head. 'It's a common thing, so don't worry.'

'You mean they follow you every time you leave home?' Sydney asked.

'Lately, yes,' Raymond said. 'As I said: it's no big deal.'

'It kind of is,' Sydney disagreed. 'Have you told Kingston?'

'Kingston will exaggerate the threat and go into full-blown lock down,' Raymond told her.

'Has he done it before?' Sydney asked.

'Once,' Raymond said. 'Not long after I became Keeper, a guy started following me around. When Kingston found out, he restricted Mother and me to the bunker until he was sure the threat wasn't serious.'

'How can he be sure the threat isn't serious?' Sydney asked. 'Did he find the guy and ask him?'

'I don't know,' Raymond admitted. 'All I know is that he said he had changed his mind one day.'

'Okay.' Sydney glanced at their reflection, spotting the man following a good ten metres behind them. 'But what if the threat really is that serious this time? These guys have approached you and threatened you.'

'I can take care of myself,' Raymond said. 'So can Mother. We're not pushovers.'

'I never said you were,' Sydney said. 'I'm just saying, what if these guys really are that dangerous? You could get hurt.'

'I won't get hurt,' Raymond assured her.

Sydney wasn't so sure of that. She was beginning to understand why Kingston was so overprotective. Raymond was incredibly sure of himself, which was never a good thing. Sydney didn't feel safe knowing she was being followed. She didn't know how Raymond and Lucille could do it. She also had a feeling that Raymond wasn't being completely honest about the threat that these men were posing, playing it down just because he didn't want to go back into lockdown.

'I don't know how you can act so relaxed,' she told him. 'I'm freaking out.'

'You don't need to worry,' Raymond said. 'I'm with you.'

'It's you they're after,' Sydney reminded him.

'And they will not get me,' he assured her.

It wasn't very assuring. As they came closer to the library, Sydney felt a sense of urgency, wanting to get back underground as soon as possible. The bunker was safe with all its extra security, and Sydney had an overwhelming desire to let Kingston know precisely what was going on. Raymond might not want to tell him, but Sydney did.

Stepping through the doors, Sydney felt almost a relief to be back on what felt like safe ground, but a casual glance behind her quickly put an end to that feeling. The man had followed them in. Sydney stuck close to Raymond's side as he led the way through the corridors and back down the stairs into the catacombs, Sydney hearing the footsteps of the man following them close behind.

'What the hell?' she heard Raymond mutter under his breath. Clearly, this was the first time they had followed him this far, and Sydney felt a wave of adrenaline pump through her.

Raymond swiped open the door that led into the bunker, ushering her through before following. As he made to close the door, a hand grabbed it to keep it from closing. Raymond growled, pushing as hard as he could onto the door and crushing the fingers of the other. It became a battle. Sydney watched from halfway down the stairs as the two men fought over the doorway. For a moment, she thought Raymond would lose as the door pushed back, only for him to throw his total weight into it.

The other man's hand vanished. Sydney was sure that his fingers had to be broken as Raymond pushed the door fully closed. There was a click as the lock engaged, Raymond finally stepping back.

'That was new,' he said, listening to the other man try to force the door open from the other side, the door refusing to budge.

'They've never tried to break-in before?' Sydney asked.

'No,' Raymond admitted. 'It's concerning.'

That was an understatement. Sydney swallowed hard, moving down the stairs and deciding straight away she had to tell Kingston.

22

He gently pushed open the door, frowning slightly at its silence. Someone must have oiled it recently. Closing it behind him, he made his way down the corridor and glanced at the closed doors, noting the light coming from the main living area ahead. He stepped around the corner, peeking in and spotting Lucille settled on the couch, flipping through a book.

Lucille glanced up, a scowl crossing her face. 'Oh, look who finally came to check on the prisoners.'

'You're not a prisoner,' Kingston said, stepping into the room.

'We are locked up and surrounded by high security to make sure no one can get in, and we can't get out,' she said. 'That is the definition of a prison.'

Kingston sighed. 'Lucille…'

'Don't you dare say this is for our protection,' she hissed. 'You know full well that we are more than capable of looking after ourselves.'

'I'm just being cautious,' Kingston countered.

'Cautious?' Lucille scoffed. 'Here you want us to keep our position secret, and then you just lock us up at the first sign that something could be wrong. Raymond and I have connections outside Kingston, with duties and jobs out there. Do you know what we had to tell everyone? That we had ovid. That we are under quarantine. Now no one will come near us in fear that we'll pass it on.'

Kingston's eyebrows rose slightly. 'That is a good cover story.'

'There shouldn't have to be a cover story,' she said, setting down her book. 'I even called my father and told him what was going on. Do you know what he called it? Overreacting.'

'Need I remind you that your father is the only Barry to retire from the job,' Kingston replied, 'and that's because he knew when to keep his head down.' He raised a hand as he saw her face darken, knowing she was about to bite his head off. 'Look, where's Raymond?'

She shot him a glare, picking up her book again. 'His office. And he's even less pleased about this than I am.'

'So I imagine.' Kingston hesitated, wondering if he should say something else, but Lucille had already returned to her book. He sighed, turning and moving in the office's direction, finding the door slightly ajar and pushing it, noticing that it too had been oiled recently. Undoubtedly, the Barry's had been performing some much-needed maintenance on their home to combat their boredom.

Raymond was at his desk, chin resting on his hand as he scrutinised the computer screen. There was a pile of books sitting next to him, but his attention now seemed to be on the Solitaire game. Kingston moved further into the room, watching the back of Raymond's head as he pushed the door closed.

'Turn around and walk right back the way you came,' Raymond said without turning.

Kingston sighed heavily. 'I just had this conversation with your mother. I'm doing this because–'

'Why?' Raymond spun his chair around, leaning back in it and crossing his arms over his chest. 'Do I have to remind you that the role of the Barry family is to protect the Kingston family? Not the other way around.'

'Right now, they're interested in you,' Kingston said. 'Not me.'

'Has it ever crossed your mind that they're probably after us so they can get to you?' Raymond raised a hand to keep Kingston from replying. 'Yes, they want the portal, and exactly where does that lead?'

'I am not taking any chances,' Kingston leaned back against the door, observing the other. 'Raymond, your grandfather is the only member of the Barry family not to be killed doing this job, and I'm not about to lose you.'

Raymond's eyes narrowed. 'Need I remind you what happened last time a Kingston ignored a Barry?'

Kingston set his jaw. 'That's not fair.'

'It's true, though.' Raymond leaned forward slightly. 'That Kingston decided he didn't need protection and wound up dead. Right now, you are unguarded because you're being a stubborn arsehole and letting personal feelings get in the way.'

'That has nothing to do with it,' Kingston shot back.

'Doesn't it?' Raymond leaned back again. 'Exactly how long are you intending to keep us locked up?'

Kingston sighed. 'As long as it takes.'

'I see.' Raymond nodded, his jaw tightening. 'And given that these guys are here in Melbourne and you're in Adelaide, that's going to take some time, isn't it?'

Kingston had to fight to keep from rolling his eyes. 'I have Jake going over all the security footage. Rita is tracking the names he comes up with, and Sydney is observing for anyone who seems suspicious.'

'Great,' Raymond said, sarcasm thick in his voice. 'I feel so much better now that you have the Scooby Gang on the case.'

'Look, Raymond,' Kingston could feel his patience waning. 'We're working on it. As soon as we work out who these people are and take care of them, things will return to normal. And just so you are aware, until we sort this whole thing out, I will restrict myself to the hotel.'

'Pleased to hear it,' Raymond said, turning back to his computer. 'Let me know how that goes while you swim in the pool and socialise in the restaurant and bar.'

Kingston rolled his eyes this time as he reached for the door handle, glaring at the back of Raymond's head. 'Sometimes I don't think you appreciate how much I care for you.'

'Well, I know you definitely underestimate what I am capable of,' Raymond countered.

Shaking his head with annoyance, Kingston left him alone.

* * * * *

'Do you think Raymond might be right?' Sydney asked Jake and Rita. 'That Kingston is overreacting?'

'A man tried to break into the bunker,' Jake reminded her.

'I know, I was there,' Sydney said. 'But what if Lucille and Raymond really can take care of themselves? They've done well up to now, haven't they?'

'Things haven't been this serious,' Jake said.

'I just can't help but feel guilty,' Sydney admitted. 'Like it's my fault we've locked them up.'

'They haven't been "locked up",' Rita told her. 'They've been isolated.'

'But isn't that the same thing?'

'They can leave whenever they want,' Rita said. 'It's just highly recommended that they don't.'

'Rita's right,' Jake said. 'If they wanted to just walk out, they could.'

'Couldn't they just come to Adelaide?' Sydney asked. 'The guys after them are in Melbourne, so wouldn't they be safer here?'

'The bunker is the safest place,' Jake said. 'Between the security and the location, there is nowhere better for them to be.'

'I'm not sure they agree with that,' Sydney said. 'Judging from their reaction.'

'Raymond's just a drama queen,' Rita said. 'Don't mind him. And his mother is just as bad.'

'I'll say,' Jake agreed.

'But there must be something we can do,' Sydney said. 'What if we find out who is behind the men coming after them?'

'And do what?' Rita asked. 'People like that don't negotiate. From what we've seen, they're used to taking what they want, and by any means necessary.'

'What about the key Raymond found?' Sydney asked. 'Are we just going to pretend like it doesn't exist?'

'We'll get it,' Jake said. 'At least when Kingston says we can. Right now, with us being watched, I wouldn't recommend it.'

'So we can't do anything,' Sydney said, feeling dejected.

'I wouldn't say that,' Rita said. 'We have security footage to go over. We have a man watching the hotel that we can try to identify.'

'It's something,' Jake agreed. 'Better than nothing.'

'I guess,' Sydney said, fidgeting.

'Until Kingston says anything, it's all we have,' Rita told them. 'We have to trust him.'

Yes, Sydney thought to herself. For now, that was all they could do.

* * * * *

As Sydney walked home from the hotel, she couldn't shake the feeling that she was being watched. It was the same feeling she'd had in Melbourne before she realised they were being followed. This time, she couldn't see anyone following her. She'd checked a few times, but no one was behind her. At least, not obviously so.

Then she remembered the conversation she'd had with Marcus about the security cameras. Looking around, Sydney spotted several cameras in her area and wondered if maybe someone was watching her through them. She doubted that would be the case. Nothing about her made her special enough for them to hack security cameras and watch her walking home.

Still, she felt safer when she finally got to her apartment and closed the door behind her. Her adrenaline was pumping and her heart racing even though she had seen no one. She wondered if maybe she was just becoming paranoid about the whole thing. Being followed in Melbourne had shaken her up. Her paranoia might be a side effect of what happened.

She remembered how Kingston had reacted when she'd told him

about being followed in Melbourne and how the man had tried to break into the Barry residence. She swore he'd gone a little pale. He'd immediately headed down to confront Raymond about it. Sydney wished she could have been a fly on that wall. All she knew was that Raymond and Lucille were under even tighter surveillance than before. She felt a little sorry for them.

It made her wonder, though – with Raymond and Lucille locked away, could the people who were going after them now be following her, Jake, Rita and Kingston? When one door closes, another opens after all. Kingston had said he wouldn't be leaving the hotel, and Jake had confirmed with Sydney that the hotel's security was indeed on its own network and not connected to the internet. There was no way that anyone could watch Kingston, which left her, Jake and Rita.

Sydney made a mental note to ask Jake and Rita about it the next chance she got. She wanted to know if she was the only one with this feeling. Maybe she was going a little crazy because of everything. She honestly wouldn't be surprised if she were.

23

RAYMOND WANTED TO beat his head against his desk in frustration. He had almost finished the work he had brought home, leaving him with nothing better to do than search Redmond's journals for more clues. It was doing his head in. Rubbing his hands over his face, he took off his glasses, cleaning them. He scowled down at the journal before he slid out of his seat, putting his glasses back on as he headed for the door.

After a quick search of the apartment, he found his mother in her office, settled into her beanbag chair, reading. He didn't disturb her. Instead, he went to the kitchen to make himself a coffee. He sighed as he waited for the kettle to boil, leaning back against the counter and glancing at the clock. The lack of windows made it hard to keep track of time in the bunker. He couldn't tell if it was midday or midnight. Raymond rolled his eyes, knowing that he had been down there too long either way. He was feeling claustrophobic.

Hearing the kettle switch off, he poured the coffee, wincing slightly as he took a sip and scolded his tongue. He usually liked a little cream in his coffee, but right now, he needed it dark. It was the only thing keeping him awake during his long working hours. Taking another sip, he frowned as he heard the phone ring.

Picking it up, he answered. 'Hello?'

'*Raymond, it's Andrew.*'

Raymond perked up a bit at his voice, although something about his tone sounded off. 'Andrew, what's wrong?'

'*It's Olivia,*' Andrew said. '*They took her.*'

'What?' Raymond felt his stomach plunge through his feet. 'Who did?'

'*Some men. They snatched her out of the front yard,*' Andrew said. '*They said if we want her back, we have to bring you.*'

'I'll be right there,' Raymond said, looking up as he spotted a movement out the corner of his eye and saw his mother watching him from the doorway of her office.

'*Hurry,*' Andrew said. '*Please.*'

'I will,' Raymond hung up the phone, abandoning his coffee as he headed for his room to grab his shoes and jacket. He could sense his mother shadowing him, and glancing at her; he saw a worried look on her face.

'You're walking into a trap,' Lucille said.

'I know,' Raymond said, looking at his mother. 'But I have to go. They took Olivia.'

'Go,' Lucille said, reaching out to grab his arm. 'Just be careful.'

'I will.'

Without another word, he left the bunker.

★ ★ ★ ★ ★

Raymond didn't stop until he was pulling up outside Andrew and Tanya's house, the two of them appearing at the door as soon as he got out of the car. They ushered him in, Andrew closing the door behind him.

'What happened?' Raymond asked.

'They just snatched Olivia out of the front garden,' Andrew said. 'We didn't even have time to react.'

'They just took her,' sobbed Tanya. 'They said if we wanted her back, we had to meet them at a certain location this afternoon and bring you.'

'Well, I'm here,' Raymond said, stepping forward and embracing Tanya in a firm hug.

'This is a trap,' Andrew said, shaking his head as Raymond hugged him next. 'You realise they're going to want to trade?'

'I know,' Raymond said. 'Me for Olivia. I'll do it without a second thought.'

'Raymond, you don't have to do this,' Tanya cried.

'Yes, I do,' Raymond said. 'Olivia's my daughter. I will trade my life for hers without hesitation.'

'Don't talk like that,' Andrew said. 'You will not die.'

'Did they say anything about the police?' Raymond asked.

Andrew nodded. 'That if we contacted them, we wouldn't see Olivia again.'

'Thought as much.' Raymond sighed, looking from one to the other. 'All we can do is go to this exchange. If it goes the way I expect, the second you get Olivia back, I want you to take my car and head straight for Melbourne. You need to let Kingston know what's going on.'

Andrew nodded, wrapping an arm around Tanya's shoulders. 'We can do that.'

'You're sure we can use the portal?' Tanya asked.

'I'm sure,' Raymond assured them. 'That time you met Kingston and shook his hand. He tested you. You should both be able to access the portals, and by default, so should Olivia. You'll be safe there.'

'But what about you?' Andrew said.

'Don't worry about me,' Raymond said. 'Just get to Kingston. He'll know what to do. Now, when and where are we supposed to meet them?'

Andrew handed him a piece of paper. 'Here. They left directions. I looked online, and it seems to be an old warehouse out in the North.'

Raymond checked his watch. 'We've got under an hour to get there, so we should go now.'

Without another word, they exited the house, heading for the car. Raymond slid into the driver's seat with Tanya and Andrew climbing into the back. Raymond programmed the address into his GPS, following the directions to the industrial district and along a road that didn't look to have been used for some time. They eventually found themselves at a dilapidated warehouse, another car already waiting for them when they arrived.

'Remember the plan,' Raymond told them as he pulled the car to a stop. He handed the keys back to Andrew. 'Drive straight to Melbourne.'

'We will,' Andrew said, the three of them sliding out of the car.

As they approached the other car, they saw four men get out, one approaching them. He raised a hand for them to stop.

'We're here for you, Barry,' the man said. 'We can do this the easy way or the hard way. If you come peacefully, you can have the girl back, and we won't disturb your little friends again.'

'I understand,' Raymond said. 'Show us Olivia.'

The man gestured to his comrades, one of them opening the car door and reaching inside. After a second, five-year-old Olivia appeared, looking confused but happy to see her parents.

'Okay,' Raymond said. 'Send her across, and I'll come peacefully.'

'No,' the man said. 'We're doing this on our terms. First you, and then the girl.'

'Together then,' Raymond said.

The man considered this before gesturing for his comrade to let Olivia go. With a little shove, he pushed her toward her parents, Olivia not hesitating to run toward them. Raymond stepped forward, Olivia giving him a confused look as she passed him and ran into her mother's arms. Raymond smiled as he watched before approaching the men, one of which reached out and grabbed his arm firmly as if to prevent him from escaping.

They led him to the car without a word and pushed him into the back seat. He cast one last look over at his friends before he climbed in, finding himself wedged between two of the men. The men wordlessly got into the car, started it up and drove away. The man held out a hand toward him.

'Your phone.'

Raymond reached into his pocket and pulled it out, handing it to the man. He felt uneasy because it was his last connection to the outside world. He looked at his friends as the car passed them, silently willing them to hurry and get to Melbourne. Raymond knew Kingston wouldn't be happy with the situation, but he would know how to handle it. Surely.

24

LUCILLE WAS PACING in the lounge when she heard the door to the bunker open. She looked up, racing to the staircase, only to feel surprise wash over her as she recognised Andrew and Tanya, the former holding their little girl in his arms, coming down the stairs. She glanced behind them, seeing no one was there, panic spreading through her.

'Where's Raymond?'

'They took him,' Tanya said, her voice cracking slightly at those words.

'They traded Olivia for him,' Andrew further explained. 'He sent us here. Said we need to contact Kingston.'

Lucille didn't even want to know how Tanya and Andrew knew about Kingston, let alone that they knew about the bunker's location. Nobody outside the select few was supposed to know, yet Raymond had told his friends everything. Lucille was going to have his ear when he finally came back.

Lucille walked over to the phone, picking it up and speed dialling Kingston's number. After two rings, he picked up.

'*Hello?*'

'It's Lucille,' she said. 'You need to get over here. It's an emergency.'

'*Is Raymond okay?*'

'No. Just get here quickly.'

Without another word, she hung up.

* * * * *

'Something's happened,' Kingston said, grabbing his coat off the back of his chair. He looked over at Rita. 'I'm heading to Melbourne. I want you to locate Jake and Sydney and meet me over there.'

'Yes, sir,' Rita said, standing from her desk. 'What should I tell them?'

'Just say it's urgent,' he said, disappearing out the door.

* * * * *

It was hard to track where they were going from the car's back seat, with two men wedged in on either side of him. The car windows were darkened to what had to be a barely legal tint, and even if he could see, Raymond knew he probably didn't know where he was. For all the time he'd spent in Geelong, it had usually been in the suburb where Tanya and Andrew lived, as well as the CBD, whereas he'd spent zero time in the industrial region of the city.

The car turned into another warehouse, coming to a stop just inside the large doors which closed behind it. The two men beside him got out of the car, one reaching in after him to grab and pull him by the arm. Raymond let himself be pulled out, stumbling slightly as they virtually dragged him out of the backseat and into the warehouse.

He cast his gaze around, finding most of the warehouse empty. There was an office just to one side where he was being led. The men didn't talk as they pulled him into the room. Upon entering, he spotted a few more men and, interestingly enough, a single dark-haired woman. She seemed smug at seeing him, a smile creeping onto her lips as she approached.

'Raymond Barry,' she said, stopping before him. 'I've been waiting for you.'

'Well, I'm here,' he said. 'I take it you're behind all of this.'

'Far from it,' she said, shaking her head. 'I'm just following orders like everyone else.' She gestured toward a seat in the middle of the room. 'Sit.'

Raymond hesitated, one man pushing him firmly in the back and propelling him toward the chair. He reluctantly sat down, unsurprised when two men stepped forward and handcuffed him to the chair; Raymond, for the first time, noticed that the chair itself seemed to be screwed into the ground.

'You know who I am,' Raymond said as the men moved away. 'Can I get a name?'

'Given how well we will be acquainted, I see no harm in that.' The woman said. 'Kendra. My name is Kendra.'

'No last name to go with that?' Raymond asked.

'There is, but you have no need for it,' she said, gesturing for the men to leave. She came to stand before Raymond, looking down at him and smirking. 'My employer has a series of requests regarding information that he would like you to provide. I'm here to get that information. How I get it will depend entirely upon you. We will start things the easy way.' She bent down, bringing herself face-to-face with him. 'Where is the location of the keys?'

Raymond chuckled. 'I will not tell you that.'

'Okay, let's try again.' She straightened, walking over to a nearby table. 'What is the code for finding the keys?'

Raymond shook his head. 'As I said – I can't tell you that.'

'I'm trying to do this the easy way, Mr Barry,' Kendra said, picking up something from the table and making her way back to him. 'Don't make me ask you again.'

'Keep asking all you want,' Raymond said, trying to see what was in her hand. 'They're not answers I can give.'

'I see.' Kendra shifted, Raymond finally seeing that she held a switch in her hands. She drew her arm back and then swiftly brought the switch down across the side of his head and sent his glasses flying. The blow stung, making his ear ring, and he could feel a welt already rising on his neck and face. 'Tell me about the keys.'

'Go to hell,' Raymond hissed.

The next blow came from the other side, more brutal than the first, and this time drawing blood. 'I can keep doing this all day,' Kendra said.

'So can I,' Raymond said, gazing at her outline with his fuzzy vision. He barely registered her moving before the blow hit where the first had. 'I will not tell you anything.'

'We shall see,' Kendra said. 'We shall see.'

* * * * *

Kingston stepped through the portal, surprised to see Andrew and Tanya standing there with Lucille. Casting his gaze around, he spotted little Olivia seated at the table, the little girl watching them as she swung her feet. Kingston joined the adults, coming to stand before them.

'What's going on?' He asked. 'Where's Raymond?'

'Gone,' Lucille answered, a slight waver in her voice.

'Where?' Kingston asked, a warning in his voice.

'A group of men kidnapped Olivia,' Andrew explained. 'Raymond offered himself in exchange for getting her back.'

'What?' Kingston felt as if someone had torn his heart out. 'When?'

'About an hour ago,' Andrew said. 'In Geelong. We drove straight here afterwards.'

'I don't understand why?' Lucille hissed. 'Why not go to the police?'

'They specifically asked for Raymond,' Andrew said. 'That if we ever wanted to see Olivia again, he had to come.'

'But why would they go for Olivia?' Kingston asked.

'Probably because…' Tanya said, glancing at Lucille. 'Raymond's her father.'

'What?!' Lucille and Kingston said together.

'Her biological father,' Andrew explained further.

'I have a granddaughter,' Lucille said in awe, casting her gaze toward Olivia as if seeing her for the first time.

'Why would he keep something like that secret?' Kingston asked.

'Because he wants her to have a normal life,' Tanya answered. 'He wants her to go to school, have friends, have a childhood. All the things he never got to have because of being the Keeper.'

'Wait, you know about all that?' Kingston asked.

Andrew and Tanya nodded.

'Raymond was not supposed to tell anyone,' Lucille growled, looking at Kingston. 'I made it clear to him it was to stay in the family. When he gets back, I'll make sure he's punished.'

'We'll worry about that later,' Kingston said, glancing back as Jake, Rita, and Sydney walked through the portal to join them in the bunker. 'Right now, we need to focus on finding Raymond.'

'Raymond's gone?' Sydney asked.

'He traded himself for his daughter,' Kingston said.

'Hang on, Raymond has a daughter?' Rita asked.

'Wow,' Jake said in awe. 'Now that's one hell of a secret. Even I didn't find that one.'

'Is that her?' Sydney asked, gesturing to Olivia.

'That's her,' Tanya confirmed.

'Oh, yes, before I forget.' Kingston gestured to Andrew and Tanya. 'These are Andrew and Tanya, Raymond's friends. That is Olivia, who is Raymond's daughter.' He gestured behind him. 'This is Rita, Sydney and Jake.'

The group exchanged greetings. Lucille stared at Olivia with wide eyes, the little girl fidgeting beneath her gaze.

'Perhaps it would be better if Olivia wasn't here for the discussion,' Rita suggested.

'I'll take her,' Lucille said. 'I have some books in my office that she might like.'

'I'll come with you,' Tanya said.

Tanya and Lucille collected Olivia, taking her down the corridor to Lucille's office. When they were gone, Kingston turned to Andrew.

'What can you tell us?'

'There were four men,' Andrew told them. 'They met us at an

abandoned warehouse. I got the registration plate of their car, if that helps.'

'It might,' Jake said. 'I can try to track the car. If you can, give me the warehouse address as well.'

Andrew handed him a piece of paper. 'This is where we had to go.'

'Did they say anything?' Kingston asked.

Andrew shook his head. 'All they said is they wanted Raymond.'

'Why would they want him?' Sydney asked. 'Do they think he will give them the location of the keys?'

'He won't,' Kingston said firmly. 'I know Raymond. He's stubborn and will take that secret to the grave.'

'It won't come to that,' Jake said.

'No, it won't.' Kingston turned to Jake. 'Get on it. See what you can find out.'

'You got it, boss,' Jake said, turning on his heel and heading back through the portal.

'Until Jake finds something, there is little for the rest of us to do,' Kingston said. 'For now, we can only wait.'

25

RAYMOND FELT HIS whole body shuddering uncontrollably in the night's cold air. Several hours ago, Kendra had poured a bucket of water over him and opened the window to the cold air, and now he was probably developing hypothermia.

There was a noise to the side. He turned his head, hearing the door to the office open. Kendra stepped in, and from how she held her arm, he knew she was on the phone. He couldn't tell for sure because of his poor eyesight. He could only make out shapes and colours, but not definite objects.

'Yes, sir,' she said, moving into the room. 'I will do it now.'

Without another word, she hung up, put the phone in her pocket, and turned toward him.

'You're looking rather cold,' she said. 'I have a nice warm blanket, dry clothes and a hot cup of coffee for you if you just tell me what I want to know.'

'Go. To. Hell,' Raymond said through his chattering teeth.

'You're making this hard on yourself,' Kendra said, picking something up from the table. She came back toward him. 'All you have to do is answer my questions, and I will let you go. That's all there is to it.'

He didn't dignify her with an answer.

'Have it your way,' she said. She reached out, grabbing one of his hands and spreading his fingers. 'I understand that your line of work requires you to use your hands. Now I would start snapping fingers, but unfortunately, I am under orders not to do any permanent damage, so we will go with something a little simpler.'

He frowned as he felt something grip his fingernail, only for the pain to blaze through his hand as she began pulling. He gritted his teeth hard to keep from screaming as she slowly and painfully ripped his fingernail free from its bed. The pain was unlike anything he had felt before, going up his arm into his chest.

'That's one,' she said. 'I have nine more to go, and then I start on the feet.' She came around to face him. 'Of course, you could give me the information, and we can end it.'

He shook his head, breathing hard through gritted teeth.

'Very well,' she said, picking up the pliers. 'Which finger should we do next?'

* * * * *

'I'm afraid the number plate was stolen,' Jake told them as they made their way up the stairs toward Kingston's office. 'It's from a 2004 Elantra Hatchback, which is nothing like the car that Andrew and Tanya described.'

'Right,' Kingston said, reaching out to open the door to his quarters. 'So that's a dead end.'

'Hello, Kingston.'

Kingston looked up sharply at the voice, instantly spotting the man seated behind his desk with his feet on the surface. Anger flashed through Kingston at the sight of him, his hands balling into fists. 'You.'

The man held a hand up as Kingston stepped toward him. 'Easy, big guy. I'm your only chance of getting Raymond back alive.'

'Who is he?' hissed Lucille as she slid into the room behind Kingston and the on-edge Jake.

'I see the gang's all here,' the man said, his feet dropping as he leaned forward. 'Come in, come in. Don't forget to close the door. Wouldn't want people to hear, after all.'

Sydney and Rita joined the others in the room, Rita closing the door behind her and turning the lock. She glanced toward her desk, judging the fastest way to reach it and retrieve her weapon should things come to blows. Sydney's eyes widened in surprise.

'Marcus?' she asked.

Kingston stared at her. 'You know him?'

'Kind of,' she admitted.

'Why don't you take a seat?' the man said to Kingston. He waited, eyes never moving from Kingston, who stood fast, arms crossed over his chest. 'Or you can stay standing. It's your room, after all.'

'Who are you, exactly?' Jake asked, sticking fast to Kingston's side and ready to follow his lead. 'I've seen you around the hotel, but you never come in. You just stand there and look in.'

'Yes, formalities, how rude of me,' the man smiled. 'Marcus Connolly. There's no need for you to introduce yourselves, as I know who you all are.' He gestured to Kingston. 'Been a while, hasn't it? July 1966, when we last saw each other, wasn't it? That was quite the eventful day.'

'Indeed,' Kingston growled.

'July '66?' Lucille breathed. 'You mean…'

'Your grandparents,' Marcus said, his smile never waning. 'Put up quite the fight.'

'You were there,' she said, eyes flicking toward Kingston. 'How could you be there?'

'Oh, he didn't tell you,' Marcus smiled at her. 'He was the only survivor. Disappeared just as things were getting interesting.'

Kingston faltered slightly under Lucille's accusing glare. 'Your grandfather pushed me through a portal and locked the door behind me. By the time I got back to Werribee…'

'Dead. All of them. And the Manor burned to the ground. Not that the authorities ever found any bodies.' Marcus shrugged it off.

'I clean up my messes. And it wasn't quick, either. They fought quite the fight and never gave up the secret of finding the keys.'

'Wait, that's over fifty years ago,' Sydney said. 'How can you both have been there?'

Marcus looked at her, pointing toward Kingston. 'How old do you think he is? Honestly.'

Sydney frowned, confused. 'Mid to late thirties.'

Marcus chuckled. 'You're about one hundred and thirty years off.'

'What do you want?' Kingston cut in. 'Why have you taken Raymond?'

'The reason has never changed,' Marcus said, returning his attention to the man. 'The portal. I want access to it and the keys.'

'Not going to happen,' Kingston said.

'What have you to gain from protecting them? All they've ever done is hurt you.' Marcus leaned forward, resting his elbows on the desk's surface. 'Just give me access and the key back home.'

Kingston frowned. 'The key home? That was destroyed long ago.'

'Says who? Your father?' Marcus gave him a measured look. 'Then how did you come through?'

Kingston didn't answer.

'Don't you miss it?' Marcus asked. 'The world where we were gods and had so much power and authority. Where people waited on us. Here we're just… common, but back there–'

'Your memory is different to mine,' Kingston growled. 'I remember death, disease, famine, the crush of overpopulation and choking on the polluted air.'

'That's because you were stupid enough to go down to the lower levels,' Marcus said. 'Among those animals.'

'They were people,' Kingston said.

'They were a burden that sucked resources away from those who deserved them,' Marcus said. 'And the same thing is happening here.'

'Wait, what do you mean "home"?' Sydney asked.

'It never crossed your mind that the portals, keys, and all of their… technology… aren't human?' Marcus chuckled. 'I believe you refer to it as "alien",' he said, making quote marks in the air.

'Alien? You mean you're an…' Sydney blinked. 'And Kingston…'

'Technically, so are you. You have it in your blood. You're a half-breed,' Marcus sneered. 'Kingston likes to surround himself with half-breeds. You could say it's his "thing".'

'It's how you can use the portal,' Kingston explained. 'And why others can't.'

'I'm part alien?' Jake asked. 'Cool.'

'Let's get back to the subject at hand,' Marcus said. 'Let me put it like this.' He leaned forward. 'If you want to see your boyfriend again, alive and in one piece, I suggest you cooperate with my people.'

'That will not happen,' Kingston said. 'And you can forget about Raymond giving you anything. He'd die before he gave up the secret of the keys.'

'If that's what it comes to,' Marcus said with a shrug. He stood. 'I've already waited for two generations of Barrys. I can wait for another. Can you?'

'What have you done with my son?' Lucille growled.

Marcus ignored her as he came around the desk, stopping briefly in front of the glowering Kingston. 'The ball is in your court, Kingston. Raymond cracks; I let him go. You crack; I let him go. All it takes is for one of you to cooperate, and the two of you can live happily ever after. But the clock is ticking, Kingston.'

'We're just going to let him go?' Jake asked, glancing at Kingston for direction.

'For now,' Kingston growled, eyes never leaving Marcus as he stepped over to the door with a smirk.

'Tick tock, Mr Kingston,' he said as he exited the doorway. 'Tick tock.'

The second he was gone, Kingston rounded on Sydney. 'You have a lot of explaining to do.'

'I didn't know he was involved,' Sydney admitted, eyes wide. 'He's just a guy I kept running into at the supermarket.'

'So he's been following you?' Jake asked. 'You should have said something!'

'I didn't realise,' she repeated. She was shaking, her skin pale. 'I thought he was just trying to be friendly.'

'What did you tell him?' Lucille asked. 'Did you tell him about the portals?'

'No, of course not,' Sydney defended. 'I'd tell no one.'

Kingston sighed, running a hand over his face as he stepped away to fall into his seat at the desk. 'We are in a terrible situation here.'

'So there's nothing we can do?' Rita asked, settling down on the couch.

'No,' Kingston said. 'Not unless Raymond breaks.'

'Which he won't,' Lucille said. 'I know my boy. He's a true Barry. He'll die with the secret.'

'We can't let that happen,' Jake said with a determined look. 'I'll keep looking. There's bound to be some way of tracing them. I'll start by looking up this Marcus guy.'

'He works in surveillance,' Sydney said. 'I know they have a contract with a local pub.'

'That's a start,' Jake said, gripping her by the arm. 'I'm going to need to pick your brain. You need to tell me everything that you know about him.'

'I can do that,' Sydney said with a nod.

'Meanwhile, we need to have a word about 1966,' Lucille said, glaring at Kingston, who gave her a tired look in return.

'You all do that,' Rita said. 'I'll keep the hotel running while you're all busy.'

'Sydney,' Kingston said, his voice measured. 'We're going to need to discuss the company you keep.'

Sydney nodded, a look of guilt on her face. Jake distracted her, pulling her toward the doorway. She gave Kingston one last look before they headed outside, leaving the others behind.

26

THERE WERE NO words for the amount of pain throbbing through his body. Kendra had kept her promise and slowly yanked out every one of his nails, only stopping to ask him to give up the information she wanted. He had stubbornly refused, reminding himself that it was his role as Keeper that kept him from voicing the answer despite how close he had come on a couple of occasions to cracking. He'd be letting everyone down if he broke, so he would continue to persevere.

Kendra had left him alone again in the cold. He knew he was probably suffering from hypothermia, especially when he factored in pain. The adrenaline had kept him warm for some time, but that had worn off hours ago. He had lost all semblance of time, but he could hear birds chirping outside the windows, so he knew morning couldn't be too far away.

Through the night, he had heard cars coming and going, leading him to wonder just how many people there were working for the man in charge. His poor vision made it hard for him to see, but his hearing heightened. What one sense lacks, another makes up for. He kept listening for footsteps on the concrete floor; though there had been some, none had approached the door to the office.

Raymond wiggled his fingers, pain shooting up his arm at the move. The blood on his hands had clotted and had cracked, causing an inching feeling, echoing the same feeling on his face and neck. He longed for a drink of water, but he had a feeling that none would come soon. He sighed, trying to shift in his chair to a more comfortable position, but the chair was one of those designed not to be sat in for long periods. Already his back ached, and his legs had started to go numb.

All Raymond could do was sit and wait, wondering what Kendra would do next.

* * * * *

'Kingston, you've been up all night. You really need to get some sleep,' Lucille told him.

'I'm fine,' Kingston said, sipping from his cup of coffee. He winced slightly at the bitterness, longing for the cafe to be open so that he didn't have to resort to the instant coffee in his kitchen. 'I can't sleep while Raymond's out there somewhere.'

Lucille sighed, casting her gaze around the room and taking in where Rita and Jake were asleep on the couch and chair, knowing that Sydney was asleep in Kingston's bedroom. Lucille herself had slept for roughly an hour, sheerly out of exhaustion and the adrenaline wearing off. Kingston, however, had been awake all night. Sometimes he had been pacing, other times, he had searched online to narrow down where Raymond could be.

'You know, I'm surprised,' Kingston said, dropping into his office chair.

'Surprised by what?' Lucille asked.

'By the lack of questions,' Kingston said. 'I was expecting questions about what Marcus said, but no one seems to ask them.'

'They have other things on their mind,' Lucille said. 'What specifically were you expecting them to ask about?'

'The alien thing for a start,' Kingston said. 'The age thing.'

'The age thing isn't of a surprise to me,' Lucille said. 'I remember you from when I was five.'

'That could have been my father,' Kingston said.

'No,' Lucille shook her head. 'You are identical to the man in my memory. My parents have also long suspected your true age. You could say it's a Barry conspiracy.'

'Did Raymond know of the conspiracy?' Kingston asked.

Lucille nodded.

'Funny,' Kingston said. 'He never said anything.'

'It wasn't our place to say,' Lucille said. 'We simply didn't discuss it.'

'I'm also surprised you haven't commented on the 'boyfriend' thing,' Kingston said, observing her.

'Also, not a surprise,' Lucille said. 'I've known for a long time.'

'Did Raymond tell you?'

'No. A mother simply knows these things.'

'It's only the worst kept secret in the hotel,' Rita said from where she was lying on the couch. 'I think even Dot, Lizzie and Kian know.'

'I see,' Kingston said, narrowing his eyes. 'Yet none of you ever said a thing.'

'It wasn't any of our business,' Rita said, sitting up. 'What you and Raymond do in your own time is your problem. Why do you think I never came in early?'

'So you never caught us,' Kingston guessed, Rita nodding. 'Seems to me that everyone knew about my secrets.'

'Not all of them,' Lucille said. 'We don't know your real name.'

'Kingston *is* my real name,' Kingston said.

'I mean your full name,' Lucille said.

'I never tell that to anyone,' Kingston replied.

'Did you tell Raymond?' Lucille asked.

Kingston didn't answer. Instead, he looked down at his desk and frowned. 'I'm guessing the alien thing was also not surprising to you.'

'The portals aren't exactly of this world,' Rita said. 'There's no other technology like them.'

'You're right. They're normal methods of transport on my planet,' Kingston said.

'What's your planet called?' Rita asked.

'Lierdan,' Kingston answered. 'It was a planet not too unlike this one; only it was vastly overpopulated. Resources were running out, so my people sought out a new planet to move to, and during the search, found this one. The scouting parties set up the first portals, and our people joined in the effort when it was found that a 'new world' had been discovered and was being colonised. That's when most of the portals were constructed. The decision to create one central portal was made, and ultimately the decision to hide the keys was also made.'

'But why were the keys hidden?' Lucille asked.

'Because some of those who came from Lierdan didn't simply want to settle on the new planet; they wanted to rule it. There were fights, and the decision was ultimately made that Redmond Barry and my father, George Strickland Kingston, would take on the roles of Keeper and Protector and place the keys into hiding. Someone killed both of them for their roles. The rest, you know.'

'But how did you become Protector?' Rita asked. 'Were you always meant to inherit it?'

'Yes,' Kingston nodded. 'I was the last person to come to the new planet from Lierdan before the home portal key was lost. I came through understanding that I would step in should something happen to my father, as he was already under threat. The problem is, he died before he could finish training me, just like Redmond died before he could train his replacement.'

'They died within a week of each other,' Lucille said. 'Redmond and George.'

Kingston nodded. '1880. Redmond died on November twenty-third, and my father died on November twenty-sixth.'

'Within three days of each other,' Rita said, awed.

Kingston nodded again. 'My father died at sea. Redmond officially died of an illness. I have my suspicions about both their deaths.'

'Does George Strickland Kingston's other family know about you?' Rita asked.

Kingston shook his head. 'They kept me secret when he was alive. Even today, I pass the name off as a sheer coincidence.'

'What of your mother?' Lucille asked. 'Did she come through the portals?'

'No,' Kingston shook his head. 'My mother died before I came here. Of the many things wrong with Lierdan, one was that it was rife with disease. Even though my family were among the world's elite, my mother set about doing charity work to help those beneath us. She became ill with one of the many plagues by doing that charity work, and it took her life.'

'I'm sorry,' Lucille said.

'She knew the risks,' Kingston said. 'She died for what she believed in and improved many lives. I was planning on continuing her work when my father, who was already on Earth, sent for me to join him. I didn't even hesitate and was able to spend a couple of months with him before he, too, died.'

'How did they choose who came to Earth?' Rita asked. 'Was it random?'

Kingston shook his head. 'They selected people from among the Elite class. They gave you a choice, and if you had family already on Earth, it increased your chances of being selected. Because of the role my father had as the Protector, it meant that I could go.'

'Do you have any siblings?' Lucille asked.

'No,' Kingston shook his head again, partly to clear it, as his mind felt foggy. 'There was a firm 'one child' policy on Lierdan because of the overpopulation. That's why many of those who came to Earth had children.'

'Do you know of anyone else from your home planet?' Rita asked.

'You mean personally? Again, no.' Kingston shrugged. 'As I said, I was the last one to come across. The only people I knew were my father and Redmond, and they both died not long after I came across. I was also supposed to meet the Overseer, but he vanished long before I came to Earth. I'm guessing he's probably dead as well.'

'Overseer?' Rita asked.

'The person who oversaw the whole operation of moving the portals to a single location,' Kingston explained, taking a long drink from his coffee and frowning as his stomach ached. 'He was essentially the boss of my father and Redmond, but he vanished without a trace. I don't even have a name, and my father and Redmond only ever mentioned him in passing.'

'So he could still be out there,' Lucille said.

'He could be,' Kingston said, frowning as he felt a slight sense of vertigo. He put it down to his lack of sleep. 'It could well be that he just wanted nothing more to do with the portals once his job was done. But maybe he was the first one to die.'

'Are you all right?' Rita asked, frowning.

'Just a little dizzy,' Kingston said, putting his coffee on his desk and slipping into his chair. He frowned as his skin warmed up, a tingling extending through his body. 'I'm probably just tired.'

'You've gone pale,' Lucille said, coming toward him.

'It's nothing, I'm sure,' he said, his stomach twisting. The corners of his vision greyed out. 'I think I need to lie down.'

'Take the couch,' Rita said, standing.

Kingston stood and came toward her, stumbling slightly as he came. He barely reached the couch, the buzzing in his ears increasing to a loud screech. White spots appeared before his eyes as his stomach cramped. He dropped onto the couch heavily as it felt like his legs could no longer take his weight, Kingston lying down just as the darkness took him.

* * * * *

Raymond looked up as he heard the door open, turning his head slightly to listen. From the footsteps, he knew it was Kendra before she came around in front of him. She was alone this time, although he knew that there were likely goons outside the door that she could call on if needed.

'Good day, Mr Barry,' Kendra said, pulling up a chair and sitting down. 'How are we feeling today? Talkative?'

He didn't answer.

'I see,' she said, reaching out to run her fingertips along the welts on the side of his face. 'You realise this will only keep getting worse the longer you remain silent?'

He knew it would. Raymond half expected her to break his kneecaps, but he kept his mouth shut. He was prepared to take the information to the grave, and he felt she was realising it.

'Okay, we'll keep doing this your way.' She said, standing again. She walked back to the door and spoke to someone outside. He heard footsteps before seeing a man enter with a tub, placing it at Raymond's feet. He frowned as the man grabbed his feet and put them in the tub; two more men entered with buckets of water and filled the tub.

When the next man entered with a car battery and jumper cables, it clicked just what was about to happen. The tub was made of metal and filled with water, and his feet were in the tub. There was only one way this was going to go.

'I'm sure you realise what's about to happen,' Kendra said as the men left the room. She picked up the jumper cables and hooked them up to the battery. 'We don't have to do this. All you have to do is tell me about the keys. Tell me what the code is to finding their location.'

Raymond gritted his teeth, preparing himself for what was about to come.

'You certainly are a stubborn one,' Kendra commented, picking up the other end of the jumper leads and hovering them over the tub handles. 'I've had men break for less than you. I admire your tenacity.'

That was worth very little, Raymond thought to himself. He let out a shaky breath, willing her to hurry and get on with it. As if sensing what he was thinking, Kendra connected the cables.

* * * * *

Sydney found it hard to focus on her job. She knew that part of being a hotel manager required her to be one hundred per cent alert and prepared at all times, but it wasn't easy with everything going on. She regretted having ever discovered the portals, longing to be naïve as to everything that was happening.

Lunchtime took forever to roll around, and Sydney moved like a zombie to the cafe when it did. Simon brought her a strong cup of coffee without her having to say a word. Sydney thanked him. She wondered what Simon would think of it all. He must have seen that something was bothering her, as he was very good at reading people.

'You look worn ragged, dear,' Dorothy said as Sydney sat at a nearby table.

'Is everything all right?' Elizabeth asked.

'Just a lot going on,' Sydney said, shaking her head and smiling at them.

'It's certainly got young Jake busy,' Dorothy commented. 'He barely even stopped in. Just grabbed his coffee and left before he had even arrived.'

'Do you want to talk about it?' Elizabeth asked.

Sydney shook her head again. 'A lot of it is confidential,' she admitted.

'Surely, there is something you can comment on.'

'Well,' Sydney thought for a second, then sighed. 'Mr Kingston is sick.'

'Oh, the poor thing,' Dorothy said. 'Is it the flu? That's been going around this year.'

'It has, yes,' Sydney agreed. 'Mr Barry has it.'

'No doubt where Mr Kingston caught it,' Elizabeth commented, Dorothy shushing her.

'It must be hard having someone sick in the hotel,' Dorothy said. 'You must be so worried about it spreading.'

'Miss Rita doesn't also have it, does she?' Elizabeth asked. 'I haven't seen her this morning, not even for her coffee.'

'No, she's fine,' Sydney said. 'But she has to work extra hard with her boss being unwell.'

'I imagine she is,' Elizabeth said. She leaned toward Sydney. 'I dare say you should try to avoid Mr Kingston's rooms.'

'I will try,' Sydney said.

* * * * *

Rita peeked in the doorway to Kingston's bedroom, frowning as she saw his eyes were half-open. She stepped inside, coming over to where he was lying on the bed.

'How are you feeling?' Rita asked.

'Like a truck hit me,' Kingston said. He rolled over so that he could face her properly. 'I wish I knew what was wrong with me. I never get sick.'

'I have my suspicions,' Rita said. She sat on the edge of the bed. 'I went through your symptoms in my books, and I think you've been poisoned.'

'Poisoned?' Kingston said, sitting up slightly. 'How?'

'I'm guessing that when Marcus was here, he laced something into your food,' Rita said.

'The only thing I had was my coffee… oh.' Kingston frowned. 'It tasted more bitter than usual.'

'That's what it is then,' Rita said. 'I'll throw it out.'

Kingston pushed himself up, pausing as vertigo washed over him and his stomach cramped at the move. 'I can't afford this,' he said, shaking his head. 'We should focus on finding Raymond.'

'Jake is still working on it,' Rita told him. 'He says that it's difficult, though. Most of the factories in the area either have closed-circuit security or no video at all.' She sighed, shrugging. 'He's traced the car some of the way, but it's going to take a while.'

'We might not have 'a while',' Kingston told her. 'We don't know what they're doing to him.'

'He's stubborn,' Rita said. 'I don't think he will crack.'

'That's what I'm worried about,' Kingston said, lying back down.

27

Rita had convinced Sydney to go home and get a change of clothing. Sydney had been reluctant to leave the hotel, but knew Rita was right. She couldn't just keep wearing the same thing. Sydney didn't want to go, though. She was worried about Kingston, especially now that Rita had told them she suspected he had been poisoned.

Sydney still felt an immense weight on her shoulders about the whole situation with Marcus. He had played her. No doubt their running into each other so often was far from being 'accidental'. She tried to work out how he could have done it. How had he known to be at that cafe at the right time? How did he know which pub she was going to so it could have a security failure? It all made her worry that eyes had been on her since she had arrived. It wouldn't surprise her if that were the case.

She stepped out of the elevator and onto her floor, looking for her key as she headed down the corridor. Rounding the corner, she stopped dead as she realised someone was standing outside her door, waiting for her.

Marcus.

Anger flashed through her at the sight of him. He looked up, a small smile on his face. She should have known he knew where she lived. He almost looked a little smug at seeing her. He didn't seem like the kind man she had met in the supermarket anymore. Now he was just a manipulative creep in her eyes. One that was hurting her friends.

'Hello, Sydney,' he said with a serene smile as he pushed himself off the door. 'You don't look happy to see me.'

Sydney shoved her keys back into her pocket and stalked over to him, bringing her hand up and slapping him hard across the face.

He barely even flinched, bringing a hand up to touch his reddening cheek gingerly. 'I guess I deserved that.'

'How long have you been following me?' she demanded.

'Since you first went through the portal,' Marcus admitted. 'Word got back to me that they saw you in Melbourne, so I knew you were let in on the little secret.'

'I wasn't exactly 'let in',' she admitted. She narrowed her eyes. 'That man that went through and died. He was yours?'

'Yes,' Marcus admitted.

'And you just let them die?' she accused. 'You had to have known that would happen.'

'Yes and no,' he said. 'I told him to get the key card. I didn't tell him to try for the portal door. He took it upon himself to get the journals. He paid the price, of course.'

Sydney wasn't entirely sure that she believed him. After all, this man had been lying to her this whole time, so how was she to know what was truth and what wasn't?

'Look, shall we go inside?' he asked, gesturing to her door.

'There is no way in hell I'm letting you into my apartment,' Sydney hissed.

Marcus paused for a moment and then turned back to face her fully. 'So we're doing this here?'

'Honestly, you should leave,' Sydney said. 'I don't want to see your face.'

'Even if I can bring back Raymond?' Marcus asked. 'If I can cure Kingston?'

'So you *did* poison him,' Sydney said.

'Yes,' he answered, a small smile on his lips. 'That was beneficial information you gave me, by the way. About the relationship between Raymond and Kingston. I'm certainly going to use it to my advantage.'

Sydney felt guilt wash over her, but she pushed it down. She'd worry about that later. 'What are you playing at?'

'Simple,' Marcus said. 'Raymond gives me the information, or Kingston dies.'

'What information?' she asked. 'The keys?'

'Their location, yes,' Marcus said with a nod. 'The keys that have already been collected. Preferably the journals and the code to decipher the location of other keys.'

'How do you know about the journals?' Sydney asked.

'It was a rumour,' Marcus said, his smile widening. 'Thanks for confirming it.'

Sydney kicked herself. He was still manipulating her, and she hated it. She knew she would need to be even more careful with what she said around him. He was fishing for information. Still, there was one thing she wanted to know. 'Why are you here?' she asked.

'Because I'm offering you a chance to rescue them both,' Marcus said. 'I'm guessing it's Raymond you have a crush on, right? He has a charm and is very pretty to look at. He might not be as flirtatious as Kingston, but he has a way of getting under your skin. Right?'

How would he even know what Kingston and Raymond were like? He must have been watching them for some time now. She hated to think how long. 'You still haven't told me why you're here,' she said.

'Like I said – giving you a chance to rescue them,' he said. 'All I want is one key. Just one. I don't care about the others.'

'Then why do you want the journals?' she asked. 'And the code to decipher them if you just want one key?'

'In case it's missing,' Marcus said. 'I don't know if the original Barry and Kingston hid it or not. A key this important, I would keep safe and not risk hiding away, so I want you to search Kingston's rooms and possibly even the Barry residence for it.'

'What's so special about this key?' she asked.

'It's the key home,' he explained. 'That's all I want. To go home.'

'To your home planet?' Sydney asked.

'Exactly,' he said. 'I grow tired of this planet. My family might not have been of high status on our home planet, but we still lived a life better than this. I didn't have to work with the dregs of society to live.'

'You were rich?' Sydney asked.

'Of course. All the elites were,' Marcus said. 'They worshipped us. Everyone below us wanted to be us. Of course, they couldn't, but they always wanted the chance to live just a little better.'

'Kingston said your planet was dying,' Sydney said. 'Overcrowded and polluted.'

'Not where we lived,' Marcus said. 'We had fresh air. There were servants. We had room to move. The lessers might have been overcrowded and living in their own waste, but not us. We had everything we needed.'

'So you're a pompous dickhead,' Sydney said. 'Who looks down on everyone because you were born with a silver spoon in your mouth.'

'More a golden spoon,' Marcus corrected. 'Everyone who came through the portal was the same. From among the elites, we were all chosen. We were builders, scientists, academics, and technicians. We were the best.'

'What were you?' Sydney asked.

Marcus hesitated a moment. 'My father brought me through.'

'So you were just a spoiled child,' Sydney concluded. 'He probably wanted a better life for you.'

'Working?' Marcus spat. 'He made me work.'

'Welcome to life,' Sydney said. 'Everyone works.'

'Not me,' Marcus said. 'I hate this life. All I want is to go home.'

'And if you get the key you want, you'll let Raymond go?' Sydney asked. 'And give the antidote to Kingston?'

'Yes,' he promised.

Sydney hesitated. She knew they were in a critical situation, but if all he wanted was a single key that would make him go away, then there was a chance to rescue Kingston and Raymond. 'And Raymond won't be injured?'

'Well, we're a bit beyond that,' he admitted.

Sydney glared at him.

'What, you think we took him just to ask him nicely?' Marcus said. 'We've been giving him plenty of opportunities.'

'And what if this key doesn't exist?' Sydney asked. 'What if I can't find it?'

'Then you better all hope that Raymond talks,' Marcus said with a tight smile. 'You're going to look?'

'I'll look,' she said, knowing it was probably a bad idea, but they were desperate. They were backed into a tight spot, and he offered an out. She'd be a fool not to take it.

'Then I better let you get to it,' Marcus said, stepping away from her door. 'If you find it, bring it to my man waiting outside the hotel. I'm sure you've seen him.'

'The man in the coat and hat,' Sydney guessed.

'That's the one,' he confirmed. 'Have a good day, Sydney.'

* * * * *

When she arrived at the hotel, she knocked on Kingston's door. There was a moment of silence before it opened. Jake appeared. He opened the door wider for her to enter, Sydney dropping her bag down beside the couch. Jake looked tired, and she wondered if he had slept at all. He headed back to Rita's desk and her computer, his laptop also open beside it. He was no doubt trying to narrow down where Raymond was.

'Where's Rita?' Sydney asked.

'In with Kingston,' Jake said. 'He's getting worse.'

Sydney swallowed and nodded. She hesitated a moment before crossing over to Kingston's desk. She started going through the drawers, finding paperwork and stationery. There was also a half-drunk bottle of whisky in one of them, which surprised her. She didn't take Kingston for being a whisky man. Then again, she still didn't know him that well.

'What are you doing?' Jake asked, frowning at her from across the room.

'Marcus just wants one key,' Sydney said, opening the next drawer.

'Wait, you've seen him?' Jake said, half-standing from his seat.

'He was waiting at my apartment,' Sydney admitted. 'He said if we get him this one key, he will cure Kingston and let Raymond go.'

'Oh hell no,' Jake said, anger flashing across his face. 'We are giving him jack shit.'

'Jake!' Sydney said, exasperated. 'It's our only chance.'

'No, Sydney,' he said firmly. 'That man is not getting *any* of the keys.'

'We can't just sit here,' Sydney said. 'If we don't, they could both die.'

'You don't know that,' Jake said.

'He's already admitted he's torturing Raymond,' Sydney said. 'And you said Kingston is getting worse.'

'That doesn't change things,' Jake said. 'We are not giving in to that terrorist's demands.'

'So we just let them die?' Sydney asked.

'No, we'll… think of something,' Jake said, looking back at his computer. 'I can do this. I can narrow down the search so we can rescue Raymond, and Rita will find a cure for Kingston.'

'But what if we don't?' Sydney asked. 'We've been given an opportunity–'

'That we are not taking,' Jake persisted.

'What's going on?' Rita asked as she stepped out of Kingston's bedroom and shut the door. 'I could hear you arguing from in there.'

'Marcus got in Sydney's head,' Jake said, annoyed.

'What?' Rita asked.

'He just wants one key,' Sydney told her. 'That's all.'

'And we're not giving it to him,' Rita said.

'Which is exactly what I said,' Jake said, an 'I told you so' look on his face.

'It's just one key,' Sydney persisted. 'And then he'll put everything right and go away.'

'We will not be the weak link,' Rita said with a firm shake of her head. 'We're giving Marcus nothing.'

Sydney guessed she could see where they were coming from, but she couldn't help but feel the moment's desperation. It was such a simple request – a single key in return for curing Kingston and letting Raymond go. She hated thinking about what was going on with Raymond. That he was being hurt made her sick.

'I just want to do something,' Sydney admitted.

'We are,' Jake said. 'By not giving in, we're doing something.'

'Exactly,' Rita agreed. 'I know it looks bad right now, but we will figure this out without giving in to that arsehole.'

'Not to mention there's no guarantee he'll do what he says,' Jake added. 'He'll probably take the key, kill Raymond, and let Kingston die.'

'That's what I believe,' Rita agreed.

They had a good point, as much as Sydney didn't want to admit it. She sighed, dropping into the seat at Kingston's desk and closing the drawer. She knew they were at an impasse. That doing what Marcus wanted might indeed not fix things.

'He just wants to go home,' Sydney told them. 'That's all.'

'And for what reason?' Jake asked. 'He could come back with more numbers and then use the portals to take over the world.'

'That is possible,' Rita said. 'We don't know where all the portals lead. They could go to highly sensitive buildings where they could get their hands on money and information and use it against us.'

Again, another good point. For all Sydney knew, Marcus could be lying about just wanting to go home to his mother. There was no way of telling, and she didn't want to be why everything ended worse than it already was.

'Okay,' she said, raising her hands in defeat. 'I won't give him the key. Not that I know where it is, anyway.'

'Or if we even have it,' Jake said.

'Kingston didn't seem to think so,' Rita pointed out.

'I don't even know where Kingston keeps the keys,' Sydney admitted, looking down at his desk.

'I think only Kingston and Raymond know that,' Rita said. 'And I know they keep them off-site. They try to keep a distance between the keys and the portals to stop people from just coming in and taking them.'

'How do you know that?' Jake asked.

'I asked,' Rita admitted. 'I thought it might be a security flaw.'

'Hell, even I didn't think of that,' Jake said. 'But it would be, yeah.'

'So basically, all we can do is sit here and do nothing,' Sydney sighed.

'We have a hotel to run,' Rita reminded her.

'I'm multitasking,' Jake admitted. 'One eye on the security, one eye on the searches to track down Raymond using the information Andrew gave me.'

'I still can't get over the fact Raymond has a kid,' Rita said, crossing the room to hover over Jake's shoulder and look down at the screen on her computer. 'How did that even happen?'

'According to Andrew, it was a drunken night,' Jake said. 'They were a threesome.'

Sydney blinked in surprise. 'Raymond?'

'Always the quiet ones.' Rita rolled her eyes. 'Considering that man's ego, it doesn't surprise me.'

'And now Raymond's with Kingston,' Sydney clarified.

They nodded.

'I'm pretty sure we already knew that,' Jake said.

Sydney felt the guilt wash over her as she remembered it was her fault that Marcus knew that. She wished now that she had said nothing to him. That she hadn't invited him out for coffee. She could just be too trusting. She should have gone with her instinct that he had been stalking her. It had seemed foolish at the time, but now she knew better; it was rather obvious.

'Look, we'll work something out,' Rita said. 'I'm looking into what poison Kingston was dosed with and how he got it. Jake's looking into finding Raymond.'

'And I'm useless,' Sydney observed.

'No,' Rita shook her head. 'We need you to put on a front that everything is fine. Keep up your position at the front desk and make sure no one makes a run for the portals. Which should be harder now that the keycard isn't kept under the desk.' She gave Jake a pointed look.

'It's safely locked up,' he assured her. 'In the security office. Fat chance they'll be able to get in there and steal it. They always staff the office.'

'Good,' Rita said. 'We just keep on carrying on. Things can't get any worse.'

'Don't jinx it,' Jake said.

Rita glared at him.

28

Raymond looked up as the door opened, barely able to keep his eyes open. He was utterly exhausted, but between the pain and sitting uncomfortably in the chair, he had found it near impossible to sleep. He had passed out sometime earlier; the pain was becoming too much for him to handle. The tub was long gone, and his clothes had finally dried out and stuck to him uncomfortably.

He heard a chair being pulled up, and raising his head; he saw Kendra sitting down in front of him.

'I see you're awake again,' she said.

He didn't answer her. It was evident that he was.

'I thought we could have a chat,' Kendra said, brushing a strand of dark hair back from her face.

It would be one-sided, Raymond thought to himself as he kept his mouth firmly closed.

'You don't need to talk,' Kendra told him, much to Raymond's surprise. 'I just have a few things to say.'

She leaned forward, bringing herself within his clear eyesight. 'I'm curious about your boyfriend, Raymond. About how much you know about him.'

Raymond didn't want to know how she knew about Kingston. They'd never publicly broadcast their relationship to everyone.

'Oh yes, I know about your boyfriend,' she said, again seeming to read his mind. 'You and Kingston have been together for what? Three years now?'

Three-and-a-half, but Raymond wasn't about to correct her. He still vividly remembered the day they had first become a couple. After months of endless flirting, Raymond had finally had enough and kissed Kingston. At first, Kingston hadn't reacted, no doubt surprised by the move, but after a moment, he had kissed Raymond back.

'Do you know Kingston has been keeping things from you?'

Of course, he knew that. Just as Raymond had been keeping things from Kingston. Even people in the most loving relationships had secrets they kept from their other half. Raymond's big secret was that Olivia was his biological daughter. As for what Kingston kept from him, he was sure the man had his reasons.

'I can tell you one secret,' Kendra said, lowering her voice. 'I can tell you he was there when your great-grandparents died.'

Not exactly a secret, as he had long had his suspicions.

'He was there because he's older than he pretends,' she continued. 'He's been on this planet for over one hundred and thirty years. Because he isn't from this planet, no, he's from another planet. Your boyfriend is an alien.'

Again, Raymond wasn't altogether surprised. It was an old Barry family tale about how the portals were alien tech and that those who had created them were of another world. It was just an old wives' tale, but there had always been clues and strange occurrences that had bolstered the stories. All Kendra was doing was confirming what he had already long known, even though Kingston had never voiced the facts himself.

'And you, of course, have your daughter,' Kendra continued. 'Who you keep secreted away from your mother and your lover.'

Mostly from his mother. He wanted Olivia to have a normal life, unlike his had been. It was one of his greatest resentments that he had grown up the way he had. He mostly blamed his mother for it and knew that if she ever found out about Olivia, she would try to do the same to her. Raymond couldn't bear the thought of it, so he kept her a secret.

Not that it mattered anymore. By now, Lucille would know about the existence of Olivia, who was hopefully safe in the underground bunker. It was the one place he had hoped Olivia would never see the inside, at least not until she was old enough to decide for herself. That was if he had lived long enough, which was why he had told Tanya and Andrew everything. That way, should something happen to him, they could pass the knowledge down to her and give her to freedom to choose her fate – a choice he had never been granted.

'What kind of relationship must you have to keep such large secrets from each other?' Kendra said, breaking his train of thought. 'That doesn't sound like a healthy relationship to me.'

Raymond disagreed. He and Kingston's relationship was perfectly healthy, even though they had been fighting of late. Kingston was way overprotective of Raymond, and he resented that. He guessed he could understand where Kingston was coming from, given the history of the Barry family and the fact that Raymond's grandparents were the only Barrys ever to survive the Keeper role, but that didn't mean that he had to like it.

'And then there is the other thing,' Kendra said, bringing Raymond's attention back to her. 'A recent development. That right now Kingston is lying in bed, sick from being poisoned.'

Say what now? That piqued Raymond's interest. He wondered how anyone could have gotten close enough to poison Kingston. Could one of them have done it? No, there was no way Rita, Jake, or Sydney would be behind it. That meant someone else had to have done it.

'My boss,' Kendra continued, 'broke into Kingston's home. Knowing how much he liked his coffee, he added a new ingredient to his jar, and sure enough, worrying about you, Kingston drank it.'

Well, that explained that. Raymond had to wonder why she was telling him this. He had a feeling he knew why.

'Of course, we have the antidote.'

There it was.

'All you have to do is tell us the information that we need, and we will give it to him,' Kendra continued. 'No questions asked. There is no way he will get better without it. If you wait too long, it could well kill him.'

So that was the latest tactic. They had worked out that they would not break him through torture, so they would use his relationship with Kingston against him. Of course, there was no way of knowing if Kendra was lying or not, and he didn't exactly trust her. He also didn't trust her to give the antidote if he gave her the information they were after.

Instead, Raymond kept his mouth shut, staring over her shoulder. He could feel her watching him as if she had expected him to react to the news. He would not give her that luxury.

'Have it your way,' Kendra eventually said, standing up from her chair. She made her way over to the doorway, pausing for a second. 'If you change your mind, you know that all you have to do is shout. Meanwhile, the longer you wait, the less chance Kingston has of surviving.'

And then she was gone.

* * * * *

'Hello, Miss Madinah.'

Sydney looked up sharply at the sound of the voice, surprised to find Kian standing before her at the hotel reception desk. 'Mr MacDowell,' she said, trying to mask her surprise. 'What can I help you with?'

'I couldn't help but overhear you talking to Dorothy and Elizabeth,' he said, his expression remaining unreadable. 'I understand that Mr Kingston is under the weather.'

'That's right, yes,' she said, wondering just what he was up to.

'Surprising, given Mr Kingston rarely gets sick.'

'It is a bit,' Sydney said. 'Although we all get sick sometimes.'

'I suppose we do,' Kian said. He reached into his bag, pulled out a flask, and placed it on the desk. 'Given how nice this establishment has been to me over the years, I thought I'd try to return the favour. I've made Mr Kingston some of my chicken soup. It has helped me in the past when I have been unwell.'

'What's in it?' Sydney asked, finding the gesture surprising.

'Nothing unusual,' Kian said. 'It's mostly made of chicken broth, but I've added a few herbs and spices for flavour. It's rather gentle on an upset stomach, and you must eat even when you are unwell.'

'Yes, you must,' Sydney agreed. She reached out and took the flask. 'Thank you.'

'You are very welcome,' Kian said, zipping his bag up again. 'Wish Mr Kingston a speedy recovery from me.'

'I will.'

29

KINGSTON WAS GETTING worse. He was spending less time awake, and when he slept, it was fitfully. He complained of stomach cramps and had now begun to vomit. As far as Rita was concerned, this was definitely poisoning. Despite knowing it had probably come from the coffee, Marcus could have tampered with anything in the apartment. She had thrown away all the food and open containers, including the tea and coffee, and made a note to buy fresh food the first chance she got. Better to be safe than sorry.

As the door opened, she looked up and saw Sydney. Rita gave her a tight smile.

'How is he?' Sydney asked as she entered the apartment and closed the door.

'Getting worse,' Rita answered truthfully. 'I've been trying to get him to drink water to flush out his system, but it doesn't seem to work.'

'I see.' Sydney set a flask on Rita's desk.

'What's this?' Rita asked, pointing to it.

'I just had Kian at my desk,' Sydney said. 'He made chicken soup for Kingston.'

'Kian?' Rita frowned. 'How does he know Kingston is unwell?'

'I was talking to Dot and Lizzie about it,' Sydney said. 'He overheard.'

'He does a lot of 'overhearing',' Rita said suspiciously. She picked up the flask, noting that it was warm to the touch. 'Did he say what was in it?'

'Mostly chicken broth,' Sydney answered. 'But he said there are some other herbs and spices in it, but it would soothe an upset stomach.'

'Right.' Rita narrowed her eyes, glancing toward the door. 'Shame Jake isn't here. He'd be the first to try some to ensure it isn't poisoned.'

'I can do it,' Sydney offered.

'Are you sure?'

Sydney nodded. 'It's the least I can do.'

Rita handed her the flask, and Sydney opened the lid. She took a sniff of the open flask. 'It smells like chicken soup.'

Using the cap as a cup, she poured a small amount into the lid, raising it to her lips. She hesitated for a second before taking a drink, then a longer one. She swallowed, feeling as if there was a lump in her throat from the nervousness, but surprised by how good the soup tasted. 'It's good.'

'No strange taste?' Rita asked.

'No, nothing like that,' Sydney said. 'It just tastes like chicken soup. Better than the instant soup that you can get.'

'Still, I would wait at least fifteen minutes before we give it to Kingston,' Rita said. 'Just to be sure.'

'Okay,' Sydney said, sitting on the couch and making herself comfortable. She felt her stomach twisting but knew it was from nerves, not the chicken soup. She pulled her phone out of her pocket and scanned the latest news headlines, absently trying to remember when there had ever been this much controversy in her life.

'Has Jake found anything?' She asked Rita.

'I haven't heard from Jake since he went back to the security office,' Rita said, returning to work on her computer. 'I assume if he had, he would have said something.'

That was true. He would have. Returning to her phone, she scrolled through her social media threads, commenting on several things and sharing a few others. She absently thought about how she needed to find more friends locally. Maybe she should ask Simon about his social media so that she could add him for a start. She wondered if Kingston himself kept up with what was happening this way as well. Was there anything like social media back on his planet?

Sydney lost track of time, only looking up when Rita called her name.

'How are you feeling?'

Sydney assessed herself. The nerves seemed to have subsided after she had distracted herself, but otherwise, she felt fine. 'I feel normal.'

'Good.' Rita picked up the flask. 'I guess I'll go see if Kingston is hungry.'

'Are you sure it's safe?' Sydney asked. 'Just because it didn't affect me doesn't mean it won't affect him.'

'It's a risk we'll have to take,' Rita said. 'Kingston needs to eat, and I threw out everything in the pantry.'

'I'll stay out here in case you need me,' Sydney said.

'Thank you,' Rita said, entering the bedroom.

* * * * *

He could feel the planet spinning. That was one of the first things that came to mind when he opened his eyes. It felt like he was on a fair ride and wanted to get off. His stomach felt like it was twisting in on itself, and he had started to shake some time ago, and he couldn't make himself stop.

Looking around to see what had woken him, he spotted Rita sticking her head in the bedroom door. 'You awake?' She asked.

'I am now,' he said, pushing himself up. 'What do you need?'

'You need to eat,' Rita said, entering the bedroom. 'And Kian brought you something.'

'Kian did?' Kingston said, surprised.

'I know, right?' She held up the flask. 'Chicken soup. Of his own making.'

'That's unusual,' Kingston said, leaning back heavily against the bed's headboard. 'I've never known Kian to bring anything for anyone.'

'He must be feeling charitable today,' Rita said, taking the lid off the flask and pouring some into the lid. 'Sydney already tried it, so it doesn't appear poisoned.'

'Sydney?' Kingston frowned. 'That's quite a risk she took. What if it had been poisoned?'

'I was there, and she only had a small amount,' Rita said, handing him the lid. 'I'm sure if Jake had of been around, he would have tried it.'

'Any word from Jake?' Kingston asked, taking a sip of the soup. He was surprised by how good it tasted. Apparently Kian could cook.

'Nothing yet,' Rita said. 'I've also been going over everything he's given me so far, and there have been no leads.'

'So we're still stuck at square one,' Kingston said with a sigh.

Rita nodded. 'They picked the right place to do their business. There are very few cameras around, and nobody seems to have been reporting anything out of the ordinary on social media.'

'Not that you can trust social media,' Kingston said. He took another long drink of the soup, his stomach complaining at the intrusion. 'Did you ever work out what poisoned me?'

'I assume the coffee did,' Rita said. 'But I threw out everything, anyway.'

'Better safe than sorry,' Kingston said.

'Exactly,' she agreed. She stood back and watched as he took another drink. 'How are you feeling?'

'Bad,' he admitted, feeling his stomach knot again. 'I can't seem to stop shaking.'

'Whatever you were poisoned with has done a number on you,' she said, shaking her head. 'I just wish I could do more.'

'You're doing the best you can,' Kingston assured her. He gestured to the soup. 'This is pretty good.'

'I never picked Kian to be much of a cook,' Rita admitted. 'He's always at the cafe buying lunch.'

'That's just one meal out of three,' Kingston reminded her. His stomach twisted again, but not as badly as it had a moment ago. 'He's a very busy man. I imagine it is probably easier for him to buy lunch than to make it.'

'He is always working,' Rita admitted. 'At least that's what it looks like. For all I know, he could be playing solitaire on his computer.'

'Do they still put that on computers?' Kingston asked.

'I'd have to ask Jake,' Rita said. She watched as he had more soup. 'You don't seem to be having any trouble eating that.'

'It's actually soothing my stomach,' Kingston admitted. 'I must have been hungry.'

'You haven't eaten anything for a while,' Rita observed. 'You haven't been able to keep anything down.'

'Hopefully, this stays down,' Kingston said, raising the lid.

'Fingers crossed,' Rita said. She sighed, looking toward the door. 'I better get back to work. Call out if you need anything.'

'I will,' Kingston promised her.

She left, leaving him to his thoughts.

30

Raymond started awake at the sound of the door opening. He'd got some sleep purely out of sheer exhaustion. His whole body ached from head to toe, and his mind was still fuzzy from exertion. He raised his head, gazing in the door's direction and spotting Kendra as she stepped inside. Two men followed her in, coming to stand on either side of him.

'Good, you're awake,' Kendra said. She reached into her pocket and took out a set of keys, unlocking the locks on his wrists. 'Get up.'

Raymond didn't ask what was going on and didn't have time to hesitate as the two men gripped him by the forearms and hauled him to his feet. His legs and feet protested at the sudden change, vertigo washing over him, causing him to stumble. He didn't fall, the grip on his arms so tight that he wouldn't have the chance.

'I've brought you some clean clothes,' Kendra said, tossing them onto the nearby table. 'Get changed. We're going on a car trip.'

Raymond frowned, stumbling as the two men dragged him toward the table. He ran his eye over it, looking for some form of weaponry and seeing that Kendra had cleaned up after herself, leaving only his clothing. The two men made no move to turn their backs as they stared him down, willing him to hurry without a word.

With trembling fingers, Raymond went about changing, every part of him protesting at the movements. After he was done, he looked up as one man held something out to him. Raymond instantly recognised his glasses. After a brief inspection to see that they weren't damaged, he put them on, relief at being able to see properly again coming over him.

He barely had a second to gather himself when he was seized again and dragged out of the room. The two men kept close to his side, Raymond stumbling on bare feet on the concrete floor. His feet protested being walked on after so long sitting down, not to mention the torture they had undergone recently.

Upon reaching the car, he was unceremoniously shoved into the back seat, a man sliding in on either side of him, much like they had the first time he had come here. In the front, another man slipped into the driver's seat, Kendra taking her place in the passenger seat. Once all the doors were closed, the man started the car, driving them out of the warehouse.

'If you're wondering why I had you change, think nothing of it,' Kendra said, breaking the silence. 'I simply didn't want you stinking up the car. We're in for a long drive.'

Raymond didn't respond. He'd had a feeling her motives had been purely selfish. It felt nice to have clean clothes, so he took that as a small win in his favour. As for where they were going, he had a strong suspicion, especially if it was a long drive.

They were going to Adelaide.

* * * * *

After her shift had ended, Sydney headed back to Kingston's room to find nothing had changed. Kingston was asleep, apparently having kept the soup down. Jake had already found his way back upstairs and was stretched out on the couch with his laptop in his lap, still running searches to narrow down Raymond's location. She could tell by the scowl that he wasn't having much luck. Rita was at her desk researching different poisons to find what Marcus had poisoned Kingston with, even though she had admitted that it would be difficult.

'And we're sure we will not find the key for Marcus?' Sydney suggested again.

'No way in hell,' Jake said, not looking up from his screen.

'You should go home for the night,' Rita told Sydney. 'Try to get some sleep in your bed. Us all being here will change nothing, and I think people have already noticed.'

'They have,' Jake confirmed. 'They were talking about it in the security office.'

'Okay,' Sydney said. She knew she still had a spare change of clothes, but honestly, having some time away would do her good. It would give her a chance to clear her head a little. 'Call me if something happens.'

'We will,' Rita assured her.

Grabbing her bag, Sydney headed out, going downstairs. She could see that Simon was closing the cafe and that the shift change for everyone was almost complete. Out of curiosity, she went to the courtyard to see if Kian was still around, but found his table empty. Clearly, he had gone home. She still wondered why he had brought the soup for Kingston. It was very kind of him to have done it.

Sydney made her way home with no incidents, noting that the man watching the hotel was still in his place. It was raining, so she had wondered if he would still be there. She hated that someone was keeping track of her; sure enough, she felt like being watched again as she walked home. She wondered if she might have taken a taxi, but then she didn't live that far away from the hotel, so it was almost pointless.

Arriving at her apartment, she was relieved to find no one waiting for her. She headed inside, locking the door behind her. She did a cautionary sweep of the apartment to ensure no one had broken in and found that everything was exactly where she had left it. Relieved, Sydney headed for the shower.

Even in the shower, she couldn't escape her thoughts. Her mind turned to Raymond, and worry once again came over her. She hated the idea that he was being hurt, and there was nothing she could do about it. It almost made her wish that she was still in New York. That they had never caught her up in this whole mess. She could undoubtedly sleep a lot easier if she were none the wiser. If only she hadn't chased that man downstairs after the key card.

Getting out of the shower, she dressed and went to the kitchen to make herself dinner. She didn't know if she could stomach anything significant, so she just made herself a salad with some pre-cut meat. Sydney sat at the table and ate, her phone sitting beside her. She almost willed it to ring and to have Rita or Jake tell her they had a lead on the cure for Kingston or the location of Raymond. Sydney was happy for either right now. She just wanted something. They needed a win.

Her stomach dropped at the sound of a knock on the door. She set her utensils down and pushed herself up, steeling herself. She had a feeling she knew who was on the other side of the door. Keeping the top lock in place, she opened it a crack and, sure enough, found herself looking at Marcus.

'Good evening, Sydney,' he said pleasantly.

'What do you want?' she asked.

'I came for the key,' he said with an amiable smile.

'I don't have it,' she told him flatly. 'And I wouldn't give it to you even if I did.'

The smile vanished. 'You didn't find it?'

'I didn't find any of them,' she told him.

'So you looked.'

'That's none of your business.'

'So we're doing this the hard way,' Marcus said, a frown on his face.

'What do you mean?' Sydney asked.

'Nothing for you to worry about,' Marcus said. 'I can tell you I was prepared to hand Raymond over. I guess that won't be happening now.'

'Just let him go,' Sydney said, a small plea in her voice. 'He will not give you what you want. You don't have to hurt him.'

'See, that's the thing,' Marcus said. 'I *don't* have to hurt him. But all of you are making this incredibly difficult to where it's inevitable that I do.'

'What are you going to gain?' Sydney asked. 'He'll take the secret to the grave. You'll be back at square one.'

'And then I'll just wait for the next Keeper to break the code, and we'll start the cycle all over again,' Marcus said. 'I will not stop, Sydney. Not until I get my key.'

'You're sadistic,' Sydney said.

'I'm realistic,' he said. 'Remember when I asked you how far you would go to go home?'

'I wouldn't kill anyone,' Sydney said.

'I guess that's what makes us different then,' Marcus said. 'Because I would. In fact, I have. And I'll do it again.'

Sydney felt a rock form in her stomach as she realised he was talking about Raymond. He was going to kill Raymond. She swallowed the lump in her throat. 'Please,' she pleaded.

'You just had to get me that key,' he reminded her. 'I guess you could say this is partly on you.'

He turned away before she could answer, Sydney watching as he walked away. She closed the door and locked it. She realised she was shaking, and as she headed back into the apartment, she cried from the sheer helplessness of it all. Dropping into a seat at the table, she picked up her phone and wondered if she should call Rita and Jake. Instead, she put it back down, not wanting to disturb them from their search.

Right now, she was alone.

* * * * *

Kingston stepped out of the bedroom, closing the door quietly behind him so as not to disturb Jake, who he saw sleeping on the couch. The man had fallen asleep while on his laptop, no doubt still searching for something to help them locate Raymond. Looking around the room saw no sign of Sydney while Rita was still working away on her computer.

Padding across the room, Kingston stopped behind Rita's chair and cleared his throat. Rita almost hit the roof, spinning around in her seat and staring at him.

'What are you doing up?' She hissed, scowling at having been caught by surprise.

'I'm feeling much better,' Kingston told her, waving down her concern. 'I don't know what Kian put in that soup, but I've been feeling much better since I had it.'

'Really?' Rita stood, reaching up to press a hand to his forehead. 'Your fever has gone down,' she said, eyeing him over. 'You also look a lot less pale. That doesn't mean you should be up, though.'

'I know, but I couldn't stay in bed,' Kingston said, shaking his head. 'Not while Raymond is still out there somewhere.'

'Jake has been working hard on it,' Rita said. 'He hasn't been having much luck, though.'

'He looks exhausted,' Kingston commented, looking down at where Jake was asleep.

'He is,' Rita agreed, stifling a yawn. 'I think we all are.'

Kingston rubbed his stomach absently as he felt it twist, still not fully recovered. He gazed around the room. 'Where's Sydney?'

'I sent her home,' Rita said. 'She was dead set on staying the night again, but I wouldn't have it. It doesn't do any of us any good.'

'Good idea,' Kingston said. He moved over to a chair, dropping into it heavily. 'I feel lost.'

'I can imagine,' Rita said, sitting back in her chair. 'But there's nothing any of us can do. Jake is working as hard as he can.'

'I know, I know.' Kingston rubbed his hands over his face, looking at Jake and feeling sympathy. 'When this is all over, remind me to give Jake some extra vacation time.'

'He'll just use it to surf and probably still come into work,' Rita reminded him.

'I'll forbid him from setting foot in the hotel during his time off,' Kingston said.

'He won't listen.'

Kingston smiled. She was right – Jake won't listen. That man was married to his job, and he loved it. That was one reason Kingston had hired Jake – because of his enthusiasm. He had been top of his class at university, and his activities in sports, plus his past part-time job as a bouncer, had made him perfect for the job as part of the security team. He'd done so well in his first couple of years that he'd quickly risen to become head of the team.

Seeing Jake's eyes flutter, Kingston smiled. 'Evening.'

'Kingston?' Jake practically fell off the couch, sitting up, having to catch his laptop before it hit the floor. 'You're up!'

'I am,' Kingston told him. 'I'm feeling a lot better.'

'Remind me to ask Kian for some of his soup next time I'm sick,' Jake said with a smile.

'It certainly has worked wonders,' Kingston told him. He nodded toward the computer. 'How goes your work?'

'Not very well, I'm afraid,' Jake told him, situating the laptop square on his lap. 'I tracked the car about a kilometre, but the trail goes dead. The fact they're stolen plates doesn't help.'

'So we've gotten nowhere,' Kingston concluded.

'Essentially,' Jake said sadly. 'I'm sorry.'

'It's not your fault,' Kingston told him. 'You've done the best that you can.'

'I just wish I could do more,' Jake said. 'I've tried everything that I know.'

'I'm not blaming you,' Kingston assured him. 'I'm blaming Marcus.'

'About him.' Jake tapped his computer. 'I did a background check on him. There are several people with his name, but none match his description, and none are in Adelaide. I searched around the local hotels to see if anyone with his name was staying there, but again, I came up with nothing.'

'It may not be his real name,' Kingston told him. 'Some of my people change their names and location every few decades to hide that they don't age very fast. He might be one of them.'

'Well, that would certainly complicate things,' Jake said. 'If he's one of those, I might never find out who he is.'

'All I can tell is that he was in Werribee in 1966. I'm not sure what name he went under then.'

'Which doesn't really help me.' Jake shook his head. 'Your people are excellent at covering their tracks.'

'We have to be,' Kingston told him. 'That's why I moved around for so long. I only came back when the Keepers could locate the keys; when they couldn't, I would travel around and check back every few years.'

'Hence why you were around in 1966,' Jake guessed.

'Yes,' Kingston nodded. 'And why I'm around now.'

'I thought that was because of Raymond,' Rita said.

'Well, mostly because of Raymond,' Kingston admitted. 'But him breaking the code was a bonus.'

'Also a curse,' Jake said. 'It put a huge target on his back.'

'Yes, it did,' Kingston agreed. 'But it told us I wasn't the only one monitoring the Barry's.'

'Do you think there could be others?' Rita asked. 'I mean, aside from this Marcus guy.'

'There could well be,' Kingston agreed. 'I doubt Marcus is the only one that would want access to the portals and what they offer.'

'So this might not be over even when we find Raymond,' Rita said.

'No, it may not,' Kingston sighed, shaking his head. 'That's why the fewer people know about the portals, the better. Many of my people had already arrived on Earth and gone off into their new lives before they merged the portals into a single access way. Many of them don't even know the location of the central portal, and we've always intended to keep it that way.'

'Marcus knows, though,' Jake said.

'He must have found out some way,' Kingston said. 'Unless he was among some of the last few people to come through.'

'Like you were.'

'Indeed.'

'So you're saying that many of your people don't even know the existence of the Keeper and Protector,' Rita clarified.

'No, they don't,' Kingston confirmed. 'It was done that way deliberately.'

'Maybe Sydney's right then,' Rita said. 'Maybe it would be better if we did not find the keys.'

'No,' Kingston shook his head. 'That would defeat the entire purpose of the Keeper and Protector.'

'But Raymond wouldn't have been taken if he hadn't broken the code,' Rita reminded him.

Kingston had no answer for that.

31

Kingston stepped out into the courtyard, taking a deep breath of the evening air. It felt good to be outside instead of cooped up inside in bed. He still felt a little queasy, but he was otherwise feeling a lot better. He wondered just what Kian had put in his soup because it had certainly worked miracles on him.

He walked around the edges of the courtyard garden, enjoying the quiet of the evening. There was a distant sound of traffic. The courtyard was lit up with the bright lights of the hotel. The cafe was long closed, so they set the seating upside down on the tables, the umbrellas folded closed. Kingston was enjoying the peace in the courtyard, with the only sound coming from the fountain.

It was certainly nice not to be stuck in bed. It was also nice not to feel as sick. Kingston stretched out, feeling his body work out some aches from having been lying down for too long. He took another deep breath of the night air as he came around the courtyard for a second time, glancing up toward where he knew his room was.

Jake was awake again and still working hard to find something, anything, to help clue them into where Raymond could be. Rita had taken over his position on the couch and was getting some much-needed sleep. Sydney, unable to stay away, had rejoined them not even an hour ago and had been relieved to find Kingston up and about, although she had chastised him much as Rita had. She had told them about the visit from Marcus. That had made it even more urgent that they find Raymond. It had undoubtedly given Jake an extra drive to keep looking.

He slowed as he thought he heard footsteps behind him, coming to a dead stop as something round pressed into his back.

'Hello, Kingston.'

Marcus. Kingston didn't bother to turn, instead slowly raising his hands as he was sure that the thing on his back was the business end of a gun. 'What do you want?'

'You,' Marcus said, pressing the gun harder into the small of his back. 'We're going for a little walk.'

Kingston didn't have time to answer before Marcus gripped him firmly by the shoulder, shoving him toward the building. He manhandled Kingston through the empty building and out a rear doorway into the laneway. Kingston kept his hands half-raised, willing someone to walk around the corner and interrupt them, but nobody came.

Reaching the laneway, Marcus pushed Kingston along, Kingston spotting a car halfway ahead. Sure enough, Marcus directed him toward the car, a man getting out as they approached.

'Into the back,' Marcus said.

Kingston did as he was told, sliding into the back seat and casting one more glance toward the building, willing Jake to check the security footage to see where he had gone. The man slid in beside him, trapping Kingston between two bouncer-esque men. His heart raced as Marcus slid into the front passenger side, slamming the door closed.

'Drive,' Marcus told the driver, who instantly started the car and drove them forward and out into the street.

'I'm surprised to see you up and around,' Marcus said, breaking the silence after they had been on the road for a while. 'I thought I would have to come up to your room and find you, but no, I found you wandering the courtyard. On your own, no less.'

'Not my wisest decision,' Kingston agreed. 'Your poison didn't work.'

'I believe it did,' Marcus said, looking back at him. 'You somehow found the antidote. Where?'

'That's a secret.'

'I see.' Marcus turned to face forward again, gazing out at the traffic. 'Not that it matters. Not where we're going.'

Kingston didn't ask him where that was. He was sure he'd find out soon enough.

* * * * *

Rita awoke from an exhausted sleep, still feeling sluggish as she opened her eyes. Once this was all over, she would request some vacation time of her own to catch up on all the sleep she was missing. Pushing herself up, she gazed around the room, finding Jake seated at her desk using his laptop while Sydney was dozing in the chair.

Standing, Rita made her way to the bedroom, taking a peek inside, and was surprised when she found no sign of Kingston. After quickly checking the rest of the flat, she approached Jake.

'Where's Kingston?'

'Uh,' Jake glanced up at her. 'He went out for a walk.'

'Alone?' Rita asked.

Jake nodded. 'He told me to keep working on finding Raymond when I offered to go with him, and he turned Sydney down as well.'

'He's still not well,' Rita said. She checked her watch. 'How long ago was this?'

'About…' Jake looked at his watch, an expression of worry creeping onto his face. 'An hour ago.'

'Where did he say he was going?'

'The courtyard.' Jake pulled up the security footage, scanning through it. 'He's not there.'

'Where is he then?'

Rita felt a sense of panic creep over her. She watched as Jake cycled through the cameras, not finding any sign of Kingston. He then rewound them, eventually seeing where Kingston had walked several laps of the courtyard. They watched as he was approached from behind and what unfolded next. Jake flipped through the cameras until he could get a clear shot of the other man's face.

'Marcus,' Jake growled.

'Oh no,' Rita said, slumping into a nearby chair. 'First Raymond, now Kingston.'

'I should have gone with him,' Jake said, kicking himself. 'This is my fault.'

'No, it's not,' Rita told him. 'It's Kingston's fault. He should have known better.'

'So should have I,' Jake continued. 'I knew better. I should have told him to stay in the rooms.'

'He's your boss,' Rita reminded him. 'You can't exactly argue with him.'

'What's going on?' Sydney asked, finally awake.

'Marcus took Kingston,' Jake told her.

'What? How?'

'Because I let him go for a walk,' Jake said, slamming a fist down on the edge of the desk. 'How could I be so stupid?'

'There's nothing any of us can do about it now,' Rita told him.

'Yes, there is,' Jake said, turning his attention back to the computer. 'I can try to track where they took him.'

'Are they still in the hotel?' Sydney asked, standing up and making her way over to stand behind Jake.

'No,' Jake said, shaking his head. 'From what I can see, they had a car standing by in the laneway.'

Rita and Sydney watched as Jake began tapping away at the keyboard, cycling through cameras, and following the car's path onto the street. He watched as it made a turn, Jake tracking it until the cameras in the hotel could no longer follow it. He then tried to hack his way into the Adelaide CCTV network.

'How long will this take?' Sydney asked.

'As long as it takes,' Jake told her. 'In the meantime, someone had better tell Lucille what's going on.'

'I'll go,' Rita said, standing up.

'I'll go with you,' Sydney offered.

'She will not be happy about this.'

* * * * *

'Kingston did what?!'

Sydney struggled to keep from shifting from foot to foot, trying not to betray her nervousness.

'Went for a walk on his own,' Rita answered.

'Why the heck would he do that?' Lucille hissed, clenching and unclenching her fists. 'That's just asking for trouble. No wonder he was taken.'

'I know,' Rita said. 'I would have argued against it if I had been awake, but I wasn't.'

'And where was Jake?' Lucille asked.

'He offered to go with him, but Kingston talked him out of it,' Sydney answered.

'He should never have let him go,' Lucille sighed, shaking her head.

'What's going on?' Tanya asked as she and Andrew joined them in the dining room.

'Kingston has been taken,' Lucille told them.

'Oh no,' Tanya said.

'Is there any way to track them?' asked Andrew.

'Jake's working on it,' said Sydney.

'We haven't been in a worse situation since Redmond and George,' Lucille said. 'Both the Keeper and Protector are missing. No doubt they'll use Kingston to get Raymond to talk.'

'Will it work?' Sydney asked.

'No,' Lucille, Tanya and Andrew said together.

'Raymond is stubborn,' Lucille clarified. 'He'll take the information to the grave. That's what it means to be a Keeper.'

'What can we do?' Sydney asked.

'Nothing,' Lucille answered. 'We will have to wait and see if Jake can find anything. Aside from that, all we can do is wait.'

32

Kingston had lost track of where they were going long ago, but he could tell they had driven out of the city. It was hard to see with the two men on either side of him, and he regretted not having his cell phone on him. It would have given Jake something to track at the very least. He tried to look out the window, but every time he did, one man would jab him in the side until he sat up again.

They pulled off the road and down a long gravel driveway. Kingston spotted the headlights of another car in front of them. As they approached it, a woman got out. Marcus exited the car as soon as they stopped and went over to talk to her. After a moment, Marcus gestured back toward the car and the two men got out, dragging Kingston out with them.

They gripped him on either forearm, causing him to stumble as they dragged him forward and toward a large hole he could see in the ground ahead. It appeared to be a tank of some sort, long-abandoned, judging from the amount of undergrowth he was being dragged through, although the graffiti told him it wasn't forgotten. That wasn't what captured his attention, however.

Two other men climbed out from the back of the other car,

dragging a third man with them. Kingston felt his heart skip as he instantly recognised the other man.

'Raymond!'

'Kingston?' Raymond called back.

'Oh, now you talk,' the woman said, leading the way toward the tank.

Kingston tried to keep his eye on Raymond as they pulled him toward the tank. Raymond looked horrible. There was bruising and gashes on his face. He was shoeless, and was stumbling hard as he was being pulled along. Everything about how he looked screamed 'torture' to Kingston, which caused rage to build up inside him.

Reaching the tank, Marcus pulled out his gun, pointing it at Kingston. 'Down, inside.'

They pushed Kingston toward a rusty metal ladder. Keeping his rage in check he slowly made his way over to it, lowering himself into the tank. When he reached the bottom, he looked for some form of escape, but a lackey had followed him down, reached out and grabbed him. They forced him over to a pipe, the lackey pulling Kingston's arms back behind him and handcuffing him to it.

Kingston looked up and saw that Raymond was getting the same treatment on the other side of the ladder. Marcus had followed them down, the woman staying at the top. The lackey that had trapped Kingston turned and headed back toward the ladder, climbing back out now that his job was done. Marcus holstered his weapon and waited until the lackey who had trapped Raymond climbed back out.

'Now then,' Marcus started. 'This is how this is going to go. This tank is connected to the water main, and it will start filling unless you tell me what I want.'

'Which is?' Kingston asked.

'They want the keys,' Raymond answered. 'The location, how to find them.'

'Exactly,' Marcus said. 'And unless I get that information, you will die here.'

'That will not happen,' Kingston said.

'Won't it?' Marcus drew his gun again, walking over to Kingston and pressing the barrel against Kingston's forehead. 'Your call, Raymond. You tell me what I want to know, and I let you go. You don't, and Kingston here is going bye-bye.'

Raymond hesitated. Kingston saw it out of the corner of his eye. 'Don't you dare, Raymond.'

'Tick tock,' Marcus said, tightening his finger on the trigger.

'Okay, okay,' Raymond said.

'No, don't!' Kingston said, Marcus hitting him with the butt of the weapon to silence him.

'It's the journals,' Raymond answered. 'On the thirteenth page, every first word gives out a message that tells you how to locate the keys.'

'And where are the journals?' Marcus answered.

'On my desk in the bunker.'

'See, that wasn't so hard,' Marcus said, lowering his gun. 'And the keys already found?'

'Also in the bunker.'

'There now,' Marcus turned and made his way to the ladder.

'Aren't you going to let us go now?' Raymond asked.

Marcus paused for a moment, then shook his head. 'You know what? I've changed my mind.'

Without another word, he climbed the ladder, pulling himself out of the tank. Kingston glared across at Raymond, who was staring over at the pipe leading into the tank. Sure enough, a rushing sound came after several minutes, water filling the tank. In the faint distance, they heard two cars start, driving away.

Still glaring at Raymond, it surprised Kingston to see a smile slowly slip across Raymond's lips until the man was grinning. Raymond began laughing.

'I cannot see what's funny,' Kingston called out over the water. 'You gave them the code.'

'No, I didn't,' Raymond called back to him. 'I gave them *a* code, not *the* code. It's useless to them.'

Suddenly Kingston realised why he was laughing and couldn't help but feel laughter build up within himself. He couldn't stop himself, joining Raymond in chuckling. The two of them laughed as the water in the tank continued to fill, coming up to their waist now.

Kingston pulled at the handcuffs, trying to see if he could slip his wrist out of them but finding that he was unable. They were trapped.

He spotted a movement at the top of the ladder, and looking up he saw someone making their way down. Surprise washed over him as he recognised the man.

'Kian?'

Kian didn't answer, fumbling with something in his hand as he approached Kingston. He reached behind him, and Kingston felt the handcuffs come free. Kian waded through the water over to Raymond, and Kingston massaged his wrists as he followed him through the deepening water. It wasn't long until Raymond was free, Kian pushing Kingston back toward the ladder.

'Get out of here,'

'Not without Raymond,' Kingston told him. 'He can't swim.'

'Seriously?' Kian said. The water was almost up to their shoulders now as he pushed Raymond toward the ladder. 'Hurry.'

Raymond pushed through the water, reaching the ladder first and hurling himself up it. Kingston followed, Kian just behind him. Upon reaching the top, Kingston spotted a lackey slumped nearby and realised that Kian had disposed of him. Without a word, Kingston reached out, pulling Raymond toward him in a firm hug.

'I thought I'd lost you,' he said into Raymond's shoulder.

'I'm not that easy to get rid of,' Raymond told him, pulling back and kissing Kingston quick.

'We need to hurry,' Kian said, heading toward where Kingston spotted a car. 'Marcus will be on his way to the bunker.'

'Why should we trust you?' Raymond said, slowing.

'You mean, aside from the fact I just saved your life?' Kian answered.

Kingston and Raymond nodded.

'Well, it's rather simple,' Kian said, turning back toward the car. 'I'm the Overseer.'

33

Kingston felt surprise wash over him at those words, sure that he had misheard them. 'You're the what?'

'The Overseer,' Kian repeated, stopping next to the car's driver's door. 'Surely your father mentioned me.'

'Isn't the Overseer dead?' Raymond said as he joined him.

'Not the last time I checked,' Kian said, opening the car door. 'Now hurry. We have to catch Marcus.'

Raymond and Kingston climbed into the back seat. Kingston absently wondered how Kian would enjoy having so much water inside his car, but he didn't seem to comment as he slid into the front. Kian waited until all the doors were closed before he started the car, the rear tyres spinning for a second on the loose gravel before they could find traction, shooting them out along the driveway.

'Where the hell have you been?' Kingston asked.

'Around,' Kian answered, glancing at him in the rear-view mirror. 'I've been in Adelaide for about a decade now, although you know how long I've been going to the hotel.'

'About three years,' Raymond answered.

'When I realised you were spending more time at the hotel, I guessed Raymond must have broken the code,' Kian told them. 'I knew someone would try to interfere, so I situated myself nearby.'

'Raymond isn't the first Barry to break the code,' Kingston told him. 'Back in the sixties, his great-grandfather also broke the code. Marcus killed him.'

'I'm sorry to hear that,' Kian said. 'I was busy in Ireland dealing with a problem there. If I had known about Marcus being in Adelaide, I would have travelled down to see what was happening.'

'What could possibly be in Ireland?' Raymond asked.

'Not all the portals were centralised,' Kian told him. 'Our people, who didn't want to lose their means of transport and power, hid a few of them. Whenever I find a rogue portal, I go about… neutralising it.'

'You destroy them?' Kingston asked.

'I deactivate them, yes,' Kian replied. 'As you can guess, people aren't thrilled about this happening, so I've had several threats on my life. That's why I've had to disappear.'

'But what about the main portals?' Kingston asked. 'We could have used your help after Redmond and my father died.'

'No, you couldn't,' Kian said. 'The central portal was in excellent hands, and while the keys were hidden, there wasn't a security risk. I knew people would watch, though. I did not know that Marcus was one of them.'

'You seem to know Marcus well,' Raymond observed.

'Of course I do,' Kian said sadly. 'He's my son.'

'Your what?' Kingston and Raymond said together.

'My son,' Kian confirmed. 'My only child. I should have realised he was a bigger threat than he was. I hold myself wholly responsible for everything that he has done.'

'He's killed people,' Kingston hissed.

'I know,' Kian said, shaking his head. 'I knew he wanted to get access to the central portal. I just underestimated how far he would go to get it.'

'Why does he want it?' Kingston asked. 'The power?'

'Nothing so nefarious,' Kian said. 'He wants to go home.'

'Back to Lierdan?' Kingston asked.

Kian nodded. 'He always hated me for bringing him through the portal. I tricked him to bring him here. I promised him I would show him the new world and then he could go back home to his mother. I didn't tell him that they would hide the keys shortly after I brought him through and force him to stay.'

'You left his mother on the other side?' Kingston asked. 'Why?'

'She refused to leave,' Kian explained. 'She was happy in her elite lifestyle and hated that by coming through the portal she would find herself a "peasant" and have to work to build herself back up again. I tried everything to convince her to come.'

'But you convinced Marcus to leave,' Kingston said.

'I did, and I regret it,' Kian said. 'He spent every waking moment longing for the life we used to have. I told him that all he had to do was work hard and he could achieve that life again, but he wouldn't have it. I partly blame his mother for giving him everything on a silver platter, but I had hoped that Marcus would come to realise that what I did was to save him. He's never seen it that way, however.'

'So that's why he's been after the keys,' Kingston said. 'Because he wants to go home.'

'Yes,' Kian said.

'But we don't have the key to go home,' Kingston said. 'We never found it.'

'He thinks it's hidden,' Kian told him. 'That the location for it is in the journals.'

'Is it?' Raymond asked.

Kian didn't answer.

'And now Marcus is heading for the bunker,' Kingston said. 'To get the journals. But the code Raymond gave him isn't the right one.'

'Which will make him dangerous,' Kian said.

'We need to hurry,' Raymond said. 'My family is in the bunker. They're in danger.'

★ ★ ★ ★ ★

'I've tried everything,' Jake told them as he sat at the dining room table of the bunker. He held his head in his hand, shaking his head in frustration. 'There's only so much I can do.'

'No one is blaming you,' Sydney assured him.

'I am,' Lucille said from the kitchen. 'You should never have let Kingston go for a walk alone.'

'No, I shouldn't have,' Jake agreed. 'That's entirely on me.'

'It's not your fault,' Sydney said, shooting Lucille a dark look. 'You've been working hard these last couple of days. More so than any of us. You've tried your best.'

'His "best" will not find Kingston and Raymond,' Lucille said.

'You're not helping,' Rita said.

'I'm not here to help,' Lucille shot back. 'I just want to find my son, and sitting here throwing a pity party will not do it.'

'She's right,' Jake said, standing. 'I should get back to work.'

'You only just stopped for a break,' Sydney said. 'At least have a coffee first.'

They all paused as they heard a commotion outside of the portal door, the door swinging open. They went rigid when Marcus strode through, casting his gaze around, reaching into his pocket, and drawing a gun.

'Here you all are,' he said, waving the gun between them. 'I was wondering where you had all gotten to.'

'What are you doing here?' Lucille hissed.

'I'm here for the journals,' he said, turning the gun on Lucille. 'Now off you go and get them.'

'What makes you think I will do that?' she asked.

'Because if you don't, your son will die,' Marcus answered.

Lucille slowly turned and walked to Raymond's office, returning with one journal.

'Now,' Marcus said, training the gun on her. 'Every thirteenth page, I want you to read me out the first word.'

Lucille glared at him, opening the journal and counting thirteen pages in. 'This.'

'Next word.'

Lucille counted out thirteen more pages. 'Is.'

Marcus gestured for her to hurry.

'Not.'

Jake began to half stand.

'The.' Lucille continued.

A dark look crossed Marcus' face. 'Hurry up.'

A small smile played over Lucille's lips as she read the next word. 'Answer.'

'This is not the answer,' Marcus hissed, slowly going red with anger. 'This is not the answer. He lied to me. Your son lied to me!'

'Of course he did,' Lucille said. 'He'd sooner die than give the code.'

'Which he will be,' Marcus said. 'Unless you break the code for me.'

'I can't do that,' Lucille said. 'Raymond was the one who broke the code. He never told me anything about it.'

'Then you better get to work,' Marcus said, gesturing for her toward the table. He turned the gun and pointed it toward Jake who was slipping out of his seat. 'And where do you think you're going?'

'Nowhere,' Jake lied.

'I should hope not.' He turned once more to Lucille. 'You had better work on the code, or I will start shooting everyone in this room. I will kill another every hour you take, so you better start working. Tick tock.'

'Marcus,' Sydney said, half-standing.

'Sit down!' he ordered her.

She did. 'You don't have to do this.'

'Yes, I do,' he told her. 'This is the only way for me to get home.'

'By killing everyone?' she asked.

'It doesn't have to come to that if this one hurries,' he said, gesturing to Lucille.

'You can't expect her to do it in an hour,' Sydney protested.

'Her son did it,' Marcus reminded her. 'And she's no doubt had training as a Keeper.'

'There's only ever been two Keepers who broke the code,' Rita reminded him. 'And they took their time.'

'Then I guess she better pull a miracle,' Marcus said. He looked down the corridor. 'Now tell me, where are the keys kept?'

'Not here,' Lucille said.

Marcus' face darkened. 'What do you mean?'

'I mean, they're kept a long way from the portals,' Lucille told him.

'Your son said they were kept here,' Marcus hissed.

The corners of Lucille's lips turned up. 'I guess that's another lie.'

'Son of a…' Marcus growled, beginning to pace. 'How many lies did he tell me?'

'He probably knew you were going to kill him anyway,' Jake said.

'And that will happen soon if this one doesn't hurry,' Marcus said, stopping to look pointedly at Lucille. 'And Kingston as well.'

A silence hung over the room at those words, Lucille looking back down at the journals. She glanced up. 'I need Raymond's notes.'

'Then get them,' Marcus told her.

Lucille hurried up, rushing for the office. As they waited, Marcus turned to Sydney.

'You know, you could come with me, Sydney,' Marcus said. 'Come back to my planet. Live a life of luxury.'

'No,' she said without hesitation. 'I'm not going anywhere with you.'

'I'll let you consider it,' he said, anger in his eyes. He was clearly not a man used to being told no. He turned as Lucille came back. 'Now, enough delays. Break the code. The clock is ticking, after all.'

34

MOST OF THE drive had been in silence. Kingston had used the time to inspect Raymond; it horrified him to discover that all of Raymond's nails had been removed. Raymond had filled him in on the various tortures he had endured, and the whole thing had made Kingston feel sick. He tightened his arm around Raymond's back, not wanting to let go.

'Marcus will probably be in the bunker by now,' Kian told them as they pulled into the laneway. There were no other cars, which meant Marcus had no doubt gone in alone. 'I suggest you let me do all the talking.'

'No complaints here,' Raymond said.

'He's your son,' Kingston agreed. 'If you can talk him down, go ahead.'

'Thank you,' Kian said.

They climbed out of the car, Kingston leading the way back inside with Raymond behind him. Kingston slowed, remembering how Raymond still had trouble walking and not wanting to leave Kian behind. They made their way through one of the hotel's back doors, then down into the Vaults and along the corridor to Kingston's storage room. Kingston found the door ajar, surprised by the lack of guards. He stopped, turning and waiting for Kian to take the lead.

'Hopefully, this goes better than I'm expecting,' Kian said.

'What are you expecting?' Raymond asked.

'Nothing good,' Kian said. 'I know my son.'

He pushed open the door, finding the entrance to Melbourne closed. With one more glance behind him, he opened the door and stepped through.

* * * * *

The group sat around the table, watching Lucille flip through the journal. Delicate beads of sweat had accumulated on her forehead as she worked. Rita knew it had taken Raymond the better part of two years to crack the code, so the likelihood that Lucille could do it within an hour was slim.

Somewhere in the homestead, Tanya, Andrew, and Olivia were still hiding, and Rita prayed that they stayed quiet so as not to alert Marcus. The man had made himself a cup of coffee and was leaning back against the kitchen counter, glancing at the clock from time to time as he fingered his gun's trigger.

They all looked up sharply as the portal door opened, Marcus dropping the cup. The liquid and shards splashed over his shoes as he spun toward the doorway and pointed his gun. 'Who's there?'

'Easy, Marcus,' Kian said, stepping through the doorway with his hands raised. 'It's just me.'

'Father?' Marcus asked. 'What are you doing here?'

'I've come to see you,' Kian said, stepping further into the room. Into the room behind him stepped Kingston and Raymond, Lucille let out a soft whimper at the sight of her son. 'Now, put the gun down so we can talk.'

'I'm done with talking,' Marcus said, waving his gun at Kingston and Raymond. 'What are they doing here?'

'I rescued them,' Kian answered. 'There is no need to kill anyone today.'

'I'm the one who decides that,' Marcus hissed.

'Now tell me,' Kian said slowly. 'Why are you here?'

'Why do you think I'm here?' Marcus shot back. 'I'm here for the same reasons it's always been. I want to go home.'

'And you think threatening the Keeper and Protector will get you that?' Kian asked.

'It'll get me the answers I want,' Marcus said. 'It'll get me the keys.'

'Keys, plural,' Kian confirmed. 'But will it get you the key that you want?'

'What do you mean?' Marcus asked.

'You want the key home,' Kian said.

'Of course.'

'What makes you think they hid it, to begin with?'

'All the keys were hidden,' Marcus said.

'Not all of them.' Kian shook his head. 'Why do you want to go home, Marcus? There's nothing for us back there.'

'Of course there is,' Marcus said. 'Mother's back there. Our whole lives are back there.'

'Not anymore,' Kain said. 'Our lives are here now. I'm independently wealthy here, so you can live the life of luxury you crave.'

'It's not the same,' Marcus said. 'It's not home. You should never have brought me here.'

'I brought you here to save your life.'

'I didn't want to be saved,' Marcus shot back. 'I was happy where I was. You tricked me.'

'Marcus,' Kian said softly.

'No, don't you dare,' Marcus spat. 'You didn't give me a choice. I would have stayed back on Lierdan with Mother if you'd given me a choice. You took that choice away from me.'

'You'd be dead,' Kian said.

'You don't know that!'

'Yes, I do.' Kian sighed. 'The planet was dying, Marcus. They were lying when they said there was a century left. There were only decades left, and they're long gone.'

'You're just saying that.' He gestured at Raymond. 'I want that code. I want the key home.'

'You want the key home? Okay.' Kian reached around his neck, tugging at a piece of cord and revealing a brass key.

'You,' Marcus breathed, staring at it. 'You've had the key all along?'

'It was the one key we couldn't afford to lose,' Kian told him. 'And as the Overseer, I took it upon myself to protect it.'

'The Overseer?' Lucille breathed, shooting Kingston and Raymond a look. Kingston nodded his confirmation.

Marcus outstretched his hand, walking toward his father. 'Give it to me.'

'Here,' Kian took the key around his neck, holding it out toward his son. 'On the condition that you let everyone go.'

'I don't need them anymore,' Marcus said, snatching the key away from his father.

'I should warn you,' Kian said. 'You are going to be disappointed.'

Marcus didn't answer as he rushed to the portal door, stepping out and crossing the hallway to the door on the other side of the room. He shoved the key into the lock, turning it and flinging open the door. Marcus stared in surprise as the door opened to reveal the storage locker. He slammed it closed again, turning the key once more and throwing it open again to reveal only the storage locker.

'What's… what's going on?'

'I warned you,' Kian told him. 'The key hasn't worked since the seventies.'

'How?' Marcus spun toward him. 'This is the wrong key.'

'No, it's not,' Kian said sadly. 'As I said – it stopped working decades ago. The portal on the other side must have been destroyed.'

'You mean there's no way home?' Marcus said, stunned.

'This is our home now,' Kian confirmed.

'No,' Marcus said, shaking his head as he fumbled with the gun. 'No, it's not. This will never be my home.'

'Marcus,' Kian said, raising his hands and walking toward him. 'I need you to put the gun down now.'

'No,' Marcus said, pointing the gun toward Kian. 'This is all your fault. I hate you. I *hate* you!'

Without another word, he brought his gun up to the underside of his chin.

'No!' Kian said, leaping forward.

Marcus pulled the trigger.

35

THE SILENCE IN the room was deafening. Lucille slipped out of her seat at the table, rushing across the room and throwing her arms around Raymond. Kian slowly walked across the room, kneeling beside Marcus and prying the gun from his hands, then reaching out to close his eyes.

'I'm sorry,' Kingston said softly.

'It's my fault,' Kian said, sitting back on his heels beside his son. 'I brought him here against his will. I should never have expected him to settle in.' He sighed, looking up toward Raymond and Lucille. 'I'm sorry for everything he's done to your family.'

'It's not your fault,' Raymond told him.

Lucille didn't answer, stepping back so she could look Raymond over. She reached up and gingerly pressed her fingers against the marks on his face. 'What did they do to you?'

'Nothing good,' Raymond told her. 'And I never told them. I never broke, Mother.'

'I know you didn't,' Lucille said. 'You're a Barry. We don't break.'

'So it's over?' Sydney asked, getting up from the table and trying not to look down at Marcus.

'It's over,' Kingston confirmed. 'For now, anyway.'

'Until the next nutcase shows up,' Jake said. He shook his head as he looked at Kingston. 'I'm sorry I didn't go with you to the courtyard.'

'It's not your fault,' Kingston assured him 'I was the one who went alone. The situation is entirely on my head.'

'Still,' Jake said. 'Next time, remind me not to let you go.'

There was a sound of a door opening, and Andrew poked his head out of a bedroom door. 'Is it over?'

'It's over,' Raymond confirmed. 'Just don't bring Olivia out here.'

'Raymond,' Andrew said, his eyes lighting up. 'You're back.'

'I'm back,' Raymond confirmed.

'So now what?' Rita asked, looking down at the body. 'You can't exactly sweep this up and throw it out with the trash.'

'I'll take care of it,' Kian said, standing.

'So you were the Overseer all along,' Lucille said. 'Where the hell have you been? We could have used your help many times.'

'Busy,' Kian told her. 'I'll let Raymond explain it to you at a later date. Right now, I need to… take care of things.'

'Let him be, Mother,' Raymond said to her. 'He just lost his son.'

Lucille nodded, tightening her hold on Raymond.

Kingston stepped forward. 'Let me help you.'

'I'll help as well,' Jake offered.

'Thank you,' Kian said. He sighed, looking down at his son for a moment before looking at them. 'We're going to need something to place his body in.'

'The table clothes from the hotel,' Rita offered, her voice shaky. 'They're waterproof on one side.'

'I'll get them,' Jake said, heading for the doorway while avoiding looking at the body.

The others dispersed to leave them to it, Raymond commenting about needing to shower and clean up. Kingston made his way to the Barry kitchen to gather some cleaning supplies. After a small amount of time, Jake returned with several table clothes. The hotel had many, so Kingston knew they wouldn't be missed. He and Jake assisted Kian in carefully wrapping Marcus' body, Kingston finding some rope from the storerooms of the hotel to help with the process.

'So you've known for some time that the key didn't work,' Kingston said, breaking the silence.

'Yes,' Kian said.

'Did you know your son was looking for it?'

'I had my suspicions,' Kian said. 'I didn't realise how far he would go.'

'Why was he so keen to go home?' Jake asked. 'It didn't sound like the planet was anything special.'

'Because of his status, I suspect,' Kian said. 'We were in the upper class. We had servants and everything we wanted. He didn't see the planet for what it was – dying. His mother convinced him that life for us was perfect. We didn't need to work, and everything was handed to us.'

'You didn't agree,' Kingston said.

'I could see the big picture,' Kian said, 'that to survive, we had to leave. But my wife didn't want to leave the comforts and privilege in her life to come here. She viewed it as a step-down. I told her we could have that life again; we would need to work for it. She said, 'why should we work if we already have it?'.'

'And Marcus agreed with her,' Kingston said. 'How did you convince him to come?'

'I tricked him,' Kian said. 'I asked him to come to see the new world. See how wonderful it was to walk in the grass and breathe clean air. I told him it was just for a little while, and then he could go home. I brought him through at the last minute, knowing he couldn't go back.'

'And he resented you ever since,' Kingston guessed.

'Yes,' Kian agreed. 'When he realised what I had done, he left. We haven't spoken to one another in over a century.'

Jake paused. 'I can't believe you guys are that old.'

'Genetic modification,' Kian explained. 'It extended our life, but led to the overpopulation.'

They finished wrapping Marcus' body. Together, they picked him up and carried him out through the door. They kept an eye out to make sure that no one was around to see them, Jake telling them he'd wipe the security footage as soon as they left. They took the body up through the back halls of the hotel to where Kian had parked his car. Kian opened the boot, and they placed the body inside before Kian closed the lid.

'What are you going to do with him?' Kingston asked.

'I'll make arrangements,' Kian said, his shoulders slumped in defeat. Yet there was something definite about him, like this wasn't the first time he'd had to clean up a mess like this. 'It will be like he never existed.'

'You can do that?' Jake asked.

'I have connections,' Kian said. 'That's the upside to being so old and being successful. You can make connections and make people disappear.'

'Remind me never to piss you off,' Jake said with awe in his voice.

'Out of curiosity,' Kingston said, looking across at Kian. 'Do you know how the Portals work?'

'I'm not the designer, but I have a rough idea,' Kian said. 'They made the portals with material from our home planet. We made them look like normal doors, but they are, in fact, technological marvels. They were the primary means of transport on Lierdan, but here they were used to establish us into positions of prominence. We used them to have an advantage over Earthlings. That is why they were centralised – to prevent our people from exploiting them and establishing themselves in positions of infinite wealth and power. We were meant to work for it – not hand it to ourselves and repeat history.'

'You're scared what happened to your planet will happen here?' Jake said.

Kian nodded. 'It's why the keys were hidden. They were never meant to be lost. They were supposed to be kept if we needed them to help any of our people.'

'Help how?' Kingston asked.

'Defensively,' Kian said. 'If anyone ever tried to use the law against them. If any of our own started killing our own.'

'Which happened,' Kingston said. 'Your son.'

'Yes,' Kian said. 'And there are others like him. Others want the keys; only they want them to get power. The portals were originally meant to help us establish ourselves. But there are those of us who see Earthlings beneath us and want to establish themselves as rulers.'

'Anyone we should be worried about?' Kingston asked.

'A fair few,' Kian said. 'But none immediately. I've been taking care of them.'

'I'm guessing the portals go to important places,' Jake said.

'Parliament, treasuries, libraries,' Kian said. 'Hotels and churches. A few private homes. Many of them no longer work, and the original buildings no longer serve the purpose they were created for.'

'Like the Medina,' Jake said.

'Exactly like the Medina,' Kian said. 'And not all the portals are in Australia. Some go to Ireland, England, Scotland and Wales. There are a couple in America and various places in Europe.'

'Significant places,' Kingston guessed.

'Significant enough,' Kian confirmed. 'And then there are those off the grid. Some engineers are still here and creating new portals. So far, they haven't connected them to the main one, but it may only be a matter of time.'

'I better increase security,' Jake said to Kingston.

Kingston nodded his agreement. 'Is there any portal we should worry about?'

'There is one,' Kian said. 'You could say it goes to a special place in Ireland. A bunker. It is where all the information on Lierdan is kept, and my notes of those I know came through the portal. I've been keeping it safe and updating that information, but there is a key to it. I don't think you've found it yet, but some want into that bunker.'

'I'm guessing the information there is dangerous,' Kingston said.

'In the wrong hands, yes,' Kian confirmed. 'Many of our people have worked their way into prominent positions of wealth and status. That information could be used against them.'

Jake blinked. 'So the New World Order is real?'

'No,' Kian said, giving Jake an unimpressed look. 'But if someone got their hands on that information, it could become so.'

'So we need to find that key,' Kingston said. 'And hide it again.'

'If you find it, I suggest destroying it,' Kian said. 'That would mean that there is only one way to access the bunker, and I am the only one with the means to do so.'

Kingston nodded.

'How can we be sure *you* can be trusted?' Jake asked.

'If I had wanted to hurt you, I would have done so,' Kian said. 'I have more than the means. My mission is to make sure secret things remain secret.'

'Are you going to be all right?' Kingston asked.

'I will be,' Kian said. There was sadness in his eyes as he looked down at the boot of his car. He rested a hand on it, as if he were touching a coffin and giving respects.

'If you ever need to talk…'

'Thank you,' Kian said. He reached out, extending a hand to Kingston, who shook it.

They watched as Kian climbed into his car and drove away, leaving them in the alley. They waited until the car was out of sight before returning to the hotel. There they split up – Jake to wipe the security footage, and Kingston to finish cleaning up the mess. Soon it would be like Marcus had never been there at all.

36

RAYMOND FELT A lot better after a shower, shave, and a fresh set of clothing. He discovered Olivia was asleep in his bed, so he kissed her forehead softly and left her there to rest. Everyone else had gathered in the living room of the flat. When he made his way in, Rita had cornered him, sat him down on the couch, and went over his injuries with the first-aid kit, quickly falling into her role as the team medic. He tried not to wince as she treated his wounds with disinfectant, his mother hovering by his side.

'Leaving you behind was one of the hardest things I've ever had to do,' Andrew said. Guilt was thick on his expression and mirrored in that of his wife. 'I hope we never have to go through that again.'

'We knew something would happen eventually,' Raymond said with a shrug. 'That's why we had the contingency plan in the first place.'

'I never thought we'd have to use it,' Tanya said. 'I thought it was a 'just in case' thing.'

'Is Olivia going to be all right?' Raymond asked. It was a lot for a little girl to go through. He worried she would be traumatised.

'She's shaken up,' Tanya said. 'She's scared the bad people will come after you again.'

'Not her?' Raymond asked.

'She doesn't seem worried about herself,' Andrew said. 'She's more worried about you.'

'I still can't believe you kept her from me,' Lucille said. 'I've had a granddaughter all this time, and you never said a word.'

'You know exactly why I didn't tell you,' Raymond said as he levelled her with a look. 'Your first thought would be to start her training.'

Lucille frowned. 'Well, she needs to–'

'No,' Raymond cut in. 'She does *not* need to. Not until she's sixteen and makes her own choice.'

Lucille blanched. 'Sixteen? By then, it will be too late.'

'For what?' Raymond asked. 'The training's not that hard. And I intend to stick around until she's well and truly old enough.'

'What is the training?' Sydney asked. 'If you don't mind me asking.'

'Nothing too bad,' Raymond answered. 'Martial arts, learning the journals back to front, understanding how the library system works, gun training – which you need to be eighteen to learn, anyway.'

'She's already doing karate,' Tanya said. 'She wanted to. We don't force her.'

'And the library system you can learn at university,' Andrew said. 'That's where Tanya and I learned it.'

'You're librarians?' Sydney asked.

They nodded.

'Tanya works at the public library, and I work in a school,' Andrew said. 'We met Raymond at University during our undergraduate course.'

'And corrupted him,' Lucille accused.

'Trust me, Raymond didn't need "corrupting",' Andrew said. Tanya smiled.

They looked up as Jake and Kingston made their way into the room before Lucille could reply. Lucille reluctantly vacated her space with her son, Kingston taking it. Jake sat on a cushion next to Sydney's chair. The room was almost too small to have this many people inside. Raymond wondered if they would be better off moving to the dining room. His train of thought was interrupted as

Rita applied disinfectant to another one of his wounds and caused it to sting.

'We cleaned everything up,' Kingston told Lucille.

'We even took the rubbish out,' Jake added.

'So, there's no blood splatter on the walls?' she asked.

'I think we got it all,' Kingston said. 'That we could see, anyway.'

'Security files are taken care of as well,' Jake said. 'Pat was on duty but didn't ask questions. He knows better.'

'I like Pat,' Kingston said. 'He's not nosey.'

'I can't help but feel like it is partly my fault,' Sydney said, eyes downcast. 'I let Marcus get close. He was using me, and I didn't know it. I should have questioned more.'

'It's not your fault,' Kingston assured her. 'You had no reason to believe anything was going on.'

'But I should have,' she said. 'He always seemed to turn up. I should have realised that he was following me. He must have seen me as an easy target.'

'Not necessarily,' Kingston said. 'He most likely saw an opportunity. He knew you were new and tried to exploit that fact to get in on the inside.'

'You can't be blaming yourself,' Raymond agreed. 'Nothing that happened was your fault.'

'He offered to let you go,' Sydney admitted. 'I just had to hand over the keys.'

'And you didn't,' Kingston said.

'No,' she agreed. 'I didn't.'

'Which proves you are far from weak,' Kingston said. 'Many would have taken him up on that offer.'

'I'm glad you didn't,' Raymond said. 'Because some things go to the grave.'

Sydney frowned. 'Isn't that a little extreme?'

'That's what we have trained him to do,' Lucille said. 'A Barry never reveals the secrets. It's part of being the Keeper.'

'Yet you were trying to break the code,' Jake pointed out.

Raymond blinked, turning to stare at his mother.

'I had to look like I was doing something,' she said. 'Otherwise, he would have shot everyone in sight.'

'So you were pretending?' Rita asked.

Lucille didn't answer.

'Mother,' Raymond scolded.

'There was no way I could do it anyway,' she countered. 'Not in the time I had.'

'Good thing I never told you the code,' Raymond said.

'But it is still my fault,' Sydney said, bringing the topic back around. 'It's my fault he found out about your relationship.'

Kingston narrowed his eyes. 'Were you even aware of it?'

'Worst kept secret in the hotel,' Rita said.

Raymond raised his eyebrows and looked at Kingston. The older man met his eye and didn't look surprised by what Rita had said. Raymond had never thought themselves obvious, but apparently, they had been. What had given them away? He also now wondered if that was why Rita never came in early to the office.

'Marcus must have liked you, but,' Jake said, 'he offered to take you with him.'

'Excuse me?' Kingston said, looking back around. 'He did what now?'

Sydney shrugged. 'He said I could come with him to "live a life of luxury".'

'First, what he said is completely overblown,' Kingston said. 'Life was far from luxurious on the home planet. Second, Jake is right – he did, in fact, like you.'

'Why do you say that?' Sydney asked.

Kingston paused, seeming to consider how he would phrase the next. 'Because of the overpopulation, Lierdan had stringent rules governing children. They permitted only one child per family. Of course, our extended lifespans still increased the population rather than depleting it, and they forbid some people from having children. Mostly those in the lower levels and those with "undesirable" traits.'

He shifted. 'Because of the single child rule, male children were more highly valued. It was not uncommon for an Elite family, upon learning they were having a girl, to end the pregnancy and try again until they had a boy. Because of this, there were significantly more men than women.'

'I bet that made marrying between families hard,' Jake commented.

'Oh no, same-sex marriages were common,' Kingston said. 'But having a wife to have a child gave you more status.'

'Because you can carry on the family name,' Andrew guessed.

'Exactly,' Kingston said.

'Wait,' Sydney said. The puzzle pieces were falling into place. 'He wanted me to be his wife?'

'That is the only explanation as to why he would want you to go,' Kingston said. 'As a woman, they would mandate you to marry.'

'Well, that's just sexist,' Rita said. 'What if you didn't want to marry?'

'There was no choice,' Kingston said. 'Also, marriages among the Elite were done for convenience, not love.'

'But wouldn't Sydney have reduced status on your planet?' Jake asked. 'She doesn't have a long lifespan.'

'It would be considered an undesirable trait, yes,' Kingston agreed. 'But clearly Marcus was willing to overlook it.'

'I think I dodged a bullet,' Sydney said.

'A massive one,' Rita agreed. 'He seems like a prick.'

'He was charming to begin with,' Sydney said. 'Once he made himself known, he changed.'

'He let you see the real him,' Kingston said. 'He was single-minded.'

Raymond hissed as Rita pressed a cloth soaked in disinfectant to his toes.

'Oh, stop being a baby,' she chastised him.

'You try getting your nails ripped out,' he countered.

'Hard pass,' she said, pressing the cloth harder against them while picking up some bandages with her free hand. 'You realise you'll have to be super careful of infection while they grow back.'

'Just give him a healing plan, and I'll make sure he follows it,' Kingston said.

'Agreed,' Lucille added.

Raymond rolled his eyes as he saw where this was going. 'I am not an invalid.'

'But you are injured,' Kingston reminded him. 'And it's my job to look after you.'

'No, it's your job to protect the keys,' Raymond said.

'To protect the Keeper,' Kingston reiterated. He tapped Raymond on the end of the nose. 'Which you happen to be.'

Raymond glared at him, knowing he would not win this fight. Kingston gave him a sweet smile and leaned forward to press a soft kiss to his lips. Hearing a couple of 'awwws', they looked around to see Jake and Andrew giving them cute looks, while Sydney and Tanya were beaming. Rita stared off into the distance while Lucille glared at them.

'You guys are so cute,' Jake teased.

'I'm going to hear shit about this, aren't I?' Raymond said, giving Jake the side-eye.

'Definitely,' Jake confirmed.

'Anyway, it's been a long few days,' Kingston said. 'We should all probably get some rest.'

'It's going to be hard to sleep,' Sydney said.

'I think you'll find you'll just pass out,' Rita said. 'Once the adrenaline wears off.'

'Maybe,' Sydney said. 'It's just… Marcus…'

'Nightmares,' Kingston guessed.

She nodded.

'Just try to get as much rest as you can,' he told her. 'If you can't, talk to Rita. I'm sure she could recommend something.'

'I have a few ideas,' Rita confirmed. 'But only if you can't sleep on your own.'

'You're welcome to crash in my room,' Raymond told Andrew and Tanya. 'We'll organise to get you three home tomorrow.'

'Where will you sleep?' Tanya asked.

Raymond raised a brow, which made Kingston smile.

'Don't expect me in to work early,' Rita said. 'Ever.'

'You never came in early anyway,' Kingston reminded her.

'Guess why,' she said, which confirmed Raymond's earlier suspicions.

'Anyway, let's break this up,' Kingston said. 'And I'll see everyone in the morning.'

37

THE NEXT FEW days passed quickly. Rita, Jake and Sydney all went back to work. Lucille and Raymond took advantage of the covid excuse to spend some time together while Raymond was recovering. Kian did as he had promised and taken care of Marcus, no one bothering to ask him just what he had done with the body.

Kian slid back into his routine as if nothing had happened. He had refused to talk about it with anyone and had simply asked for more time when Kingston had approached him to ask more questions about his role as the Overseer. Kingston had honoured his request and had let him be for the time being.

Sydney never asked Raymond about what had happened when he was gone. She was almost afraid to ask. She could see his bruises and how carefully he walked and used his hands. Her fingers ached at the thought of his nails being torn out. She shuddered, knowing she could never survive under that treatment. She had a whole new respect for the Barry family.

She still hadn't entirely wrapped her head around Marcus being gone. Sydney still had trouble sleeping, hearing the gun going off as he pulled the trigger. She hadn't been able to see him from where she had sat, but she had seen his body afterwards. She could not grasp why he would rather perish than just exist here. Was it so bad on this planet? He had been more desperate than she had realised.

Raymond had answered Sydney's questions about Kian's involvement. Sydney still didn't know why Kian hadn't stepped in earlier than he had. Had he known the full extent of the threats against the Barry family and that people had died? She almost felt like this could have all been prevented if he had. Raymond had been at as much of a loss about that as she had. In the end, she had just hugged Raymond, glad to have him back and understanding that Kian needed his space.

She again questioned why they needed to find the keys at all. Jake had eventually concluded that if they didn't, someone else would use it to gain power and money. Kingston and Raymond needed to find and move the keys before the next threat arrived. It was entirely possible that Redmond's journals weren't the only place where the location was recorded; it was better to be safe than sorry. Sydney could understand that, although she wondered if keeping the keys together was a good idea. Rita had reminded her they didn't know where the keys were held and that most of them didn't work.

There was also the question of what would happen if something happened to Kingston and Raymond, and they couldn't be Keeper or Protector anymore. Jake had instantly offered to step in as Protector, and Kingston had approved of the idea. As for Keeper, Lucille was adamant that the position remain within the family. Raymond had shot that down, saying that if Olivia didn't want to be Keeper then he would find another replacement, someone who wanted the part, or the job would die with him. Sydney shuddered at the thought and wondered if maybe, just maybe, she could offer herself to take over the role. She could probably never break the code, and it scared her she would break under pressure, but she entertained the thought. She'd have to put much more thought into it before saying anything.

It felt strange to Sydney how seamlessly things had returned to normal, as if the last few days had never occurred, with the work at the hotel mundane in contrast. She almost wished for a rowdy guest to break up the monotony.

One thing that happened was a complete failure of the hotel's security system. One of Jake's 'improvements' had caused an issue, and the entire system had to be reset back to default. Kian had all but given Jake an 'I told you so' when he had found out.

Looking up, Sydney saw a new guest entering the hotel. She put on her brightest smile and turned to greet them.

* * * * *

Raymond knew he was there the moment he arrived. Raymond hadn't heard the portal door open, nor had the other made any sound to alert him of his presence. Still, Raymond knew. Chewing his lip to fight the urge to turn around, Raymond tried to focus on the task at hand, his finger skimming under the words of the journal so as not to lose his place, but he kept forgetting what he had read almost as soon as he had read it. The eyes on the back of his head were just too distracting.

'You're making it incredibly hard to concentrate,' he said, his words loud in the quiet room.

He heard the soft chuckle and could see the smile in his mind's eye, but the other didn't say a word. Raymond returned to read the page he was on but again lost his place. He leaned back in his chair with a sigh, turning it around to face the door.

Kingston was leaning against the door frame, watching him, his arms by his side and his mask of confidence and leadership not present. He looked tired, Raymond noted. Tired and almost defeated.

'I'm surprised to see you are working,' Kingston said, breaking his silence.

'Gives me something to do,' Raymond said. 'Keeps my mind off... everything.'

'How are you, Ray?'

No 'Raymond'. Raymond felt his mask slipping at the sound of Kingston using the shortened form of his name. He stared at his hands where they rested on his thighs, noticing he had unconsciously clenched them. He opened them, pressing his palms flat onto his thighs as he spread out his fingers.

'Physically, I'll heal.'

'And mentally?'

The last of his mask fell away as he allowed the exhaustion to show. He shook his head as he stood, crossing to sit on the couch by the door. Kingston didn't say a word as he moved to join him. The feeling of the man beside him comforted Raymond.

'I don't think Mother will ever forgive me for not telling her about Olivia,' he said.

'You had your reasons,' Kingston said.

'She knows that, but I don't think she understands.' He worried his lip, thinking of the quiet anger and hurt in his mother's eyes before she had left earlier that evening. 'I'm not sure it's even because I didn't tell her she had a granddaughter.'

'Your mother has always put the job first,' Kingston said, loosely crossing his arms over his chest and staring at the floor. 'Sometimes, I get the impression she resents not being the Keeper. That she feels like you stole the job from her.'

Raymond looked up sharply. He had long suspected it, but it was surprising to hear it from Kingston. 'You think that's why she acts the way she does?'

Kingston nodded. 'She was only a little girl when her grandparents died, but old enough to understand that she would take her grandfather's place when he retired. Your grandfather thought she thought she'd still step into the role once she was old enough.'

'When did she realise she wouldn't?'

'First, when your grandfather stepped down. I think she knew for sure the day your grandfather told you he was retiring and you would take his place.'

'That was the day she changed.' Raymond thought back to that day. He'd always thought she'd become stricter with him because he was stepping into an important job. He'd never felt it was because he was filling the role she'd always thought would be hers. It put things in a new light for him and gave him a new understanding of why his mother acted the way she did.

'She is proud of you,' Kingston said, breaking his thoughts. 'She was terrified at the thought she would lose you.'

'I know.' Raymond nodded, feeling a lump form at the back of his throat and remembering how his mother had clung to him when they reunited. 'She doesn't say it, but I know.'

They fell into a comfortable silence, Raymond listening to the sounds of his home. As the library closed for the evening, there were muffled steps from upstairs. The soft hum of the fan on his laptop. The faint ticking of the grandfather clock in the dining room. He frowned to himself as a thought came to his mind.

'So you're over a hundred years old.'

'In Earth years, yes,' Kingston answered without missing a beat.

Raymond turned his head to look at him. 'And an alien.'

Kingston met his eye. 'If you mean I'm not of Earth, then yes, I am.'

'Huh.'

'Does that bother you?'

Raymond shook his head. 'No. It's… odd. But you're still the same person I met years ago.' He paused. 'It means you're going to have to watch me die.'

A dark looked crossed Kingston's face, and Raymond could feel him grow tense beside him. 'Not for a long time.'

The memory of recent days played through Raymond's mind, of how close he had come. He remembered his great-grandparents. He remembered what had happened to Redmond Barry himself. 'Edward…'

'Raymond,' Kingston said, his voice firm. 'Not. For. A. Long. Time.'

Raymond could hear the punctuation mark after every word and see the defiant look in Kingston's eyes. He wanted to argue the point, but knew better. Instead, he simply nodded, his shoulders feeling heavy as a fresh wave of exhaustion hit him. He glanced at his watch and was surprised to find it was still early.

'You should take some time off,' Kingston said, shifting on the couch and stretching back so that his arm rested just behind

Raymond's shoulders, the other on the armrest. The dark look had vanished as quickly as it appeared, Kingston again appearing relaxed and open.

'You're not eager to find the next key?' Raymond asked.

'I've waited this long,' Kingston said. 'What's a few more days?'

Raymond smiled, feeling lighter as Kingston returned it. Raymond closed his eyes and let his head drop back, using Kingston's arm as a headrest. He frowned. 'Do you ever wonder why they first hid the keys?'

'I do,' Kingston replied. 'But the fact Redmond left a record of their location means they were intended to be found.'

'Not easily. And he didn't leave any codex to find them. Just a few vague paragraphs in his journal on how to decrypt his code, and even that was hard enough to work out.'

'Do you think we should stop looking?'

Raymond opened his eyes to see Kingston watching him, a serious look on his face. He considered the question, glancing to the side to where his laptop had powered itself down due to lack of use and the open journal that lay just in front of it. 'No,' he said, turning to face Kingston again. 'We've come this far. And if we don't find them, someone else will.'

Kingston nodded his agreement. 'Then we will find them. And we will put them somewhere where these people will not find them.'

'Because that's our job,' Raymond said.

'Yes,' Kingston agreed, leaning across to kiss him softly. 'Because that's our job.'

www.ingramcontent.com/pod-product-compliance
Lightning Source LLC
Chambersburg PA
CBHW050605190726
48283CB00007B/2290